Dark & Dirty
A Dark Erotic Fantasy Anthology

D.C. STONE
KASTIL EAVENSHADE
LEA BRONSEN
R. BRENNAN

Published by Writers in Crime
Print edition
Not One Night: Copyright © 2016 D.C. Stone
Redeemer: Copyright © 2016 Kastil Eavenshade
Slick: Copyright © 2016 Lea Bronsen
Addictions: Copyright © 2016 R. Brennan
ASIN: B01MCYQ7BR
ISBN-10: 1537569880
ISBN-13: 978-1537569888
Editors: D.C. Stone, Lea Bronsen
Layout and cover art: Lea Bronsen

CONTENTS

INTRODUCTION

I loved her, not for the way she danced with my angels but for the way the sound of her name could silence my demons.
-Christopher Pointdexter

When I was asked to do the introduction to this anthology, I didn't hesitate to accept the invitation. To be asked to do this for a group of talented women writing about something that might be considered pushing the limits, was such an honor. Dark and erotic might not be for everyone, but like with all new things, you have to try it to see if you'll enjoy it. The darkest recesses of our hearts can hide the most beautiful emotions, the most frightening desires. Every day we go through life hiding something from the ones around us, from even ourselves. It might be a desire, a thought … the very make-up of our DNA. Some hide what they want for fear of what others might think, or decide to be someone else because fear holds them back. We need to learn to allow ourselves to be who we are, to love what we want, and experience what might not be considered normal. It is only within ourselves that we can accept who we are, and what we want. It is only then that we can be free and true to ourselves. So, go into this anthology with an open mind and heart. Don't let preconceived notions hinder what you could enjoy. We are our own judge, jury, and executioner. Let go and live the way you want, without thinking of what someone might think. Be free and experience. Enjoy and never look back.

~ Jenika Snow

NOT ONE NIGHT

BY

D.C. STONE

DEDICATION

When I was approached to do this anthology, I had a mixture of fear and excitement. Fear, being that this type of story was so outside of my comfort zone that I didn't know if I could do it. Excitement, being that I would be doing yet another lovely book with fantastic, talented authors.

The concept of Not One Night came to me with the characters being in opposite lights, with Johanna originally being the protector, and Brady a shady criminal. Even though I know it's possible, I couldn't get through the story in keeping to that theme, so I had to adjust a few things. The adjustments I made really got me curious and I have a big feeling these two will be showing up in other stories/series to come, perhaps even with the Empire Blue series, which is set just down the street from NYC.

I wanted Johanna to fight for something near and dear to my heart, something I've been a child-victim to, and something that doesn't get enough attention. Domestic violence is a silent and hopeless crime many struggle to get out of. There is more than just one victim in every case, especially if children are involved. If you find yourself a victim of domestic violence, please seek help. Not just for you, but for all of us who love you and want to see your light shine again. For more information on domestic violence, please visit **www.thehotline.org**.

I'd like to dedicate this story to those who stand in the shadows trying to help others.

~ Deserie

"You know, one of these days, someone is going to fuck some sense into you."

Johanna King scowled and cut a glare at Brady McBride that had him chuckling. He shook his head, both impressed and annoyed that after thirteen years of friendship, she still reacted to the shit that came out of his mouth. Then again, after what she laid on him last week, and the request made to him, he figured that astonishment could go both ways.

Humbled at that thought, he rubbed a palm across his noggin, the short hair still a shock to his senses, despite having shaved it off over nine months ago. Needing a change, but not wanting to flip his life completely out of whack, he'd taken to clippers on a whim one night, slicing off the shoulder length strands. The result: a ton of weight had been taken from his shoulders, rather than the small pile that probably wouldn't register on a scale. His partner had taken it better than Johanna, and he still had the bruise on his thigh as proof.

"Seriously," Johanna said, "I shouldn't be surprised, I mean really, look at where you work. They say sailors have some mouths on them, but the colorful language I've heard coming out of the precinct is enough to make my Uncle Bob blush, and he's more perverted than any other I know."

"And that's saying something," he added, grinning at her repeated scowl.

"But," she continued, rising her voice in a deliberate show of talking over him, "each time I think I have you figured out, you go and do something to smash through those perceptions."

Brady lifted the corner of his mouth, let out a short chuckle, and faced her. "I don't know why. There's not much about me that says I follow any rules."

She lifted her brows.

"What?" he asked.

Her gaze went up, and he fought the urge to rub his shorn hair again. Instead, he shrugged and leaned back in the seat, taking a glance outside the town car, but didn't focus on anything.

"Not by the rules, huh?" she asked, her voice unusually gentle. Yet another thing that had changed, something he put a finger on. Why things seemed to be shifting since *the* question. He hated that despite not giving her an answer yet, their friendship may have changed. He didn't want that. Didn't know how to get it back to before. But apparently, the decision was out of his hands.

He rolled his head on the leather seat and looked at her. "Do you have a point you want to make?"

One sleek brow arched. How had he never noticed the classical features of her face? The soft curve of her jaw, the high angle of her cheek bone. The bow shape of her lips. He forced his gaze away.

"You're a detective, Brady. And not just any detective, the new face of the homicide squad." She snorted. "If there's any job outside being a soldier that follows rules, um, honey, I think that's it."

"Jesus," he muttered.

"Whaaaaaat?" she asked, and the attitude that always lurked behind her tone hinted its appearance.

He resisted grinning. Barely. Instead, he spoke to the window. "You have no idea what kinds of rules I play by. There's the rules that are accepted by society, and rules that I operate on my own… However," he said, drawing out the word, "after your question last week, I figured you'd want to jump all over that answer." He met her gaze. "Literally."

Pink rose in her freckle-covered cheeks. He wanted to shout in success. Instead, he smiled. He could spew all the bullshit he wanted right now, when it was still just Brady and Johanna. Soon enough, too soon, things would change between them, and call him a sadist, he just wanted to draw this banter out a little longer. Wanted to remember the time when he still had his friend. Because later…well, there was a completely different agenda for the night.

She'd been waiting all week for him to answer her question. And while most men would have jumped at taking her up on her offer, he'd hesitated.

"I want a lover, Brady. But I can't take one on at my age with the lack of experience I have. I need you to take one for the team here. Teach me. One night. Show me everything you can about sex."

Jesus. That moment she'd smacked him with that question still wrung his stomach in knots and butterflies. How he could both have the hardest boner and want to shrink inside of himself at the same time was a feat he had to give to Johanna.

As a lead detective for New York City's Homicide Squad, he had faced some of the most violent offenders, gruesome murder scenes, and horrible endings to life. After all, when you stuffed close to nine million people on an island thirteen miles long, things were bound to get interesting.

But after hearing Johanna ask that one thing, he'd almost fallen to his knees. Had to reach out to palm the wall, if his memory served him correctly. Embarrassing for a man his age. Deadly for someone in his profession to be caught off guard by a slip of a girl.

But rather than push it off and ignore the question altogether, he'd arranged for them to go out, somewhere their regular crew wouldn't be, which was usually scattered across bars in the city. A place where they could focus on each other, and he could give her an answer to the question without any of their friends picking up on weird vibes.

He was fooling himself, though. Was such an asshole for what he planned to do tonight. He had his damn answer already, but didn't know if he could step over that line of their friendship. He was curious, sure, and once she'd opened that line of thinking, the thought of falling between her sweet milky thighs and teaching her all the naughty things he wanted to do...wouldn't leave his head.

Beams of lights flashed through the tinted windows of their town car. Yet another extravagance Brady wouldn't have voted on, but Johanna insisted. Taxis would cost an arm and a leg anyway, so it was just as well. Although, at the rate they were going, they'd get across town by dawn. He checked his watch. Ten o'clock.

"So where are we heading tonight?" she asked, nervous energy thrumming off her through her fidgeting. She gave him a pained look. "Maybe hanging inside tonight would be better? I feel like a fool."

A fool? He completed a slow perusal of her. A bite of something fruity filled his lungs, sweet, tasty, reminding him of a peach. She looked good, he'd give her that. But Johanna had always been athletic, someone who kept her body in top shape and could take probably half the guys in his squad. He didn't like why she did it, the late nights, the fights, the reputation she'd gathered doing her version of a vigilante, but with her childhood and everything she'd witnessed from her father beating on her mom, Brady didn't expect anything else.

And as much as he hated it, the public's perception of her was a big deal, especially since she'd become the face of domestic violence. He'd tried for years, over and over again, to get her to stop her night time gig, had used threats, anger, and silence treatment. He'd even mock-arrested her a few times, but she wouldn't stop. Then trying to get her to stop turned into keeping her name out of the public, the media, news outlets. In the end, it took one picture, then everything went downhill. And since she was this little woman, all of five foot three inches, beating on men sometimes twice her size and over a hundred pounds heavier doting out her own brand of justice, no one had told her to officially stop.

Beside him.

But then again, she had never listened.

The red dress tonight had been a shock. All she wore lately was drab clothing, yet another topic of their arguments. Those clothes made her look like some dark, bitter woman, someone others would be scared to approach. But he saw them for what they were: armor. A way to keep everyone at a distance, to not stick out in a crowd. But that was the problem. There was no way to mute her presence. A hum of energy always surrounded her. And her glow, despite the dark clothing, stood out from others.

But that dress. It was nothing like what he'd seen her in before. Hell, he couldn't remember her wearing a dress when they were kids.

The top fit to her body, snuggled and pushed up generous breasts. It cut wide so a lot of cleavage was on display before wrapping around her neck in a halter hold. At her waist, the cloth fell over the curve of her hips in what looked like strips cut precisely to give the outfit a jagged appearance. When he'd mentioned as much, she stated something along the lines of a handkerchief dress.

Whatever it was, the look of it, of her, did things to his body *she* had never done before. And combined with her long, black hair tumbling down to her waist in thick curls, her makeup a subtle smoky, and her several inch-high stilettos, he fought between panting, admiring, and cursing her.

"Because," he said in response to her earlier question, "then there wouldn't have been a reason to wear that dress. And, sweetheart, that's one hell of a dress. A fool is the last thing you look like in it."

She crossed her arms. The movement pushed her breasts up more, the material of the dress straining to keep her contained. He bit his tongue and looked outside, not really seeing the pedestrians still lining the sidewalks despite the hour, but knowing they were there.

Johanna was his closest friend, for Christ's sake. He wouldn't be able to offer anything outside sex. Hot sex, but still just sex. And even though that was all she asked for, the thought that their friendship could be cut off because of sex had him double guessing his decision.

Even the assessment had him fidgeting. And he never fidgeted. He'd faced down knife wielding combatants without batting a lash. But it'd been like this since he decided to go through with her proposition. To introduce her to what he liked. He swallowed hard. Knowing she'd only had one other man made him nervous as ever.

He wasn't built like most men, and despite who he was, what he craved, he worried she wouldn't accept him after she learned the truth. A truth he planned on setting out in the open tonight. And after that, what would that mean for their friendship?

But, goddammit, he took another glance at her cleavage. He could only be pushed so far. And that dress...

"Besides," he said once he could speak without desire clogging his throat, "you already agreed to come out. You're here. We're almost to the club. Your nightly vigilante duties are going to have to wait. There's no reason for you to go home, so stop bitching, let your hair down for once, and try to have some fun, yeah?"

Silence.

Shit. He rubbed the area between his eyes. They used to be able to rib each other, after all, their relationship was formed on the building blocks of laughter. But for the past few months, there'd been no smiles, no laughter, no joking, no nothing. Just a shell of a woman who used to live such a bright and blinding life. Especially to a dark soul such as him. And that's how he saw them, with the ugly he witnessed day in and out, versus what she'd broken out of to become. She was a bright light in his otherwise fucked up world.

And despite everyone warning him that a man and a woman couldn't remain just friends, he hadn't wanted to put them in the same box as countless other horror stories. The ones where two friends let a night of drunken sex ruin years of friendship. But here he was, sitting next to sin in silk, running her question over and over, and anticipating the night to come.

Don't get him started on the come-hither looks he could swear he'd seen from her. He wasn't one hundred percent sure, as one minute she'd look like she was about to jump him, the next, like she wanted him out of her life for good. Shit was hot and cold with her lately.

"My hair is down in case you haven't noticed, jerk."

He snapped his head up. With one long leg crossed over the other and a sly eyebrow arched, she looked every bit as prim, proper, and strong as she let everyone see. But there was a gleam in her chocolate eyes. One that gave him hope, and one that made him want to mess her up.

He curved his lips. "Believe me, I noticed. I'd be hard-pressed not to."

A wink of the street light showed narrowing eyes. "Stop that."

"Stop what? What am I doing?"

"That," she said and uncrossed her legs to lean forward. Her knee touched his. Contact. Damn if he didn't like the touch, no matter how innocent. The low flip of his stomach surprised him. Contact between them never crossed to anything sexual, nor did he think she intended the brush of her knee to be erotic. But the pressure ran a straight invisible line right up to his cock. Perhaps he was starved for her touch. Perhaps he knew somewhere in the back of his mind, after tonight, that touch would go away forever. "Flirting," she finally answered. "Being charming. Acting like you do with all your little fuck buddies."

He laughed, the sound coming from his gut and filling the car. "You're hilarious. One, you'd know if I was flirting, trust me. You've never had the full impact of it. Two," he said and fingered one of her curls that dropped over her bare shoulder. The tendril was softer than it looked, and the damn thing looked like silk. "You'd never be one of my fuck buddies."

Despite her trying to cover it, he saw the flinch. He waited for several silent seconds, trying to beat back a burst of annoyance. He didn't understand what was up with her. Why she seemed to have changed despite him not answering her.

Wait... The answer hit him like a two-by-four over the head. He still hadn't told her he agreed to her proposition, had he? "You'd be a hell of a lot more, Joey. You already are." He gave a soft tug on the strand, then released her and turned back to the window, needing to break the too-intimate moment, to stop teasing himself. Another part of him really wanted to know, though. "It's all a moot point, anyway."

Several agonizing minutes passed in silence, the stop and go of the car, the stifling heat the driver had set, and the forewarning of how this night would end. His stomach turned sour. He cracked a window and tilted his head toward the cool rush of air. It washed over his damp skin with a refreshing wave.

"Why not?" She lay her hand above his knee. That small contact shot up his leg like a bullet slamming into its target. His cock swelled, although he fought going fully erect. He grabbed her wrist and yanked it off.

Johanna's eyes widened. *Shit.* What the hell was happening to him? That damn dress. That had to be it. Could he go through with this tonight?

To cover the violence of his reaction, he turned her wrist up and pressed a soft kiss below where he held. The sweet smell was stronger there, her pulse a steady beat under vulnerable skin. It'd be so easy to mark her, to stain her skin with the touch of leather...

Her breath hitched. Even if he'd been in a rock concert at Barclay Center, he wouldn't have missed it.

"Because I don't want to lose your friendship," he said. "You mean a lot to me."

She flinched—again.

"Goddamnit, stop doing that," he said, annoyance making the words come out sharper than intended.

"Doing what?" she asked and pulled on her wrist.

He tightened his grip. "Flinching or being shocked at something I say or do. That isn't us and it's beginning to piss me off." How much worse would her reaction be later? When she learned the sordid, awful truth of what being with him entailed.

"Well, maybe that's the problem," she said through a hiss.

The car pulled to a stop in front of the nondescript club, but he couldn't get out until they got this clear. "What are you talking about?"

"Maybe I have no idea if we're friends or not anymore." Her arm shook beneath his hold, but he still refused to let go. With flushed cheeks, a heaving chest, and fire behind her gaze, her anger licked in the air and pushed against him. *She's beautiful.*

"What the hell does that mean? Of course we're friends."

A wrinkle appeared between her eyebrows and she frowned. "Really? Why is it you barely come over anymore? And when you do it's just for a quick dinner."

He reared back, taken off center by her accusation. Where in the hell had this come from? "What?"

"And you never hug me anymore," Johanna continued. Despite his anger, happiness flooded his system. She hadn't been shying from his touch. Her ire, though, this complete change in her, took him off guard. The door at her back opened.

"Give us a minute," he barked to the driver. A second later, they were back in their cocoon of muted city sounds. He tried to get his thoughts in order. Wanted to respond without biting her head off. And he really wished she'd stop trying to pull out of his hold.

"Stop that," he ordered and tightened his grip around her fragile wrist. She was so damn small, not in the sense of her size. Of that, she was a healthy, curvaceous woman who had a running schedule she stuck to every morning. Compared to him, she had a small stature. At six foot four, two hundred and thirty pounds, and used to working and speaking with his hands, he wasn't one made for soft touches or gentleness.

"One...I love hanging with you," he said and yanked her toward him when she tried to pull away. Not a gentle move, as again, he wasn't that type of man. She tumbled into his arms with a gasp. He wrapped one around her waist, and threaded his fingers into her lush, thick hair, tilting her back to meet his gaze. "And two," he said, his voice a lethal blade, "I have no clue where the rest of that bullshit is coming from. What's going on with you?"

She flinched again and his control snapped. He leaned down and bit her sharply on her plump lower lip. She sucked in a breath, but he held her between his teeth and kept his eyes on her widened ones. A low growl rumbled from his chest, and the sound was apt. She made him act like, feel like an animal. A feral one half the damn time.

Within his arms, her body was stiff, as if she'd frozen solid. He hated this fear, this uncertainty she not only stated with her posture, but also in her words. How could they have gone so far off track with their friendship?

Needing to deal with one thing at a time, he focused on Johanna in his arms. Lush breasts pressed against his chest. For a moment, he wanted to growl again, his suit jacket and dress shirt an annoying barrier. But he held in the sound and tightened his grip on her hair. Her accelerated breath skipped out of her mouth and washed across his face in a soft tease. Very much the sound he'd come to associate with a woman just before she went over the sweet ledge of pleasure.

This time, he didn't fight anything happening between his legs. There was a point he'd make here in less than thirty seconds. Then, hopefully, they'd move on and get back on track.

Closing his lips around her plump lip, he held her gaze. She was a little blurry being so close, but he had a feeling even with his eyes closed, he'd still be aware of every reaction she gave. Their intimacy wouldn't be lessened. He scrapped his teeth over her lip, then sucked it into his mouth.

She whimpered and rich iron coated his tongue. Peach lip gloss. So, obviously, the smell was a favorite to her, too. He'd have to remember that when he missed her.

Just one more taste… He took what he wanted. He always did—except when it came to Johanna King.

Brushing his lips across hers, once, twice…okay, he'd give it three times, he pulled back and took his arm from her waist.

There was nothing to do but wait for what came next. The inconsistencies in the past few months, along with the teasing touches, had pushed him too far. He needed to be clear on his intentions, and it would all come out anyway, so it was time to get started. For her to think he didn't want to be around her, that he shied from her touch, wasn't acceptable. Nor had any of her reactions to him been right tonight.

He took her hand, his thumb pressed to the center of her palm, and guided her to his straining erection. Her touch had an erotic hiss escaping him, but he wrapped her around him firmly, then pressed his hips up so she stroked him once. A shudder tickled down his spine.

"So let's clear a few things up," he said, but didn't release her hair, or her hand around his cock. "The next time you question our friendship, there's going to be consequences. You may be the big bad ass at night, but between you and I, it's just Brady McBride and Johanna King, two friends who actually talk to each other rather than you trying to railroad your way over what we have."

He gave her a few moments to let his words sink in. "Unzip me," he demanded and pulled her closer.

"Wh-what?"

Her lips were right there, blood pooling in at the plushiest part. A damn tempting sight. To take her, say fuck it to the entire night, would be so easy. But he'd held himself back this long, what was a bit longer? He wanted to draw this out, make the anticipation last for as long as he could. Have some fun with her. She'd end up hating him for being unable to give her anything more than an orgasm. A relationship between a psychopath and an angel of justice was like having the sun shine at night…it'd never happen.

Instead, he had to deal with this strife between them to move them along. He couldn't have her dancing around his touch all night. Not if he was to do this right. "Unzip me. Take your hand off my cock and unzip me."

She removed her hand, but didn't do anything else. He let out a heavy, annoyed breath. "You forgot something."

Wide eyes on his. "Brady, I don't think—"

"So help me, if you don't unzip me right now I will not be responsible for my actions."

Her eyes watered, but whatever kind of tears they were didn't fall. Johanna had a tendency to cry when she was angry, something that pissed her off more. He thought it was pretty comical. But he couldn't tell what kind these were.

She reached down with a flickered glance and unzipped him. He was a bastard, would hate once she realized that, too, but there was nothing to do for this. He was at his wit's end. Plus, he was a selfish son of a bitch, and he wanted her touch, it'd be the highlight of his miserable life.

He set his mouth next to her ear, but instead of speaking, he drew in a deep breath. Her hair always smelled the same, a fragrance of some sort that included cleanliness, and a soft, sweet musk that reminded him of tumbled pillows after sex. She never told him what kind of shampoo it was, nor did he ask, but he'd get close at any opportunity to take it into his lungs again. A fragrance that could intoxicate, make him drunk on the smell until he became an alcoholic just for another whiff.

"Touch me," he whispered in her ear. "Take me in your hand again."

"Brady, please," she said with a hint of vulnerability. Her skin barely moved against his mouth, and the slight touch did its trick again—caused his cock to swell further. This was too intimate, his mind screamed. But fuck, he couldn't turn away.

The vulnerability in her voice was a bit of a slap. Yeah, he wasn't just a bastard. He was an asshole. "Do it."

Her hand pushed inside the opening of his pants and brushed against the length of his erection. Damn, he wanted her to free him from the confines of his pants, was tempted so much, he didn't protest when she did. Cooler air, but still warmer than outside the vehicle, wrapped around his length before her hand encircled him.

"Stroke me," he rasped out. She did. Damn her, but she did. His eyes rolled back in his head, and he sighed as pleasure lit in a million sparks beneath every inch of his skin. He breathed heavily against her cheek, nuzzled his face against hers, and moaned when she tightened her grip.

It'd be nice to let this play out, to rip off her panties, slide her over him, and sink his cock inside the warmth of her pussy, but that would be cheating. There'd be time for that later. Right now, he had a point to make.

"Does it feel like I'm shying from your touch?" he asked. She paused in the middle of a stroke, but he wrapped his hand around hers, squeezed until he winced, and used both their hands to stroke him, this time tighter and faster.

"Brady, stop, I'm going to hurt you."

"Answer the question." He clenched his hand and leaned back against the seat, his hips now pushing into the movement. The pain was there, but minimal. Something she wouldn't understand. Yet another thing he'd hidden.

"What?" she asked, her wide gaze on their joined hands.

As much as he didn't want to, he froze, but kept their hands where they were.

Johanna placed her free hand against her mouth, the limb shaking, taunting him. Her reaction called him all kinds of a bastard. Even worse. *She's practically an innocent, you dick.*

"Obviously, I have you in my hand, so I know you're not shying from my touch. There. Are you happy now?"

He narrowed his eyes. "Next time, do not fucking insinuate that I don't want to touch or hug you. It's you that's been shying from me, but you've also been throwing out some other vibe, babe, that we're going to get to the bottom of tonight. You brought this up and put it between us."

"You don't have to be a dick about it," she said through clenched teeth. "You could have very well told me rather than do this little side show."

"Baby," he said, amused by her words, and hopeful, because she sounded more like the Johanna he knew, "I am a dick, you have your hand around my dick, and honestly? I think you stroking me is much more fun."

She snorted, and he grinned.

"So…what now? Do you want me to finish you off"—his cock jumped at that option—"so we can go inside without you sporting a woody?"

He laughed, and she scowled again. "You said woody. As much as it sounds like a great idea, I have a surprise for you tonight and I'd rather keep with what I had in mind."

He removed his grip around her hand, but she didn't move. Instead, she looked down, and swiped her thumb over the bulbous head. He swallowed hard. "Why? We both trust each other," she said with a sly glance up at him, before resuming her study of his dick and her hand.

This was the back and forth he'd been talking about exactly. "Because," he said and gently removed her hand, then pressed a kiss to her palm. He tucked himself away and willed his body to get under control. "You're special. And I hope you'll remember that later tonight. Plus, I won't risk going there until we sort some shit out."

"What shit?"

He tilted toward the window and the dark building outside. He planned to show her, rather than tell her.

She frowned, and he rubbed the small wrinkles between her brows. "I don't agree entirely with everything you said, but I understand. However, I think you're making too big of a deal out of whatever this *shit* is. We're friends, you're one of the closest friends I have, and seriously, you didn't have to do all of this." She waved her hand toward the entrance. Her words made his heart kick. "You forget I know you…probably better than you know yourself."

If she only did…

"Christ," he said and scrubbed his face. "Let's go inside. And yeah, you're my BFF, too, and all that mushy shit."

She laughed and opened the door. The driver helped her out while Brady exited his side of the vehicle and rounded the trunk of the car. He kept a watchful eye along the length of the building, hating that he couldn't see in the dark alleyways. Streetlamps cast a buttery glow on the wet asphalt.

He took her hand. "I have an idea…if you're willing to open your mind a bit."

She flashed him a smile, and his heart tumbled into his stomach. Shit, he would miss her.

* * * *

The easy entry into the club surprised Johanna. While this nightclub setting, or whatever it was, hadn't ever been her scene—she was more of a bar girl—her curiosity pushed her to overlook the somewhat eerie and dank feeling at the door. The low lighting that told her the occupants who entered didn't want their faces seen. And the lack of a line called questions into legitimacy.

So instead of pointing all that out, she ignored her gut feeling, an instinct that had always done her well, and allowed the beefy looking bouncer dressed in a black suit and white open neck shirt—*trying to blend in much?*—to run his hands over her waist and at the small of her back in a professional, distant way, without rolling her eyes.

"Really now," she said with a huff of disgust. "What can I hide in this dress? A whole lot of nothing, that's what." The guy ignored her outburst. And even if she hadn't been sucking in her soft gut already, it still wouldn't have stopped her from trying to suck in some more. Because while she was a professional kick-some-asser, and the bouncer a hired security head, she still felt as if she needed to be the bigger badass here.

Whatever.

Brady took her hand with a smirk, his eyes dancing, and shook his head as if he knew what she'd done. Resisting the need to check and make sure all her girly parts were still tucked in, she lifted her chin, tightened her grip around his, and ignored the flutters in her stomach as well as the calluses on his palm. There hadn't been much opportunity to ever hold his hand, but seeing as she was proficient in handguns, she recognized the rough patch of skin. Those calluses told her he worked with his hands outside being a cop, too. There were groves in the middle of his fingers that matched the same on her dominant shooting hand. His skin seemed rougher, thicker, yet his hold was strong in a sense of she never wanted to let go.

How in the hell had she missed this? But before she finished silently asking that question, she knew. She never held his hand, had never been intimate, always kept this thin barrier up between them as if she somehow suspected things. Dark secrets. Dirty thoughts. Nefarious activities.

And no one wanted to believe someone they loved could be a master of disguise. In everything. A tough lesson she had to learn at such a young age when her father revealed he was more monster than man.

Brady tugged on her hand, pulling her into an open room, effectively pushing the unease to the back of her mind. Wide, cathedral ceilings stretched across a large room. Dark couches, of which she wasn't sure the color due to the muted lighting, were spaced throughout the room. Tables and benches lined the walls. One wall not covered to her left held the bar, and behind that, a built-in fish tank filled with exotic fishes of every color. A DJ mixed stimulating music across the room in a dark corner. A melody that whispered late-night promises made between two lovers. She had an urge to smooth her hands over the soft silk of her dress, just to feel any sort of sensory touch. Instead, she continued to take in the rest of the room. The only thing left was a dark wood dance floor in the middle.

That was it, a few pieces of furniture, some music, a bevy of drinks, and muted lighting. Yet she'd never been somewhere so sensual, so sexy, so promising that she couldn't help but epitomize the same feelings.

She didn't want to acknowledge her mood, but all of this was odd in the sense that she didn't consider herself anywhere near sexy or sensual. She was too manly, too strong, and too overbearing, all things she needed in order to be good at her job. Plus, she held an additional fifteen pounds since college, weight she'd never been able to kick no matter how many miles she ran, how many crunches she did. She blamed those fifteen pounds on her love for chocolate. If she could get away with it, she'd put the decadent treat on everything.

And don't get her started on her nose. The damn thing had been broken more than once. All of this should have made her feel inadequate, and they actually did, especially when she was in her friend's presence for some reason.

So, wanting to lean into Brady's body when his arm curled around her waist, wanting to rub against his face with hers, wanting to put a little extra swing in her hips, wasn't anything she expected. Yet, she had to fight against all those urges and allow him to lead her to the bar.

The heavy weight of curious gazes landed on her shoulders like a cloak, kissed the back of her neck as a long-lost lover would. She hated it all, and tried her best to avoid situations such as this; ones where she'd been in the middle of a strange crowd, in an unfamiliar location, and out of her depths with what to do. She didn't like people in her space, tried not to draw attention to herself, and had no idea how to deal with this situation.

Brady tugged on her hand, drawing her up between him and the bar, then sheltered her much smaller frame by setting heavy arms on either side of her. Yeah, he caged her in, and pretty damn well, she'd give him that. She couldn't help being both a little grateful and a little turned on. With his long, lean body barely brushing the back of hers, him playing the protector and not allowing others to reach her, as well as feeling the brush of silk against her skin… Well, he'd managed to take away every bit of her insecurities from seconds earlier, and make her feel very feminine.

It'd been so long since she'd felt anything other than responsibilities in taking care of her mother, of acting as the city's last line of defense against men who got off on kicking women around. For one night, the temptation to let go beckoned.

Be free.

Be anything other than who she was.

So, rather than curving in on herself in order to avoid any contact with anyone, Brady included, she subtly arched her back, and pushed her chest out, while at the same time her rear-end came ever-so-slightly in contact with his hips.

He jerked and stilled. The oddest sensation came over her. His entire focus centered on her. But more than knowing all that, a sinister type of tendril wove its way into her awareness. Almost like she'd poked a sleeping lion and was about to learn the meaning of boundaries. Either that, or she was a chocolate cake at a weight loss clinic meeting. She couldn't tell which, but both scenarios exhilarated and scared the absolute shit out of her.

Brady scooted closer so his groin came into full contact with her ass, the fit as if he'd been born to be there. He rapped two knuckles on the bar and caught the attention of the tender, who was dressed in a black tee with purple letters over the left breast, reading "Phuckit". He flashed two fingers at the young male, then pointed to a sign. Seconds later, two Coronas settled in front of them, and she snatched hers off the counter before her next blink.

A quick exchange of cash occurred, and she held her breath, waiting for him to move back and establish the friendly distance. It never came. Instead, he wrapped a big hand around his bottle, and she felt, rather than saw, him curve over her.

"Joey, have a care to who you're rubbing against." His voice rumbled low, causing her to shiver. Hot breaths puffed against the naked skin of her neck. She tilted toward his face, straining to hear what he'd say next, seeing as he hadn't moved away. "I'm all for teasing games, but there's a time, and there's definitely a place. You need to get taken care of, I'll make sure that happens. And I'll get you to that place keeping your safety in mind. You just gotta say the word."

Well, that was ominous. "What—" she tried to ask.

His free hand landed on her hip and squeezed. He pulled her toward him and pressed forward. *Holy shit!* Not only could she feel a very sizable erection slide between the crease of her cheeks, but the move caused her to arch her back even more to where she was almost bent over the bar counter. Surprising, seeing as he'd manipulated her with one movement of his hand. Hot because of the position, their surroundings, and because it was *him.*

She knew this position was doable for sex, she just never realized how much she wanted to try it until this moment.

Why now, she couldn't answer. Maybe it was the music. Maybe the atmosphere. Maybe it was just the time.

"I won't lie," he said against her ear, drawing her attention back, "and say I've never thought of getting you in bed. Even now, I want you. But there's more than just friendship coming between us and that happening. You need to understand a few things."

"What does that mean?" she asked, staring ahead at the dozens of exotic fish moving around in the tank. Such a simple life. Get fed. Swim around. Have someone else clean up your mess. Simple.

"Mr. McBride?" a throaty voice asked next to them.

Johanna tore her gaze away from the fish and focused on a woman in a long, skin-tight black dress. She was Brady's height, causing Johanna to look way up in order to catch her gaze. Beautiful, too, with long, rich mahogany waves slipping over her shoulders, tickling around a pair of smaller breasts.

"Finish your drink, Joey. I'll grab new ones before we head back." He released her and stepped away, far enough that they weren't in direct, intimate contact anymore. Cooler air brushed along the exposed skin of her back, his retreat making her bereft. She turned and found his dark head dipped low and talking to the newcomer, his voice too quiet for her to hear. She finished the beer, her eyes watering from the harsh carbonation, but her nerves singing in gratitude. She wanted something stronger, but had a feeling she'd need to keep her wits tonight. Brady wouldn't let anything happen to her, but for some reason, he seemed as much of a threat to her as the rest of the strangers in the room. Physically she didn't fear for her safety. But the feeling that she missed something, or rather, *was* missing something, still settled in her tummy.

He replaced her empty bottle for a fresh one, then grabbed her free hand and led her from the bar. They followed the woman through the crowd and to a door at the back wall.

"Where are we going?" Johanna asked.

The woman turned to both of them, one hand on the knob, the other holding a black keyless card. She ran her gaze down the length of Johanna, then turned to Brady. "Remember, guests are your responsibility. They break the rules, you'll be held accountable. It's in the contract."

"I understand. She will be fine."

"Wait, what?" Johanna asked. "What rules? What contract?"

The woman raised a brow, but kept her gaze on Brady. "This is interesting. You've never brought a guest before."

He matched her eyebrow. "Keeping tabs, are we?"

The woman shrugged. "It's in your file. Morgan is very particular about members. Especially those that act out of the norm for their regular activities."

His back went straight. "I'm not certain I like your tone. The only difference tonight is my guest. That's it. If Morgan has a problem with what I do, then both he and Bennett can ask me themselves."

The woman arched her brow. Brady didn't say anything, only stared back. Who were Morgan and Bennett? Owners, probably. But of what? Why the shady, secret conversation? The code talk?

The woman flickered her gaze to Johanna and back. "Can we assume she'll join you?"

Wait, what the hell was all this? Cryptic much? "Of course I'll join him," she inserted. "I am his guest."

Brady's brows cut down in a sharp vee, his hand squeezing hers in a warning. "She thinks we're having sex, Joey. Or rather, will have sex tonight."

"What? What business is it of hers to…" Johanna asked, at the same time the woman said, "I see."

"Like I've said, tonight is no different from any other. Just a friend accompanying me. I would think Morgan would be happy to have the possibility of more members," Brady said. "But if this is going to be a problem…"

"There's no problem. I'm glad we've cleared that up," the woman answered, her voice smooth, then turned and used the key card. An audible lock clicked, and she pushed open the door.

Johanna looked at Brady, whose face gave nothing away, then through the door, unable to see anything other than the fall of dark sheer drapery. "What's going on?"

He stopped, one foot inside the door, one out, and looked at her. "Do you trust me? This is just one part of tonight. I need to know you trust me."

She studied his features, looking for anything to give her a clue. Like always, though, his face gave nothing away. It was like he wore a mask, one he refused to take off. He had no tics, no tale-tells, no emotion. He stood there looking deadly handsome and so confident it was almost cocky. Their friendship swelled past thirteen years. He'd been there for her through so much.

Did she trust him? Trust not knowing what she was walking into?

She took a deep breath, bit her lip, and plunged off the cliff, stepping into the room behind him.

Where the music in the other room teased with sensual strokes, the melody floating through this one spoke of the deed. Of hot, sweaty sex with no shame.

Brady pushed through the drapery and paused for a moment before stepping aside.

The heavy weight of his attention landed on her, but she couldn't tear her gaze away from the room. There must have been a good twenty to thirty people standing around, some paired, others standing solo. Fog drifted along the floor and seemed thicker at the sides of the room. The scene would have looked ridiculous in any other room, but in this one, with the music floating through the air, the soft moans and smacking flesh, the added silliness provided exactly what it should have…a reticent mood. As if one would never know what could jump out from the mist and touch you.

The focus of everyone was on a stage about three feet higher than the rest of the floor, located at the back of the room. A couple moved together in ecstasy, the woman's lithe form bent over a bench, the male taking her from behind. And despite the ball in her mouth, despite Brady and Johanna being fifty feet from the stage, the pleasure this woman took was written all over her face.

Johanna gasped and set a hand high on her stomach, feeling a warmth curl deep within. That was pretty damn close to the position she'd been thinking of at the bar. Her skin tingled, her body turning on in a flash. Watching others engage in sex should be something forbidden, but it didn't feel that way. While it was a shock, she couldn't look away. Didn't want to. Instead, she imagined herself up on that stage, so free, so wanton, able to stand the stares of others on her skin. To see the desire etched in their faces for her, as they did now. To submit her body to the care and pleasure of someone stronger than her, someone who wouldn't let her down.

Someone she could trust.

The female screamed her release, and the male stiffened behind her with a harsh groan. Several in the audience moaned as well, the timing too coincidental, but very real. Johanna's breath caught.

The lights on the stage plunged into darkness as the room's overhead turned up a bit, though not much, and just like that, her connection to the stage broke. She looked around, then up at Brady. He studied her, his face inscrutable, as if waiting, or bracing, for her reaction. Why her best friend would bring her to a place like this was beyond her. She couldn't seem to keep up with any rational thought process in order to try and figure it out. She'd never given him a hint—hell, she hadn't even known she'd want to—that she'd want to attend a place like this. Sure, she'd heard of sex clubs before, knew that in a city the size of New York there'd be plenty of them around, but she'd been with one man, one time, and that experience hadn't had her wanting to jump back into bed again anytime soon.

Pretty sad for someone who was twenty-six years old.

Sure, she'd given herself pleasure, but that wasn't the same as receiving one from another's hands. Instinctually, as if her body was curious, she took in Brady's hands. Long fingers, a wide palm with calluses that would surely catch on the fragile material of her dress. Would he build her up slowly with those hands, or would he work her into a fast frenzy over and over again?

What was she thinking? This was Brady.

"Why did you bring me here?" she asked.

"Hold on a second. What just went through your mind?" he countered, instead of answering her question. She tilted her face. His gaze was still on her. She wished for once he'd give something, anything away with his expressions. His hand tightened on hers.

"I—I…" She tried to find the words that wouldn't disclose what she really felt. That the scene turned her on more than she'd ever been before. That she wondered what it'd be like to have Brady take her to that stage. That her mind was having these betraying thoughts. That tonight had cemented a pivotal change in their relationship. Things would never be the same, regardless of them having sex or not.

Not that she thought he brought her here to have sex. No way. He'd never given her any indication that he'd be interested in her like that.

"Joey," he murmured and drew her closer, "don't overthink this. If you're uncomfortable, we'll leave. Just say the word."

"I'm not uncomfortable," she said. A sound drew her attention back to the stage. It seemed to be rotating, and instead of the bench and chair, this new room had a bed covered in a thick, lacy white comforter. A woman sat on the bed, her head bowed, while a man stood off to the side. As soon as the stage stopped rotating, the man stepped forward and brushed his fingers along the woman's face. Her sigh reached across the room. The audience held their breath, anticipating what would come next.

"What's happening?" she whispered.

"Come," he said, tugging on her hand. He drew her into the crowd, gently easing past bodies. Her attention darted back to the stage time and time again. The female still sat on the bed, but now her head tipped back. The man leaned down and kissed her, the act anything but normal. There was a sensuality in the kiss, a need driving the scene, rather than acting things out. What the couple engaged in seemed normal, as if they were in the privacy of their own room, not in a club full of strangers. And still, even in the objectification of the scene, the trust between the couple was a visible string tying them together.

The man pulled back and eased the woman from the bed, then led her to the wrought iron pole at the end. He stepped into her and kissed her. Johanna's heart sighed. This was what she wanted to experience again. Not necessarily just sex. But the story that was told in the act. This was why she wanted to take a lover. To build a deep connection to someone.

Brady shifted behind her and set their linked hands on her stomach. So in tune with the scene, she hadn't realized they stopped moving. She risked a quick glance over her shoulder, but found his attention on the scene as well, his lips parted ever so. Again, nothing in his expression told her what he thought.

She faced forward. The man had pulled the woman's arms over her head and tied them to a railing that held sheer drapery around the bed. Her white negligee rode high on her legs with the pose, something the man paid attention to if his hands teasing along the top of her thighs were any indication. He inched up the negligee, baring the woman's skin so slowly Johanna thought she'd scream. Instead, her breath punched out with harsh pants and she squeezed her nails into the only thing she could find, Brady's arm.

He hissed and gently smoothed her grip. His hand, though, now lay against her stomach, his palm so wide the pinkie reached the top of her pelvis and his thumb brushed beneath her breasts. She should feel embarrassed, with his hand over her stomach, where extra weight lingered, but Johanna couldn't feel much of anything but hot and turned on.

Her nipples tightened. The area between her legs grew moist. And tingles spread low in her tummy.

"Do you like watching?" Brady's voice rumbled in her ear. The vibrations sent an erotic shock down the length of her spine.

"Why did you bring me here?" she asked inanely again.

Silence sounded loud from behind her while moans from the stage filled the air. The man had pulled the woman's negligee up until the material covered her eyes, and he had his dark head dipped toward her chest.

"You need an outlet," Brady finally said, his mouth next to her ear. "I've seen you wind yourself up tighter than a helix these past two years, and more recently with taking care of your mom. You need to find someplace where you can be who you need to be, a place where you can let go. I think," he said and seemed to hesitate for a few seconds, "that you might find yourself in a place like this."

She drew her brows together in thought, unable to take her gaze off the stage. "So you thought a sex club was the place I should do that? You know me so well you honestly think I'd want to let go in a place such as this?"

"Don't get your damn panties in a twist. It's not like that. There's something deeper that goes on here."

"Then what is it? Because for the life of me, I can't seem to understand how you would think it'd be appropriate for me, someone who has had sex once, who has built this larger than life reputation in the city, the face of domestic violence? You think bringing me here would somehow be what I need. And really, with everything I'm dealing with, did you think this would be the place I'd want to spend my free time out?"

"You know I'm just as upset about your mom, Joey. Her mind is deteriorating, and because of the abuse she's been through, it's progressing pretty fast, but you have her in a home now, so that isn't any excuse you can use tonight. And don't get me started on your vigilante justice bullshit. When's the last time you've been with a man? Even to just let him touch you." His lips brushed below her ear.

She shivered. "I don't think my orgasms are any of your business."

"I didn't ask when the last time you pleasured yourself was. I asked when was the last time you let a man between your thighs. When you laid with someone that wasn't a piece of vibrating plastic. Someone who had a heartbeat, that could generate heat like you, that could make you moan with surprise."

Her core clenched at both his words and the erotic scene unfolding before her. The man on the stage was on his knees, one of the woman's legs over his shoulder, his face buried between her thighs. "Why are you doing this?" she asked, out of breath.

"Sometimes people need to be pushed into something that's best for them. And if you want an answer to your question, you need to understand this."

The woman on stage arched her back and cried out her release. Johanna gripped Brady's thigh behind her. Someone next to them groaned low. A shadow stepped up to the right of them and whispered something in Brady's ear. She couldn't tear her gaze away. Her body held on the precipice of something, as if she would orgasm watching. One touch and she'd go over the ledge.

"And this," she said with a nod toward the stage, her own back arching, her hips pressing back into Brady's, "this is what you think I need? To watch couples fuck each other in front of a crowd?"

"No," he said and brushed his lips over the shell of her ear. An extreme contrast to his fingers biting into her hips. "There's something deeper I think you need. And more, understand. This is the only way I could think of to make you understand."

Her heart slammed against her chest. He was going to say yes. The attraction, the teasing, the liberties she'd taken with him had all be in good fun. Okay, she wasn't being truthful. She'd always been attracted to Brady, but hadn't ever acted on it. First, for obvious reasons. Then, it'd seemed like something that could never be. That was until the past few months when this urgency had built, almost as if time was ticking away until any shot they had for a friendship or more would slip through their fingers. She didn't know where this feeling came from, but she didn't like it, and needed to act before it was too late.

Then again, she was curious to see what would happen between them and used her inexperience as an excuse to open a line of communication on the topic. Having him confirm he'd known what she'd been doing, and having him put the go-ahead in words sent a thrill of excitement up her spine. But it made her nervous as ever, too. Butterflies took flight in her stomach, and a buzz encompassed her head, almost as if electricity sparked across the surface.

"This?" she asked, and her breath caught. He tightened his arm around her waist. A band of steel entrapping her.

He nipped her ear, and she somehow knew it was a disciplinary action. "Don't play coy. We're past that. You want to jump off this cliff, I'm willing to take you up on what you've been offering."

Her spine stiffened, and she wanted to turn, but he still held her in place.

"I'm through hiding," he strangely stated. "We do this, you know it all. This"—he motioned toward the stage—"is just one part of me. If you understand after watching, and explain to me how you understand, then I think you'll be ready for my answer."

An uncomfortable feeling settled in her stomach. The back of her neck prickled. "This? That you like to watch?"

"And be watched. I like control. I like for others to see that control."

That uncomfortable feeling turned sour. She stared at the stage, at what a moment prior she had thought was beautiful. Now she pictured Brady up there and felt despair. How often had he done this? How often did he take women up there?

The shadow at their right shifted, reminding Johanna they weren't alone. Brady bent toward the figure, the shadow turning out to be who had grabbed them from the front. They had a conversation too low to hear, but both nodded and shook their heads in answers to some questions she wished she knew.

The woman said something. Her gaze darted to Johanna quickly and Brady tilted toward her. He straightened. "How much longer?" he asked the woman.

"Ten minutes, at most fifteen."

He nodded. "That should work. I shouldn't need any more. I'll take the penthouse. One female. Samantha if she's around. Melissa if she isn't."

The woman stared at Johanna. "And her?"

Brady kept his gaze ahead, not sparing her a glance, and that ugly feeling was back, dirtier than before. What was going on? "She'll sit to the side at a private table. Have Henry watch over. And no one, absolutely no one is to go near her. Matter of fact, bring Henry to me and I'll explain myself."

Her stomach turned. Was he thinking of... And what did he mean, someone watch over her? She could watch over herself, thank you very much. But first... "What's going on?"

The woman's eyes narrowed just a bit. Not as if she were mad or annoyed, but merely curious. "Mr. McBride does a scene here every other week. One of the more popular shows we have. We're discussing the preparations for that scene." She paused. "You didn't know?"

Johanna swallowed the remaining fluid in her mouth and immediately wished she hadn't. Her stomached roiled in protest. Rather than open her mouth and risk throwing up, she shook her head.

"No?" the woman asked, her brows flying high. She waved her hand around to encompass the room. "Look around. Look at how the crowd grows even now. As if they are waiting for him."

Johanna did. The crowd grew thicker, feet shuffling closer to the stage as if they slid through syrup.

"There's no other scene more popular." The woman tilted her head. "And yet, here you two looked so close. I'm surprised you didn't know."

"Enough, Francesca," Brady said in a low warning.

"Why else did you come tonight if not to watch him?" Francesca asked.

"I didn't...know."

"You didn't know? What did you—"

"Francesca," Brady barked.

"I didn't realize this was a sex club, okay?" Johanna snapped, trying to pull herself out from below the sinking water of humiliation. The water filled higher and higher, her head a chaotic mess. Pretty soon she'd be submerged.

Francesca tapped a long red nail atop the same shade of plump lips. "But you're King, am I right? You know everything that goes on in the city? Or at least, if the rumors are true, you should."

She was not wrong. This club should be something she knew. But she hadn't. Sure, her mind had wondered time and time again, but she'd never had any reason to come inside, nor had she ever been allowed past the front door.

Until tonight.

She shrugged. "Well, you got me. Apparently, I don't know everything going on."

Francesca curved her lips slightly. "So now that you know, what are you going to do about it?"

Brady's spine snapped. "Stop."

"What? You mean you didn't invite her? Tell her?"

"Tell me what?" Johanna asked.

Francesca turned wide eyes and a wide smile toward her. "You could join him." Johanna's heart slipped up her throat. "Either taking Samantha's spot or joining them both."

"Goddammit, stop it!" Brady roared.

The crowd around silenced and turned toward them. Johanna felt every one of their gazes on her skin. Calling her a fraud. Unworthy. A coward. Heat blistered across her face and chest. She wanted to hide or leave, but she couldn't get her feet to move. Not knowing what was coming on that stage in ten to fifteen. Okay, okay, bad choice in words, but still…

"She won't be joining me on stage," Brady stated firmly to Francesca. "You can only push me so far tonight, Frankie. I'll advise you to stop now."

Frankie? Just how did he know this woman so well to have a nickname for her? Did he frequent the club that much? She spread her free hand across her stomach, trying to will it to calm down and not upchuck the chicken enchiladas they'd had for dinner. Her joining Brady on stage wasn't an option she'd normally consider, especially with how much she and her body didn't get along at present. Had she been anyone else, in any other city, she might consider it. Especially with the option of doing something so daring and wicked with him.

"Why not?" Francesca asked. "Why not let her up on the stage with you? Isn't that the real reason you brought her?"

"No," he answered immediately. Yeah, okay, that was starting to bug her. His quick and adamant refusals to let her participate.

Participate?

What was this, some kind of recreational town sporting event now?

Jeez.

"What…why don't you let her answer for herself, McBride? Perhaps she'll shock you," Francesca antagonized.

"No."

"Why not?" Johanna asked.

Both pairs of eyes turned to her and both sets of brows raised.

"See," Francesca said at the same time Brady asked, "What?"

"Why can't I…" She would not say participate. She would not say participate. "Why can't I be in the scene? With you?"

He jerked back and eyed her with speculation. She was not some damn bug under a microscope, yet that look, the "you have got to be kidding me" plastered all over his face made her feel about one-foot-tall, and as appetizing as a liver and onions. "How many reasons do you want?"

She flinched. *Ouch. That hurt.* She tried to tug her hand from his, but he held tight.

"I didn't mean it like that, dammit. Shit." He scrubbed a hand over his scalp and scowled as if he'd forgotten something.

"Yeah, pal, you look like Mr. Clean the past few weeks." Teach him to get friendly with clippers.

His scowl increased and he shook his head. "Brat." He heaved a heavy sigh. "I simply meant that doing a scene isn't something for everyone, Joey. I didn't bring you here for this. I brought you here for you, and for you to understand."

She couldn't help but look over. The stage had rotated again. Now, a sheet of dark glass stood between her and the stage. Through the glass, a masculine living room decorated the area. A long and simple black leather couch, a glass coffee table, and a china buffet with various bottles inside. How many scenes did this stage hold?

"Three," Brady answered. "With additional props they can use to switch out. The larger furniture stays, though."

Had she spoken out loud? "But what if I want to try?" she asked, voice soft.

"What if I don't want you to?" he retorted, just as soft. She looked at him then. Turbulent feelings finally flittered across his face, and a world of worry sat in his eyes. Fine time for him to show her something. He'd gone back and forth with her tonight, one minute his hands all over her, sexy talk coming out of his mouth. The next, as cold as a glacier in Alaska. She didn't know what was real. There was one way to find out. And that was to push.

"Then I'd ask you to try, too," she answered.

He sighed and bit his lip. She honed in on the move. Blunt teeth that even looked strong. The pearly whites scraped over a plump lip and left behind a trail of moisture. Way too sexy a move for a man.

He growled her name and her eyes shot up to his. "That look did it." He didn't seem happy. "Fine. But don't say I didn't warn you."

* * * *

This is a bad idea, McBride. And he wasn't talking about just bringing her on stage. Bringing Johanna here tonight had been the stupidest thing he could have done. But again, things hadn't been quite right between them, something that over the past few months had gotten worse and worse. And then she talked about never going out anymore. His dumb ass just had to tell her about a club he knew. One that in the deep recess of his mind he'd fantasied about bringing her to many times before, but that's what those thoughts should have remained. A fantasy. He should have never followed through.

He'd really stepped in it this time.

Now here he was, minutes from having full control over Johanna, the ability to touch her, to pleasure her, and to take his pleasure as he saw fit from her lithe little curvy body. A body he'd jacked off to more times than he could remember while lying in bed during the darkest hours. Curves he'd imagined tasting. On a woman who was cleaner than he'd ever be.

Dammit, why couldn't he have offered a nice night out to dinner and maybe some quiet music? There were things they needed to talk about. Things they should have discussed way sooner than minutes before baring themselves to about a hundred strangers on the other side of the wall. *Fuck.*

He roughly massaged the area between his brows, trying to quiet the throbbing pain. Sharp, almost like a gremlin sat inside his head and chipped at his skull from the inside out using an icepick.

He blew out a heavy breath. Shit, maybe it wasn't too late. Maybe he could still grab her, take her somewhere else, and tell her everything she needed to know. Maybe then she wouldn't hate him as much as she would if they went through with this.

Yeah, he had to tell her. There was no denying the need to get it all off his chest. To just have her know how much he liked to give pain and receive it during sex. Not in the masochistic sense, but more to heighten the peak of pleasure. That he had to have the pain in order to orgasm because he was a fucked up man.

Decision made, he crossed the room, scanning through the few people standing around. A hint of red popped up in his peripheral, and he cursed under his breath as Johanna slipped around the corner leading to the stage. There was still time to catch her before the lights lowered in the crowd.

He picked up his steps, and rounded the corner, then stopped in his tracks as if he ran into an invisible wall.

Frankie was good at staging a scene. And with the sight that greeted him, she had definitely staged. Johanna had her back to him, facing what was supposed to be a window that would generate a picture of the skyline at night from their side. On the other side of the glass, the audience would just see them.

Her legs were shoulder length apart, her hips tilted back. All of that was great in any normal circumstance. Her dress made it even better. But what made it out of this world was that Frankie—or Johanna, he wasn't sure—had positioned her to pull the dress up until just a hint of cheek peeked out. Combined with her world class legs and her long hair trailing down her back, she looked very much the wanton vixen waiting for her lover.

And that's all it took.

He wanted her. He'd have her.

He was a selfish son of a bitch.

The lights in the crowd lowered and the murmurs evaporated until only the sound of his heavy breaths echoed through his ears.

Fuck. Go to her. Give her one more chance, asshole. Call off the scene.

But he couldn't get his feet to move. Instead, he was captivated, caught in the spell of sexual hunger and long denied cravings.

The lights came on in front of Johanna, and while it was all fake, it still looked good. The membership fees at the club were nothing to baulk at, and Morgan didn't make any qualms about showing everyone what he put the money to use for. This skyline shot was done from an angle at midtown, high in the sky. Beautiful. And despite all the darkness, he loved his city.

Even knowing it was fake, that all of this wasn't actually placed in a penthouse somewhere secret, the crowd around faded away. All he could concentrate on was her. The soft rise and fall of her shoulders. The slight movement of her hair tickling her lower back with a teasing caress. The fingers of her hands clenching the silky material of her dress.

She shook slightly, and had he been in any other frame of mind, that might have made him pause. Instead, he decided to draw out the anticipation a bit more. To make her wait for his touch, his voice, his command.

Him.

Soft gray notes of light caressed her hair. Even the light wanted in on their affair. A private rendezvous with two lovers looking forward to a night of raw and dirty fucking.

She couldn't possibly know the affect she had on him. If she did, she'd run.

She'd run fast.

* * * *

Johanna swore she was going to throw up. Her stomach heaved and twisted, as if it was scraped over an old washboard in an elaborate attempt to cleanse every dirty little thought she'd ever had in reference to Brady.

Standing on a stage with unknown how many eyes on her, practically begging to be used, to be fucked by a man she'd once considered the closest friend she'd ever had, was like baring her soul to Dracula. And why she was thinking of references such as the Prince of Darkness was beyond her. Perhaps it was because she was prey to a big, bad demon who would end up sucking her dry in the most delicious way before the night was over.

Why had she agreed to this? Her throat burned with the need to either cry or puke, she couldn't decide which, but neither would be very attractive. And therein lay the root of her problem.

She'd never seen herself as attractive. Sure, she had the confidence to do her own version of vigilante justice, but that was the extent of where her confidence went. Otherwise, her thighs were too thick, her stomach too round, her breasts burdensome, and her face too dull. She'd never been one to stand out on the street, or get the construction workers worked up in a frenzy of cat calls. No. She'd never been that girl. And so baring herself to this scene with Brady, knowing that others were counting on her to turn them on, had her seriously questioning whether she could go through with this.

If she walked off now, maybe everyone would give her a pass. After all, nothing had really begun yet…

"Don't move," Brady whispered next to her ear. She gasped and clenched her hands on her dress. How had he approached without her knowing?

"What?" she asked, even though she'd heard him.

"I said," he replied, trailing a finger down her cheek. Goosebumps popped up across her body, and she shivered. "Don't move." This time, he spoke in a low voice, but somehow his words carried across the space. She looked around, careful to not move her body, seeking any microphones. Nothing was visible. But she knew what she'd heard.

"Brady, I don't know if—"

He tsked her. "You had your chance, Johanna." Her full name on his lips was a shock to her senses and told her she was definitely out of her element. This man only had to utter a few words and she both heard the command and knew who was in charge.

Him.

Fingers trailed across the curve of her right butt cheek. The touch went from the outside of her hip to the inside of her cheek. Her lower stomach clenched, and she craved more of his contact, perhaps his whole hand. And even more than that, she craved his touch to move to where she wanted it most. Anything to relive some of the pent-up pressure that had gathered. She sucked in her lower lip and tilted her hips into his hand.

He chuckled beneath his breath.

The sound broke her out of the moment. Was he laughing at her? How pathetic was she to allow such a simple touch to reduce her to putty? She sucked in a sharp breath and straightened.

Before she had the chance to turn and confront him, she found the front of her body plastered against the glass partition.

"Do you have a problem following commands?" he asked, his voice laced with bafflement.

"What?" He had never handled her like this, nor did she know how to respond. Her first instinct had been to fight back, but she didn't want to hurt him.

"I told you not to move, and then you go and pull away from my touch. What...is that it? Do you want to be punished?" His hand at her waist tightened. "I don't believe it."

She shook her head. "I don't understand. I don't understand any of this. Let me go."

"No. I already told you that your time has passed. We're moving on from that. What I want to know is why you pulled away from my touch. What went through your head?"

She gave short shakes. "Don't."

He sighed and pressed his forehead against her temple. "You should have run from me, Joey." These words were spoken so low she almost didn't catch them. But she did, and their meaning were baffling, utterly confusing. He, a man who'd grown from a young protector and hidden her away when the beatings at home became too much. A man who'd always had her back, even when he opposed everything she stood for. A man who had always been such a dear friend to her.

And yet, she'd put him in this spot.

Shame washed over her. She'd manipulated the situation to her advantage to get what she thought she wanted. He'd come here for whatever his reason, which was obviously sex, but more than likely not with her. She hadn't listened when he said no. Hadn't done what he asked and sat by until he was finished. Even though the shame filled her until she felt poisoned, still the thought of him touching someone else made her feel nauseous.

"I'm sorry I've put you in this situation." She blew out a heavy breath, fog creating a round, little glow against the glass.

His hand curved over her hip to lay flat against her stomach. He pressed her toward him and nuzzled her face, brushing his lips where his forehead had been. "What situation? Talk to me."

"Well…" she hedged and bit her lip, all kinds of a coward. She wanted to be looked at as a grown woman, it was time she started acting like one. "Making you bring me up here. I've ruined your night, so I'm sorry."

The hand at her hip ran up the length of her spine to fist in her hair and pulled back. Not a tug or a yank, but with steady pressure until she was forced to look at the ceiling. Brady ran his nose along her neck. Her breath jumped.

"Making me bring you up here?" he asked, his voice holding a slight edge.

"Yeah," she said on a shaky gasp. He removed his hand from her stomach and reached across her body to slide the strap of her halter over her head. The dress pulled hard against her. He held the strap in front of her face, then dropped it. Being so tight against her at the bodice, it didn't fall. Small favors. "Brady," she called. What was he doing?

"I've never been one for following orders. Haven't we had this conversation once tonight?" He nipped her throat and she jumped. "Stay still, Johanna."

She swallowed. "What are you doing?"

He wrapped his palm around the top of her throat, then inch by slow inch, slid it down the length until his hand splayed across her exposed cleavage. An unsteady breath in her ear, his mouth hovering. Then he grabbed the front of her dress, his intentions clear as if he screamed them.

"Wait," she said.

"How much do you like this dress?"

She frowned. "What? Please don't rip it."

He tightened his grip of her hair. "I want to. I want to rip this fabric off you so goddamn bad."

Her breath burned out of her lungs. "Why?"

"Because I never want to see you in it again."

"What?" she choked out.

"Because," he said, almost talking over her, "if I see you in it again, it's just going to remind me of that time I fucked your brains out."

Her stomach flipped.

"And then I'm going to want to fuck you all over again. I don't know if I could be held accountable for my actions."

"Brady…" she said, but nothing more came out as he gave a steady pull again, this time on the front of her dress. The material strained, something tore at the side, and then her breasts were freed. Cool air drew her nipples into tight peaks, and behind her, Brady's whole body shuddered.

"Fuck," he said. Hot breaths pushed across her temple, his hands holding her hips tight. The night had definitely taken a turn she didn't know how to process. This was the whole problem, why she asked him to teach her things about sex. Well, at least that had been what it was originally about. Now? She had no clue. Did she interact with him? Touch him? Could she move yet? Or was this part of his foreplay? Because if it was, it wasn't doing much of anything but making her too self-conscious.

There was no way she'd forgotten that the room was nearly full of individuals watching them. And since she faced them, they probably had a pretty good view of her breasts, not an image she supposed was sexy like the skinny vixen that had been on stage before her.

And the longer he stood behind her not moving, the more her exposed breasts shamed her. They were too big. Heavy. And outside tonight, always wrapped with sports bras. The image in her mind turned uglier and uglier. What the crowd had to think of her. What Brady had to think of her.

Her sinuses flared, her eyes burned, and humiliation washed over her in a tidal wave. How had she ever believed she was good enough to be with Brady. To actually turn him on.

She turned her face away from his mouth and her breath hiccupped.

"I don't know if I can be gentle," he said low, strained.

She swallowed a hard lump, trying her best to hold everything inside until she could escape. She brought one arm down and over her chest, wanting to shield herself, or help block the ugliness of her body from the crowd, she couldn't decide which.

"I'm sorry," she said. "I shouldn't have put you in this position. I feel so embarrassed." She turned, barely making it around before finding her back against the wall again. He hadn't moved an inch.

He stared down at her incredulously. "What the hell is this? What are you talking about? What position? Why are you embarrassed?"

She clenched her teeth. Damn if she would say it. "Don't. You don't have to play dumb. It's okay. Let's go get Samantha, or whoever you asked for earlier."

"The fuck we will."

His vehemence took her aback. She met his gaze. An alarm licked across her skin. The man in front of her was no longer the protector she'd known, the friend who'd made her laugh until her stomach hurt, the colleague who'd had her back more than a hundred times. No, he was danger personified. A living, breathing predator who was extremely pissed off. And all that anger focused on one thing.

Her.

"You had your chance," he said and unbuckled his belt. He whipped it out of his pants. Leather snapped and licked through the air. "I told you there was no longer an option of escape. You had that slim moment, and I gotta tell you, Johanna, I don't even think you'd have been able to escape then, either."

She slid down the glass wall, moving away. She couldn't help it. His words bled fury. His gaze jumped down to her feet and back up again. Then he cocked his head in a very animalistic move "You going to try to run now, Joey? After what I've just said?"

His tone mocked, but his words held an undercurrent of warning.

"Don't try and tell me you wouldn't prefer someone else?" she hissed out. "That they"—she gestured toward the crowd with her free hand—"wouldn't prefer someone else."

His eyes narrowed. "Are you deaf tonight? Or is the dumb routine part of the scene for you?"

Her spine snapped straight. "Fuck you."

He grinned. The bastard actually grinned! "No," he said, amusement lacing his words, "I'm going to fuck you."

Then, he lunged.

She tried to turn and run, but came up short. Before she knew what happened, her hands were bound by his belt and held over her head, hanging from a large hook that had come down from the ceiling. He gathered her dress and pulled. The fabric tore, then the cloth fell to the floor, baring her body with the exception of the tiny, French-cut thong.

She froze, shocked to her core at the depth of violence Brady had meting out in under thirty seconds. And to her, no less! He'd never raised a hand to her. Never hurt her. Never manhandled her in such a way.

Yet...if she were being honest, he hadn't hurt her now either. But he had definitely manhandled her. There was no doubt about that.

She ignored the slight thrill that gave her, to know he could throw her around as if she weighed nothing. Instead, she turned furious eyes toward him. He didn't meet her gaze. No, the *a-hole* had the nerve to slide his inspection across her exposed flesh.

"Let me go," she demanded.

He brought his hand down on her exposed ass cheek. The *smack* echoed in her ears. "No. And each time I hear you say something idiotic, you'll be punished to my choosing."

"Idiotic?" she said, seething, her ass stinging. "How dare you?"

He turned and hit a switch. The lights lowered. His hands on her waist turned her to face the glass again.

Stretched out, she had to admit, her reflection was shockingly erotic. Almost beautiful. From here it looked as if she had long, graceful legs, when they were anything but. Only an appearance because of the cut of her underwear, the way she had to point her toes to reach the ground.

Even her breasts looked shapely, her dark nipples a stark contrast against her creamy flesh.

Her hair trailed down her back and over her shoulders to curl enticingly above her cleavage.

But still, no matter how scandalous the look, it was an illusion. Not who she really was.

Brady stepped in front of her, blocking her view. She wasn't complaining, though. He'd removed his jacket and shirt, and had only his dress slacks on with the top button undone. He'd even removed his shoes.

Hair long enough to pull dusted his chest. He was broad shouldered with strong pecs and abs that weren't necessarily model perfect, but fit him to proportions and no less beautiful. He was perfect to her. Every inch of him a piece she wanted to touch, taste, and lick.

Above her head, her hands clenched.

"Look at me," he demanded. The blue gaze of his irises burned into her with a stunning intensity. "I don't know what to do with you. I have to give you that, Johanna, no one has ever done *that*. And yet, at the same damn time, I want to punish you, but also hold you in my arms. It's fucking driving me insane."

She lifted a brow and tried to stop focusing on the lush pad of his lower lip. It looked bitable. "What?" She thought over his words. "Now that you have me tied up, you don't know what to do with me?" She laughed without humor. "Please."

He shook his head and rubbed his chin. "No, you missed my intent. I'm torn between fucking you silly, or marking your body with my touch or the kiss of leather. How is it you can drive me toward violence and gentleness at the same time?"

Her entire body clenched in questionable fear. "Like that BDSM shit? You're into that stuff?"

He gave a slight nod, almost unsure of himself, which wasn't like him.

"You want to beat me." She couldn't figure out if she said it as a statement or a question.

He took it for a question. "Not beat you. Mark you. Bend you to my will." His attention narrowed on her lips. "Fix that smart little mouth so you stop talking back...before I put it to other uses."

"Hurt me."

He drew up so quick she hadn't seen him move. His face was centimeters from hers, his hand wrapped under her jaw. "Never." His chest brushed against her nipples with each ragged breath. "Don't you get it? My touch on your body, whether it be soft or hard, is never designed to hurt you. Do you honestly think I'd ever do anything like that to you or any woman?"

She thought over his question. There was no need. She'd already known the answer as well as she knew herself. "No."

"Do you think any of the men or women in this room would allow me to do something that hurt you? In a way that wouldn't bring you pleasure? Have you lost your faith in humanity that much?"

The reminder that they weren't alone slapped across her senses. Brady had her complete attention. She'd forgotten everyone else, a feat she would have called impossible. But it'd happened. The dark glass behind him beckoned. "They can see me naked."

"Of course they can."

She turned her face away, shamed all over again.

"Hey," he said and turned her back with a hold under her jaw. "What is going on with you? What's this?"

"Please," she said, her voice shaking.

He frowned. "Please what?"

"Take me down. Don't make me do this."

He froze and stared at her for several seconds. "I thought you wanted this. You asked for this. You wanted me to teach you."

The hint of vulnerability took her aback and showed a different side of him. "I'm just...I'm not like the other women up here. My body...it's just not..."

His lips tightened. "Stop."

She looked up at him again. *Uh oh.* The anger was back.

"Stop what?"

He didn't answer, or rather, he didn't answer with words. His mouth crushed against hers and his tongue thrust into her mouth. His kiss laid a claim on her, his tongue the skillful puppet master. He stroked her to respond, urged her to participate. And did she ever. How could she deny him anything? How did she think she ever could?

She tangled her tongue with his, matched his rhythm and thrust, lost herself in how to feel. How he made her feel. There was nothing she could compare it to, the feel of his mouth rubbing against hers. The soft nips with his teeth, the soothing licks to take away the hurt. His fingers holding her head in place, yet at the same time moving in an erotic massage against her scalp. She couldn't explain it, but each tiny motion he made with his hands sent sparks of pleasure across every inch of her skin. As if her body was waiting in breathless anticipation for him.

And his taste...the sweetest nectar to her parched soul.

He broke away from their kiss with a rough sound, then placed his mouth next to her ear. "I'm going to fuck you now."

Her thighs clenched, and instantly, she was drenched. Ready. He pulled back and grinned at her, as if he knew. The bastard.

He turned behind her and faced the darkened window again. In their reflection, she watched as he dropped his head. The sight of him combined with the feel of him biting at her hip had a moan tearing up her throat. He dropped down, then looked up, holding her gaze as he pulled her thong off using his teeth.

Rising to his full height, he moved slowly, as if he had all the time in the world. The silence, his lack of words or erotic lines sounded too loud. She fidgeted, unable to easy the coil inside her.

"Brady," she said on a breathless moan.

He paused. "Yes, baby? Something you need?"

She narrowed her eyes while her stomach flipped with the endearment. He knew what she needed. The proof visible with liquid running down her leg and in the hard tips of her nipples. She tried to pull her hand from its binding, but no matter how strong she was, there was nothing to be done.

Instead, she dropped her head back on a gasp. Something was going on with her body. Something she couldn't control. This deep, deep ache built inside of her, almost a restless kind of animal that wanted to be set free.

She bit down on her lip, both scared and a little daunted by what she'd gotten herself into. She didn't understand this feeling. Didn't understand this need.

Brady grabbed her hair and yanked her back even more, thrusting her chest out to try and follow the movement. She had to curve her spine into the shape of a C, and held her weight by her tippy toes. "I asked you a question, Johanna. I expect an answer."

Her mind worked frantically back in time, trying to remember the question. Oh…what did she need.

"I don't…" How could she put this into words? Did he expect her to voice what she wanted? Him. Hadn't she already said so? "What?" She tried to get her thoughts in order.

But instead of asking her another question, he let go of her hair, wrapped his arm around her waist, lifted, and stepped forward. The hook she hung from rolled along some track high above. She couldn't see it, but she could sure hear. The sound stopped just before her body jerked to a halt with a tug on her hands. Brady pushed forward and pressed her against the glass wall.

The coolness of the glass was a shock to her senses, especially since she felt overheated, as if she'd combust from the inside out.

He stepped away and the sound of rustling cloth followed, the rip of something. A grunt. She tried to see him behind her in the reflection, but being so close, the angle wasn't working. Slowly, something else began to happen. With each breath she took, her stomach pressed her hip to and fore against the glass, creating a slight friction with her skin. Not enough to get her off, but enough to remind her of a sensual little dance that could follow.

The glass also gave off a steady hum, almost a vibration, but it wasn't steady at all, she realized. No, it was vibrating to a beat. And her body subconsciously tried to get closer.

Brady stepped up against her again, and this time there was no mistaking him being stark naked. Coarse hair from his chest and legs brushed against her back and thighs. The proud jut of his erection slid between her legs to run against the lips of her core. She spread her legs as much as she could, seeing as she was still on her tippy toes. It wasn't much, but it was enough.

He chuckled and hissed, his erection making contact with the hottest part of her. Instead of changing the angle of his hips and thrusting inside, though, he kept up a deliciously slow pace, running the length of his erection over her entrance and clit. Her eyes rolled back in her head as sparks of pleasure erupted over her skin, from deep in her belly.

She moaned his name.

He paused, grabbed her hips, and pressed her legs together. His cock stayed nestled against her clit, unmoving, but right there. "What do you need, Johanna?" he asked again, his breathing heavy and erratic.

"You," she answered without missing a beat.

He tapped the outside of her thighs. "Leave these here."

Before she could ask why, he cupped her breasts and resumed moving his hips back and forth, but this time the pace was even slower. She groaned in frustration.

"What do you need, Johanna?" he asked again.

She tried to move her hips, wanting to speed things up, but his erection slipped out from between her lips and she made a frustrated sound. "Brady! Please!"

He pinched her nipples sharply, the pain causing her to cry out.

He grabbed her hips again, then held her in place as he slowly slid back in place. "I asked you a question you still haven't answered," he said, his words gritted.

"What?" He ran an agonizing slow ride across her clit. She gasped. "I did."

"Listen," he said and slapped her once across her backside. The crack sounded through the air and heat spread from the center and out, adding to the haze of pleasure. "One more time, Johanna. What do you need?"

She could feel the ridge of his cock change. Where the head of him passed over. How wide he'd be inside of her. How he'd be a patient lover, but one who'd make sure she knew who was inside her. He'd rule her body, of that she had no doubt.

And it was a little scary.

But a whole lot exhilarating.

Exactly what she needed.

"I want you, Brady. Inside me. Your cock, please, put it inside me. Fuck me here. Fuck me now. Take me until you can't take me anymore."

His fingers tightened on her hips and he stopped moving. "Impossible," he said before the angle of his hips changed and he slammed inside her.

She cried out at the sudden invasion. Big was an understatement when it came to him. He was huge, and instead of giving her any time to get used to him, he angled her hips back and proceeded to do what he'd promised. He fucked her against the glass.

It was glorious. Wild and raw. His grunts said more about his control than anything else. A little voice inside her shouted in victory, knowing she could affect him so.

She flew over the peak within seconds, screaming her release, but he didn't give up. No. he wouldn't. She'd issued him a challenge he took her up on.

He wrapped his hands around her waist and cuddled her closer to him, his mouth right next to her ear. "Johanna," he said, and something changed. He pulled out, turned her around, and released her hands from the hook. They fell into position over his shoulders, and he lifted her up and pressed her back to the glass. He slammed inside of her again at the same time.

Holding her gaze, he thrust deep and steady, his eyes communicating something his mouth wouldn't, or couldn't, she didn't know. She tried to read the message, but it seemed even Brady was having a hard time understanding exactly what he wanted to say. Confusion almost, was awash over his handsome face.

He thrust one hand in her hair, tilting her head back. She tightened her legs around his waist. A deep burn built low in her stomach again.

"Johanna," he said again, his voice rougher, deeper.

"Brady."

He spun and laid her on a table. Her shoulders fell off the side, her breasts bouncing with each deep thrust he made. He licked and sucked at her nipples, a low growl sounding with every movement of his hips.

"Joey," he said, his voice holding an edge. "Jesus, Joey."

He sat himself to the hilt and ground his pelvic bone against hers, and it was the right fit. What her body had been waiting for. She flew over the edge on a gasp.

"Thank, fuck," he said and slammed in and out of her. Her orgasm went on and on, her screams ebbing over the sound of Brady's grunts.

She collapsed back on the table in a heap, out of breath and feeling as if she could just sleep for hours.

Brady dropped his head to her chest and she absentmindedly ran her fingers through the back of his hair.

The lights changed then, growing brighter as the lamp above them dimmed until she realized where they were. She tensed and he lifted his head. "Don't," he warned, but she couldn't help it. She tilted back to stare through the clear glass now, and out across the dazed crowd.

* * * *

"They think I'm beautiful," she said, but the words sounded sad, painful.

"Of course, gorgeous."

"They think I'm beautiful," she repeated, her words coming from a distance, as if she was talking to herself. "Everyone but him."

Brady thinned his lips, the *him* in her statement clear. The *but* screaming in his face. The entire sentence slapped him hard. Almost as hard as his orgasm had caught him off guard. He'd never been one to get to the peak without pain, but with the growing tension in Johanna's body, there was no time to examine that now.

He made quick work of the condom, disposing it in a hidden bio container, then tucked himself away. It was a futile hope that he could calm the sting of her words before returning to her, but all of that took less than a minute to achieve. Returning, he wrapped her in a black blanket and gathered her in his arms.

A heavy need to attend to her ran through his veins like a drug. To take care of her, remove her lush body from the gaze of others. Their staring rubbed him wrong, made his skin crawl with an insane jealousy he didn't understand. He'd have to set aside a conversation and explanation of her statement for later. Maybe that'd give him enough time to calm to speak and think rationally.

Her weight was slight, and it wasn't until he stepped into a hidden hallway at the back of the room that a warm liquid hit his shoulder, and she sniffed.

The sound about broke his heart and made his stomach twist in pain. He had a feeling he knew the reason for her tears, her earlier twisted statement making it abundantly clear. And he wanted to talk about it, would even chance doing it now, but he couldn't. They didn't have enough privacy, nor did he want to have this conversation here.

Instead, he stepped into a small room and set her on her feet. "Your dress is on the table, and I asked Frankie to bring you a trench. It's late. You've had a long night, so don't argue and just put it on. I'll be back in a couple of minutes."

He never denied being an asshole, but his words even sounded cruel and curt. She could do much better than him, but despite his previous reluctance at committing to anyone, he didn't think he'd be able to deal with Johanna seeing anyone else. Nor did he think he'd fulfilled his hunger for her yet.

He grabbed the rest of his clothes and his phone, then made a call to have the car ready outside.

With that taken care of, he stepped up to the closed door and stopped, dropped his head against the dark wood. His hand clenched and released, the emotions of the night sending him on a rollercoaster of feelings. Up and down, over and over again, he couldn't come to a conclusion of what he felt, how he'd expect to deal with this evening.

Then the door opened and all that fell away. The uncertainties. The confusion. The anger at her earlier words. Everything slipped away until the only thing left was a driving need to determine when he could get inside her again.

She lifted red rimmed eyes, drew in a breath, pulled back her shoulders, and lifted her chin. His strong girl. It made him so fucking proud. His heart swelled with a protectiveness that overwrote the earlier need.

She gripped the ties of her jacket, drawing his gaze down her body to long, smooth, perfect legs. Perfect like her body. Like her face. Like her.

He froze, his hand lifted to grab hers.

He loved her. One hundred percent, knock 'em on their ass, super-size it loved her. *Shit.* How could this have happened? When did it happen?

Johanna took his hand. "What's wrong?"

Tossed back into the moment, he shook his head, and interwove their fingers, then led her outside and to the car. They didn't speak for the ride to her apartment, nor did she say anything when he stepped out with her. They entered her home in silence, he breaking off to grab a beer, she sliding behind her bedroom door without an explanation.

He was finishing the last of his brew when she walked in. She'd changed from the trench and dressed into a pair of capri black sweats, a white camisole, and a turquoise sweater that hung past her waist.

"I'm exhausted." She didn't meet his eyes, and this distance she attempted started to piss him off. "I'm going to lock up, take a shower, and go to bed."

He nodded, finished his beer, and set it down on the counter with a loud *clink*. The fridge rotated ice and fed water through the line. A clock chimed somewhere down the hall. But he didn't say anything, at a loss for words, and still a bit shocked and pissed that she'd somehow managed to trap him into her web. He didn't know if he was more pissed at falling in love with her, or that he hadn't figured it out prior to making love to her. Because that's what it was. Making love. The first time he'd ever done so, too.

What an odd feeling, this combination of wanting to wrap his hands around her neck and kiss her at the same time.

"I think you should go," she said. "We'll catch up tomorrow."

As if he'd let her brush him off so easily. Not after what she'd done. "No."

She blinked, and dammit, that was cute, too. "No?"

He nodded once. "We need to talk."

She pulled her sweater over her chest and crossed her arms. "It's late. I need to shower. To sleep. It's been a long night."

"I'm staying the night, Joey, so you might as well go take a shower. I'll lock up. Then, we can talk either in the shower, or in the bed. I'll be nice since it seems you're having a hard time following orders tonight, and offer those choices. But you're not getting any others."

She swung her arms out the sides and leaned forward. Dark tendrils slid over her shoulders and wrapped around the curve of her breasts. She was magnificent. "What do you want to talk about? I think we've said all that needs to be said, or done, tonight, haven't we?"

He tried breathing through the pulse in his ears. One…two…

"Or did you not get enough with round one, Brady? Looking for round two? Well—"

She didn't get to finish. He was across the room in a flash, trapping her against the kitchen island, and tunneling his hands in her hair. "Why the fuck did you push this between us tonight, Joe?"

That cute little wrinkle formed between her eyes again. He wanted to lick it, but couldn't allow himself to get distracted. Short, choppy breaths pushed her breasts against his chest in little erotic beats. He fought to keep his mind on the right task.

"I…I didn't…"

He gave her a slight shake, using his hands in her hair. "Don't you lie to me. After everything we've been through. With how much our friendship means to each other, don't you do either of us the injustice by fucking lying. Not about this."

Tears pooled in her wide doe eyes, but he ignored his clenched gut and waited for an answer. She couldn't have played him like a fool. Couldn't be blind to what was going on…right?

"Johanna," he said.

"I—" Her breath hitched and a lone tear spilled over her lid and down the curve of her cheek. He swiped it away with his thumb, and she smiled. He'd seen her smile thousands of times, but this time was different. It was as if her eyes sparkled, but still held a hint of uncontrolled sadness. She tilted her head so the same cheek he wiped her tear from cradled in his hand. "I love you, Brady McBride." The words were utterly heartbreaking.

He sucked in a sharp breath.

"I couldn't imagine you going on that stage with anyone else because I love you. I've loved you my whole life." Another tear fell down her cheek. For some reason, he couldn't catch it before it dripped off her jaw.

"Christ," he whispered.

She grabbed his wrists, held him in place…to her. "I didn't plan on where we were going tonight, but once we were there, I just…I couldn't let you get up there with someone else. It would have butchered me."

"Jesus," he said, trying to catch up.

She let out a half laugh, half sob, and more tears tracked down her cheeks. "I love you." Another small hiccupping sob. "I can't help it."

She loved him. She'd said it more than once. She'd said it to him. There was no refuting it. There was also no denying that he felt the same way. He couldn't help but feel a little anger at how much time they both had wasted by not realizing this sooner, but then again, who knew where they would be if they hadn't made the decisions they did. But to think he could have lost her any number of times she'd been out doing her vigilante stuff. To think…

"Say something," she said, her voice trembling.

His attention snapped back up. He opened his mouth…and kissed her. She released his wrists to circle her arms around his shoulders and returned his kiss with as much passion. Long, deep licks back and forth. Tongues tangling. Hands groping. Bodies pushing closer and closer. He pressed her back to the wall and lifted his head, panting as if he'd run a marathon.

"What…what does that mean?" she asked.

He didn't hesitate. "I love you, too. That's what it means."

She laughed. Where he thought she was beautiful before, he knew he'd been mistaken. That was nothing on her when she laughed. And beautiful was too tame a word. He doubted he'd ever be able to do her justice with words alone.

He kissed her again, wanting to fall into her for days, and even knowing he'd never get enough. Lifting her up, she wrapped her long legs around his hips. He turned toward her bedroom.

She broke her mouth away. "Again?" she asked, a mischievous glint in her eyes.

He lifted a brow and cocked the side of his mouth up, pushing through her door. "Complaining?"

She shook her head.

"Although," he said and set one knee on the bed, then lowered her to her back, "we need to talk about your night time activities from here on out."

She set her hands on his shoulders and matched his eyebrow. "Way I see it, is there's nothing to talk about."

He winced. "Beautiful, maybe we can talk about you dialing it back a bit."

Her face turned soft at his endearment, and he made a point to remind himself to make sure she heard it every day for the rest of her life. Despite the soft face, she shook her head, pulling him down to her again. "No way."

Then, she kissed him.

And just like earlier, for him, everything else melted away.

The End.

REDEEMER

BY

KASTIL EAVENSHADE

DEDICATION

To my parents for always believing in me.

To the ladies of the Dark & Dirty antho for letting me come along for the ride.

Last, but not least, for my readers that make me love what I do.

~ Kastil

CHAPTER ONE

Gianni's fingers traced the contours of the plaster walls in his small townhouse. The bass of music pounded a heavy vibrato through every square inch. Lights dimmed, the swirled colored lamps splashed a rainbow revealing technicolored skin as his party revelers danced. While his family preferred the northern end of the city, the south side was his solace. His family's roots started in the 19th century brownstone. When his father's power grew within the seedy underbelly, he abandoned the small dwelling for something more extravagant. Yet the man refused to give up one inch of wealth. Gianni was more than happy to take up residence. Narrow, secret passageways allowed him to enter and leave with discretion. The size of the rooms gave an intimate vibe to epic parties with his closest acquaintances.

Cups littered every corner table. The sweet perfume of alcohol laced with drugs tickled his nostrils. Sweat-drenched and lost in the frenzy of gyrating bodies, he guided through the throng of guests. One person caught his eye— Tina Cooletski. Her red satin dress opened in a perfect 'V' toward her navel. She dragged him closer to lay a kiss on his cheek. Tina had shared his bed, along with a kilo of cocaine, on numerous occasions. The memories faded except for the tangled sheets. His hands on her cheeks, he kissed her. Heat wafted from her, pulsating and inviting. His tongue mingled with hers. If he lifted her dress and fucked her against the wall, no one would bat a lash. One of the perks of being a Bencivenni. No one dared to question your actions unless they had a death wish.

She jiggled a vial in front of his face. He paused. The white allure inside tempted. The powdered heaven cascaded onto her cleavage. Gianni needed no invitation. Head first, he dove in between her breasts and inhaled. Euphoria gripped him as he lapped the remains. She encouraged him, her fingers clutching his dark curls tight.

A gentle touch tickled his side and he turned. His friend Shannon smirked. His stark, strawberry blond hair seemed a beacon to the dark-hair beauty he'd sandwiched against the wall. Deep-seeded hunger sparkled in his emerald eyes and spoke of a decadent night to come.

"How about we take this party upstairs?" Tina's tongue ran along her lips. Gianni traced the seam of her dress and grasped the hem. His fingers danced up her thigh to the delicious heat of her pussy.

"My friend's going to join us, Tina." Gianni nipped her earlobe. She squirmed.

"I wouldn't have it any other way." She slipped under his arm and headed upstairs.

With a glance at Shannon, Gianni followed. Each step stiffened his cock as Tina dragged her hand along the rails and bounded up to the third floor. He might open his home to friends and acquaintances, but that hinged on one rule. No one dared go to the top floor without his invitation.

Gianni had converted the once-attic space to a spacious master bedroom. His bed, adorned with golden silk sheets and soft restraints dangling from the wrought-iron filigree above the headboard, hugged the back wall. The floor had plush, dark carpet with light gold accents along the perimeter. Sconces spaced on the wall gave a soft glow. An oasis away from the chaotic madness of his family's business of racking up a body count. If the need to launder money hadn't been thrust into his hands, the allure of drugs wouldn't have grabbed hold. The gene at the root of the blame game was a deep-seeded DNA in his lineage.

He stripped off his shirt. Tina's hips swayed as she sauntered to the bed. Out of the corner of his eye, Shannon paced near the large armoire in the corner. Almost predatory. Tina's fingers traced the contours of his bare chest. Gianni shivered. He blinked away some of his cocaine haze and palmed her breasts, so perfect and conforming to his touch. She worked the buckle, and his pants fell to the floor. One kick and his legs were free. Shannon unbuttoned his shirt. A fine sheen of sweat dampened the soft light curls on his chest. As Tina sank to the floor, Gianni grinned. Her plump, ruby lips kissed the fat head of his cock. With the drag of her teeth on the smooth silky underbelly of the shaft, he hissed. He held out his hand as Shannon advanced.

"Wait your turn. We've got all night." He chuckled. "Don't you want to watch her suck my cock?" Shannon's narrowed gaze and clenched fists almost had Gianni spilling his load between Tina's lips. He refused to avert his eyes, challenging his friend to defy him. Each loud, wet suck unpuckered the man's mouth. He yanked Tina to her feet and gripped her jaw. Lipstick smeared her swollen lips. He smoothed his thumb across the raised surface.

"I'm going to fuck you so hard, you're not going to remember." He kissed her. Eager, her tongue invaded his mouth. Tumbling to the edge of the bed, her satin dress caressed his skin. Shannon stood behind her and lifted the material away. He smoothed his hand over her ass. As he slapped her tender flesh, she jumped. Tugging the narrow band of her panties, he let it go with a satisfying snap before removing them.

"This is going to be one wild ride." His friend smirked.

"Yes." Gianni cupped Tina's cheeks. "Such a good girl."

"Wha—" Her eyelids drooped and Gianni pushed her off to the side. Shannon, his erection bobbing, stood at the foot of the bed waving a syringe in his hand.

"Are you fucking crazy? I wasn't done with her."

"Yes, you were, you fucking tease." Shannon stalked over to the side and set the syringe on the nightstand.

"You better have a good god damned reason. I haven't had a good dick suck like in a long time, asshole."

Shannon chuckled. "The things I do for a good fuck." He climbed on Gianni, kissing him madly. Gianni grabbed his hair and yanked back.

"What the fuck to do think you're doing?" He shoved him away and slid higher on the bed. "Tie me up and suck my cock first. I want to taste me on you."

One by one, he secured Gianni's hands with the restraints hanging above the headboard. Any other time, Shannon would be the one at his mercy, but treating his voracious lover after a long absence had been a promise. With little control on his life, the bedroom was his to manipulate to his pleasure. He regretted leading Tina into thinking they'd fuck, but in the morning, she wouldn't remember a thing.

As Shannon straddled him, Gianni closed his eyes. Warm kisses trailed along his neck and he groaned. Farther south, his lips traveled until the wet mouth of his lover encompassed his rigid cock. Down to the base of the shaft, he almost came. Family meetings and keeping up his image in public had kept him away from Shannon's glorious lips and ass for too long. The last stint in rehab hadn't helped, either. Six months of sneaking around to jack off had done nothing to sate his appetite. His family built their extortion business on fear and intimidation. A little cocaine to fuel the crazy added to that in Gianni's opinion, yet his brothers tried to cow him at every turn.

He opened his eyes. His masterful boyfriend worked the shaft better than Tina could dream of doing for him. The flaming locks on his head matched the fiery method. His tongue slathered Gianni's shaft. Pussy only satisfied him when his lover couldn't find a way to sneak into his home.

"Missed you." Shannon kissed the tip of his cock. "You don't know how many times I climbed down that trellis in the back when your family made a surprise visit. Fuckers. That apartment I'm living in is shite."

Gianni loved the Irish lilt in his voice. The tone made their intimacy taboo, considering his family thought Shannon's ethnicity beneath their standards, except for manual labor. Not that he didn't enjoy Shannon laboring over his cock masterfully.

"Yeah, well, my old man is sending me overseas for a bit to some resort or something in Switzerland. Deep woods shit." As Shannon dragged his teeth on his balls, he sucked in a breath. "So you won't have that problem. I plan to see you bent over every night."

"I'm going to suck your cock all night long." His lips slid down slowly before hurrying his pace.

"Take it all." Gianni jerked against the restraints, regretting his decision. He wanted to feel the top of Shannon's cropped hair, and come all over his face. Letting his boyfriend have some measure of control was worth it. Shannon's perfectly swollen lips milked his cock, but he held back, savoring the moment.

His and Shannon's relationship had started more as animalistic need than mutual attraction. Shannon was a warehouse worker for his father, barely making by on his salary. When he'd stormed out on a family meeting regarding expanding their business to include illegal imports, Gianni had wandered into the storage area of the warehouse. He'd gone into the worker's bathroom to get away from his brothers in case they'd come after him. Whether their failure to locate him was on purpose or Gianni's luck at hiding, he used the out-of-the-way place as his sanctuary. One day, when his brothers teased him incessantly on why he hadn't found a wife to knock up yet, he'd run into Shannon. He had been relieving himself at one of the urinals and Gianni couldn't keep his eyes off the impressive cock. Not fully erect, veins pulsed beneath the surface of the smooth shaft. Gianni had gone stiff in his pants from seeing such a specimen, and beautiful visions of his tongue slathering the tip with his tongue sprung in his mind. Shannon met his blatant gaze, and instead of running out, Shannon locked the door. With a shove against the wall, he kissed him. A bold move, but one Gianni welcomed.

The memory of bending Shannon over the sink spent his cock. Ravenous, his boyfriend milked every drop into his mouth while massaging Gianni's balls. One swipe of his finger along his ass had him gasping. An invitation for things yet to unfold. True to his word, his lover crawled up and kissed him to share his taste. His stiff cock pressed into his belly. "Do you want me to fuck you, Gianni?"

"In the nightstand. Lube." Breathless, he watched Shannon rifle through the top drawer. His lover smirked, holding a small purple bag of powder up first. He dumped a portion on his tongue and kissed him again, hard and forceful. The surge of that drug in his system propelled him to regret the restraints. This was Shannon's turn to shine before their roles reversed. One night to let go.

With Gianni's legs in the air, Shannon spread lube on his hole and used his finger to penetrate. "I've been wanting to do this for so long."

"Do it before I change my mind. Fuck me good and I'll find some rent boy for us to play with in Switzerland."

"A threesome?" His grin widened and he plunged in. Fast and hard, Gianni rocked on the bed. Euphoria, more from Shannon's urgency than the cocaine, had him soaring. The simple dock worker owned his hole with precision. Shannon slowed, gasping for breath. "I never want this to end. Your ass is heaven." He gyrated, thrusting forward quickly when his cock slipped deep. Masterful, he hit a sweet spot.

"Oh, fuck, Gianni. I can't hold it. Fuck." Strain on his face, Shannon finished with two hard strokes. He tumbled to the bed beside him. "Thank you."

Gianni stared at the ceiling, never wanting this feeling to end. "She's going to wake up in about an hour. Let's get cleaned and put her in bed. Tomorrow, we'll have the house to ourselves." Restraints loosened, Gianni padded to the bathroom. Shannon grabbed his ass most of the way. Their shower was brief, a touch-and-play to release any tension lingering. Shannon gave him a calm that most of his past boyfriends never managed. Not that he had any serious relationships. His last steady fuck had been a man named Johnny. When that affair ended, Gianni wanted nothing to do with another man in his bed for any more than a twenty-four hour period. Deep down, he still wanted his ex-lover, but Shannon was flesh and bone, not a ghost from his past.

Back into the bedroom, they positioned Tina naked in between them and drifted off to sleep. In the morning, she could tell any story she wanted of their prowess. It kept his cover from his family. If he didn't leave this country soon, he'd be dead by his family's hand for having someone's *dick* in his ass. Never mind a man in his bed was exactly what he wanted.

* * * *

A crash woke Gianni. Sitting up, he tried to rub the piercing headache from his eyes. How long had he slept? His hand searched the satin sheets for the familiarity of Shannon's muscled abdomen, but the bed was void of his lover. He hated not being able to spend the morning with Shannon. Most likely, his grand party had garnered the attention of his family and Shannon had to sneak away again. Even with them living on the opposite side of the city, someone always seemed to contact them when Gianni had a little fun. At least, Tina had served her purpose as a decoy.

The clock on the nightstand blinked neon blue. Sometime after three in the morning, the power had gone out. He wouldn't have to deal with bodies strewn along the hallways downstairs. Darkness had the tendency to make his friends scatter. Without music and cold beverages, the parties ceased.

Footsteps on the steps made him groan. He had hoped his brothers would leave him in peace for one day before busting his balls again. To his surprise, two cops entered his room.

"Gianni Bencivenni. You are under arrest for violating the terms of your release." One of the cops had his hand on his cuffs and held a fold of papers. His partner wavered toward his gun.

"Fuck off. You got nothing." He lay down, biting back a curse. Out of the corner of his eye, the curtains to one of the windows billowed from the breeze outside. Shannon's getaway route.

"Does this jog your memory?" Behind the cop, a plain-clothes detective held up a purple baggy full of Gianni's cocaine stash. "Get dressed, asshole."

Did his brothers loathe his presence so much that they'd rather throw him back to prison than deal with his behavior? "Mind if I piss first?"

"Let's save that little sample for downtown, shall we?"

With no energy to argue, Gianni gathered his clothes and dressed. The boys in blue kept their distance, yet never gave him a clear path to bolt out the bedroom. Not that it mattered. If there wasn't a convention of the pricks downstairs, he'd be shocked. At least, Shannon had left. Gianni's family, or at least his mother, wasn't going to be happy that he couldn't stay clean. Out of all his blood relations, she never lost hope that he would overcome his addictions. He tried to make her proud, but white lines on a mirror appealed to him greater than staying sober. His escape from a world he wanted no part of. Escorted down the stairs, he was ushered outside and into an awaiting car. At least, the paparazzi hadn't shown up. Not that wind of his arrest wouldn't get a front page mention in the city paper anyways. They reveled in seeing Niccolo Bencivenni's youngest being dragged off in cuffs. Another stain to earn a beating as soon as his brothers got ahold of him.

One of his worst fears reared its head when the car pulled up to the station. His father stood at the entrance. No manner of excuses would save his hide from wrath. When Gianni was helped out of the car, Niccolo advanced.

"You useless prick." He backhanded Gianni. "What you do to your mother." Another slap stung. Throwing his hands up, his father walked away. The cops did nothing to stop his small measure of punishment. For his mother, Gianni should have tried to detox his body. The allure of cocaine overrode any sensibilities he had. No judge was going to use any type of leniency if his father had any influence. His chances had been used up in rehab after rehab to cleanse his body of drug addiction. Lies had flowed from his lips at other court proceedings on how he'd remain sober for another chance. No judge would be stupid enough to believe him now. He'd burned that gambit a long time ago. Prison would be his home soon. His heart clenched at not seeing his mother, but the rest of his family could rot in hell for all he cared. He could hide under the guise of Tina sucking his cock in a room full of people, but his family wouldn't believe he was straight, A gay son deserved one thing in his father's eyes—a bullet to the head. If his mother ever died, that was exactly what they'd give him in his grief.

Fingerprinted and the condemning sample given, Gianni reflected on his last night free. Beyond his mother, he'd fucked up with Shannon, too. Even if conjugal visits were allowed, his deviant relationship would shame his family and end Shannon's life. The latter he couldn't bear.

CHAPTER TWO

Gianni watched the tremor in his hand grow. Sweat trickled down his brow. He spat out a curse. The words in the book he tried to read blurred again. His stomach twisted in pangs not borne from hunger. Outside his open cell, chatter from the other prisoners warped. Maddening whispers gnawed through his skull. A crumpled letter—the only one his mother sent when he was locked away for his third offense of being under the influence in less than a year's time—poked out of his book. He read the beautifully scripted note at night before going to bed. All the hurt and pain in each word still didn't stop him from doing whatever he could within these concrete walls to get high. The crushing reality of what he was for the majority of his family necessitated his habits. He was an unwanted son to an empire that wanted marriages of convenience to strengthen ties.

His two brothers—Salvatore and Luciano—married with gusto. Their ceremonies had been chaste and all a good Italian Catholic family could hope for. But the way they showed up and handled themselves at the reception was anything but chaste. Both had ground their crotches against the bridesmaids during the dance floor frenzy like they were their property. Not that their brides had a virginal bone in their body. Gianni had a taste of how well they'd be faithful in their marriages. In trying to adhere to his father's strict standards, Gianni had drunk a bit of liquid courage and done a bump of cocaine one night with Salvatore's future bride-to-be Lucy far before their engagement was announced. The soppy aftermath did nothing to curb his true desire: a hard, long cock rammed in his ass. He'd kept Lucy's alleged virginity by taking her backside with gusto.

In secret, his family scorned him, but so long as his preference for a bedmate didn't get out to the general populous, his punishment was crass jabs instead of a back alley beating. Nevertheless, his family had done their best to protect him when he was sent to jail in the past. Not that he needed or wanted their help. Their reputation was the one reason they aided him in his legal troubles. The extended hand in solidarity was born of necessity, not compassion.

He closed and tossed the book on his cot. Prison wasn't going to curb his drug use. The quantity, however, was less than desirable. His supplier was going to have to give him more than a small portion that, on the outside, amounted to a pregame warm-up for the cocaine show.

To appease his family, Gianni hid his lover away in a small apartment uptown. When his father was going to let Shannon go because he didn't need him, Gianni stepped in and asked if he could be his personal driver after his license was suspended from a DUI. In the deal, Shannon fed his father any bullshit story they concocted about where he'd driven Gianni in a log book. Oh, Shannon drove, all right. All day and as often as he commanded. Gianni loved his Irish accent and the feel of his fingers around his throat. More importantly, Shannon had a discreet drug supplier. When he got released, he planned on snorting a little white powder off every inch of his lover's skin. But without a joyous party, where spies of his father could hide under the guise of being a friend.

"Bencivenni, you little prick."

Gianni yawned, scratching his chin before flicking his fingers at the large inmate who entered his cell. Frank had been stupid enough to believe his lie he'd share the pilfered drugs if the dumbass parted his cheeks. "Fuck off, you piece of shit." He offered one finger to the two men with the hulking brute.

"You took my share." Frank towered over him, spittle dribbling from his mouth.

"I took what was mine all along. You were the idiot who believed I'd give anything to you." His palm slammed into Frank's crotch before gripping his balls tight. Standing while the cowed man screamed, Gianni grinned. His tongue snaked out and licked the side of Frank's face. "Or is it that you hoped I'd drop to my knees and suck your cock, lover boy." He ground his crotch against his victim's. "Maybe you'd prefer the feel of my cock in your ass."

Frank's skin reddened and, before Gianni could move, the brute snapped his head forward. The cartilage in Gianni's nose snapped and pain exploded in his face. The sting spread, but he laughed and squeezed harder. He pushed Frank away. One swing at the blurry image to his right didn't connect and he lost his balance. Frank's goons took turns kicking his sides. Blood smeared on the floor and each blow radiated agony through his body, yet he laughed louder. If only his brothers had the stones to bestow such a beat-down, he'd think higher of them. He cursed at the sounds of the guards breaking up the fight. The drugs did nothing to make him feel something beyond dead inside. One thing branding him more than a walking corpse were the delightful scars of his scraps inside and the pain that accompanied them.

He staggered to his feet. The room spun and warped. His fingers smeared the something wet and sticky across his cheek. "Why does it still smell like bitch in here?"

"I'm going to fucking kill you, runt." Frank's blurry image broke free of the guards. Gianni smiled, although brief. The world tilted around him as he hit the floor.

* * * *

In Gianni's muddied state, the sterile, white environment reminded him of clouds. Sweet morphine coursed through his veins to stave off the wonderful ache his body promised once the drip ceased. Touching his nose, he bemoaned that a spark of pain hadn't spider-webbed along his face. The bandaging wasn't as thick as he'd thought needed.

"Fuck," he grumbled.

"In due time."

He shifted his gaze to the left. One of the guards from the prison sat beside his bed. The chiseled specimen no doubt had been paid by his mother to protect him inside. That came with a price larger than lining his pockets. Too numerous times to count, Gianni had gotten into trouble and tossed into solitary for a special visit from these assholes. All it took was a small malfunction of a camera in the hallway and a well-timed arrangement for the brutes to fuck him senseless. Though the sex lacked the passionate flair Shannon brought, the drugs the fools thought he needed to perform deprived acts made up for it. On rare occasions, they draped a black mask over his head that exposed nothing but his mouth. He heard them joke about how much money they made in the fetish porn industry with movies starring his mouth while he jerked his cock. One of the few times he could indulge his fantasies without outing himself to two men who seemed to enjoy fucking a man over their alleged girlfriends or wives. In this sick and twisted environment, an alpha mounted the beta no matter what the outside world thought. In here, fucking a man was more about dominance than sexual preference. Showing that you enjoyed it would land a beating over a nice reach around. Gianni never counted on his name precluding him from any mercy. If that had been the case, he wouldn't be in this stink hole.

"You'll have to find someone else. I'm busy." Gianni closed his eyes. Sleep would take his mind off the fact the edge from the morphine faded. Pain from getting the shit kicked out of him broke the dull edge of deadness in his soul. Soreness reminded him he'd survived one more day. But the agony of withdrawal was altogether different. A poke at his side brought him back to reality.

The first guard's buddy had joined the party. Gianni never bothered to remember their names. If he got called to testify, he could pick their cocks out of a line up any day. Not that his accusations would amount to anything. Their name tags were always missing when they visited. In his world, they were Crotch and Ass respectively.

"No one's here to care what you think." Crotch adjusted the front of his pants with his obvious erection ready to break free. "Besides, your jaw isn't broken and that's all you'll need in the next few minutes."

Ass stood and turned off the drip. "Don't worry. We got your kick. You'll just have to work for it." Gianni groaned as they lifted him from the bed after stripping his gown. Bruises littered his body. If these guards put another on him, no one would notice. Across the room and into an exam area, they closed the curtains. Slumped on the floor, Gianni waited for the inevitable. Crotch shook a bag of white powder in his face. Undoing his pants, he sprinkled a little along his erect shaft. Snow from heaven to take Gianni away from this world. Ass took the bag next.

"Let's go, Gianni. Be a good little fuck boy and we won't let it get back to your family that you've failed every drug test in this place. It's awful hard to switch the results and I think you should reward us. Come on. I've sugar coated it for you."

White glistened on the cock before him. To feel the smoothness of the skin coupled with the rigid hardness beneath. His cock hardened, but he couldn't make it obvious that he wanted this more than the guards did. For them, it was feeding another cock sandwich to some little rich punk who got caught inside.

"Maybe he wants me to fuck him with a night stick again like the first night." Ass laughed.

Gianni leaned forward and took the cock in his mouth, more to hide his own erection than the prospect of that rigid tool gliding effortlessly inside him. They weren't videoing their exploits today, or the mask would be on him.

"Yeah, take it all." Down to the base, Gianni gagged. The sweet powder absorbed into his system and he licked the residue clean. He couldn't run from his addiction, nor did he want to. Ass yanked his head back and shoved his white-laced cock in. More forceful than Crotch, the guard fucked his mouth hard.

"See? I told you he liked a good mouth fuck. Get the condoms." Ass slapped him on the cheek withdrawing. "I'm feeling generous." He cupped his balls. "How about you clean these off for me."

Gianni dove in. Smooth as silk, he devoured the guard's sac. In the three years he served, his protectors had enjoyed his body more than he'd allowed any of his lovers. For all their gusto, both of them did this for the perceived power it brought them over the youngest of the Bencivenni family. A personal high five that meant nothing when their recipient enjoyed the ride.

"Get him up." Crotch ripped open a condom.

Tossed on his stomach, Gianni hung off the other end of the examination table. Ass slathered his cock with more cocaine before shoving back in his mouth. Crotch spread his cheeks wide. A thick smear of lube prepared his puckered hole to receive a stiff latex-covered shaft. Gianni thanked whatever caused them to position him belly down. Hiding his erection had become a tuck game as of late. Facedown, his fuck buddies would never see how much he enjoyed their alleged demeaning behavior. As Crotch penetrated him, Ass slapped his head again.

"Better suck better than that, boy, or we're going to see if anyone else wants to split you open."

As pleasurable as his proposition was, Gianni didn't want this fetish to spread like wildfire. His assailants might keep a tight lip for their own good, but another guard brought in might leak this venture into the general population. Gianni could only fight his way through the masses for so long. Each slam from the rear brought him forward toward the cock in his mouth. He sucked and lapped, his tongue snaking out to lick the base.

"Fuck yeah. That's better. He could give my girlfriend lessons."

"He's probably given you more blowjobs than her." Crotch laughed, digging his nails into Gianni's hips. Animalistic grunts echoed of the walls with each thrust.

"He never says no." Ass fisted his hair, slamming his dick further in with loud moan. Cum filled Gianni's mouth, and he swallowed all of it. As the shaft withdrew, he suckled on the tip to draw the remaining semen out. Ass stroked his cock. "Oh, I'm not done with you, pretty boy. We both took a little blue pill to make this session last." Foil tore and the pressure in his ass ceased. Switching, Crotch peeled his condom off and worked his shaft. Deliberately, he shot his load onto Gianni's face. The thick liquid clung to his hair, and the smell of ammonia filled his nostrils.

Ass took over at his backside. As furious as his mouth fuck, the man leaned over and grabbed Gianni's shoulders. Exhaustion nearly took Gianni.

"What are you?" The guard taunted him. "Say it." Flesh slammed into flesh and the table groaned against the strain.

"Your bitch." Gianni cried out as Ass crashed into him one last time. The erection he'd hid faded without climax. An empty feeling swept through him. The brief high from the drugs was never enough. The two guards dragged him to the shower area and dumped him on the floor. Pain flared from his wounds, both from the beating and his treatment from the guards. He had precious few days to recover before they threw him in the hole for fighting again. After spraying him down, they returned him to his bed. Like clockwork, the resident doctor came in.

"What are you two doing in here?" He tossed his charts on the table. If the morphine hadn't dulled Gianni's senses, he would have laughed. No doubt the man took a cut to disappear at all the right moments.

"Here to tell pretty boy here he's being released early. Bereavement." Crotch smacked him on the leg. "Congratulations. Your mother's death is your ticket out. Just waited until he woke up to give him the good news."

Gianni's soul crushed to the farthest depths of his mind. The tears she shed for his fucked-up life. She was the one family member who tried, and failed, to save him from addiction. He'd pissed away every opportunity she'd ever given him. So much so, she'd stopped sending letters two months into his sentence. These two assholes were her last calling card. They said she paid them to protect him from the inside, but his brothers paid more to see that he suffered. Closing his eyes, he choked back the rage. When he got the opportunity, both of the guards would die. Every bone in their body would shatter with a sledgehammer.

CHAPTER THREE

Butcher stood in the far corner with his hands folded in front of him. Chatter and static crackled through his ear piece. For the most part, he ignored it. His duty had ended when Rosalia Bencivenni passed away from the cancer eating her bones. If he was honest about the manner of her death, the disease had nothing to do with her demise. Day by day, he watched her wither. Her frail hands penned letter after letter to someone who would never receive them. Under instruction from the patriarch of the family, each letter was to be burned until even the ash disappeared into the wind. With eyes constantly on his movements, Butcher still managed to save the letters and burn blank pages in their place. None were mailed, though, because of the risk. He'd witnessed her son, Salvatore, crumple up her work and toss it into the trash by her hospital bed. Each badgering word from the whelp's mouth sent her spiraling down a path she'd never returned from. Butcher had thrown him out of the room. Niccolo had almost discharged him from service until Butcher explained what the man's offspring had blasted to his mother. Disrespect to his employer's sons was one thing, but for that brat to dishonor his dying mother? Butcher took no pleasure in seeing the boy get backhanded.

Niccolo stepped in front of him, nodding. Not a tall man by any means, the patriarch of the Bencivenni family stood as if ten feet tall in his finely-tailored Brunello Cucinelli suit. His short-cropped hair had enough gel to reflect the sun and kill a few insects in its path.

"She left a letter saying you are to help lay her to rest. I appreciate the comfort you offered her in her final moments."

"It was my duty, sir." Butcher remained passive. Niccolo disgusted him. For a man who showed respect in the public eye, he alone was the driving force behind locking Rosalia from sight. Once the interment was dealt with, Butcher was out of a job. A blessing in disguise. He planned to take a trip far away from this family. Although good at his profession, the burden of serving a family who scorned one of their own wore on him. The anguish of a mother pining to see her youngest son again before she died burned a raging fire inside him. In his head, Butcher had enough vengeance to tear the Bencivenni family to pieces. If not for the promise to Rosalia, they would be six feet under just as she.

His conscience gnawed at him as the funeral processed on. So many in the room, but he recognized so few. In life, people rarely came around when sickness lingered. In death, no remorse overshadowed the guests. What they saw was their own mortality in the form of a peach casket littered with huge bouquets of white roses. Taking his place as a pallbearer, Butcher noticed the narrowed eyes of Salvatore. The boy still hadn't gotten over his bruised ego. The rest of the funeral went by in a blur. He stayed by the grave after most had left. His duty to Rosalia wasn't over yet.

Mature trees shaded her grave site. A light breeze rustled the leaves. He moved away and leaned against a large trunk. His sense of purpose seemed lost in the void, even with the directions within the letter tucked in his jacket.

"I asked to be cremated. Leave it to Niccolo to ignore my wishes one last time." Rosalia's image wavered beside him. As she neared death, his visions of her spirit intensified. Alcohol had been his liberator from the haunting specters of the dead, but his family had forced him sober when his work ethic turned macabre. The namesake earned during that time had stuck.

"He never understood you." Another bad habit was actually treating his symptoms as real human flesh before him. Rosalia didn't exist under the cool shade of the tree on a hot afternoon. Yet her form, as vibrant as when he first started caring for her, smiled at him. He'd endure the visions instead of the deadly effects of addiction. A penance for all the black sin that coated his soul.

"Promise me you'll save him."

He nodded and closed his eyes, willing her to disappear. Her voice haunted, yet soothed.

"What are you hanging around for?"

Butcher's gaze focused on Salvatore. Next to the older son of Niccolo were two of his private goons. "Paying last respects."

Salvatore shook his head, smirking. "Aren't you forgetting something at the end of that sentence?"

"My employment ended with the death of your mother. Call it a favor to Mr. Bencivenni." Butcher noticed the movements of the two bodyguards. Their hands casually slid into their jackets. "I would prefer if blood isn't spilled on Mrs. Bencivenni's grave. She doesn't deserve disrespect." He remained passive, though the sweet lullaby of his piece against his ribcage called.

"Then show me the respect I deserve." Salvatore puffed his chest, a childish display that didn't impress Butcher. The man would cow before him if not for the ones standing to his side.

"As I already said, I don't work for your family anymore." As one of the bodyguards started to withdraw his gun, Butcher pointed a finger at Salvatore. "You shame your mother's good name, boy. Back off before I do something that requires a thousand Hail Marys and Our Fathers."

Salvatore waved his goons off. "He's not worth the bullets. You're washed up, Butcher. A has been."

"Keep telling yourself that, kid."

Salvatore walked away with his bodyguards. Even at this distance, as the little prick weaved in and out of the trees and tombstones, he could still put a bullet straight through his skull. End the life of the son Rosalia had been the most ashamed of. Telling, considering the way his own family conducted business. That a man could beat his wife for disobeying his wishes so long as she didn't end up in the hospital within the Bencivenni organization was acceptable. But stray from that holy Catholic union of marriage? Hell had no fury like a shamed Italian mother. Salvatore needed to be put to ground, but that wasn't Rosalia's last request, unfortunately.

The vibrating of his phone refocused his thoughts. He fished the earpiece out and tossed it to the ground. His employment was at an end. He answered his phone.

"Are you available to have dinner with your old family?" His father's familiar baritone voice crackled through the phone. Butcher hadn't spoken to any of his family since his isolation with the matriarch of the Bencivenni clan. His own family business dealt with the clean-up of what families like the Bencivennis dabbled in.

Butcher walked to his car on the other side of the cemetery. Thankfully away from Salvatore, lest his thoughts stray again. "I have no immediate plans."

"Meet us at that old Italian place on the south side."

Butcher cursed as he closed his phone. The one person Rosalia wanted at her funeral had been strangely absent, and Butcher pieced two together why. His father referenced the old Bencivenni home. Last he knew, Gianni used that at his residence. He clenched his teeth. If Butcher's family was called in, the scene had to be pretty messy. His sick, twisted family had to have killed the one child that brought an embarrassment worse than Salvatore's infidelity. Gianni had his faults, but he didn't deserve to be brutally murdered. Nobody did. Rosalia was going to haunt him from the grave for not protecting her youngest.

"Dammit."

The drive took over an hour. Twice, Butcher swore he'd been tailed. For what reason, he couldn't make out. Niccolo held no ill will that he knew of. Rosalia's care had been a special circumstance that he would have refused had his family not been close to her. She was the real cogs in the engine of that machine, more ruthless in life than any other person his family had served. He'd been called to numerous places at her private demand to dispose of a corpse. Men who partnered with her husband often took her as a meek woman they could molest with impunity. Their calloused hands on her silky thighs were the last memory before she put a bullet through a vital organ.

Unease settled into his stomach, and he switched the car for his motorcycle at home before getting to his destination. Having an escape route without being seen was a must in his profession. After the altercation with Salvatore, he trusted no one until he left the country.

At the old brownstone house, his big brother Jimmy ushered him through the back. The big lug still sported his long brown hair tightly held back by a piece of leather. His tattoo collection had expanded as well, but socializing would wait until their grim task was complete. A hazmat suit was draped over the chair in the back room. Butcher dressed, the silence in the house eerie.

"Who is it?"

Jimmy shrugged and adjusted his mask. "No clue. We got the call and came. Usual transaction. Why?"

"Because this is Gianni Bencivenni's house." He pulled his facemask on. No one's identity would be known if the one who did the job came back for any reason. The blue lettering on his suit—Henry's Termite Service—let most of the hitmen know they were off limits. A good cleaning crew was hard to find and getting on the wrong side could potentially start a war they would never win. Butcher's family never got in the middle of a turf war, but they didn't take kindly to be pushed around, either. Each of his clan could wield a gun better than some of the goons making the messes they cleaned up.

"Pop wants to talk to you topside about your absence." His brother pointed upstairs.

"Not this again." He headed toward the stairs and up. His father had a thing for Rosalia in his youth and never got over her picking Niccolo. If not for the code, Butcher was sure his father would have told him to make the old man have an accident. At the third floor landing, he paused. Most of the work had been completed except for the bloody mess on the bed.

"You're late." His father tapped his shoulder. Dressed from head to toe in the same gear, Butcher would recognize his large frame at any distance. He pulled down his mask, revealing more gray in his beard than Butcher remembered.

"I was tailed." Butcher side-stepped as one of their crew moved out of the room with a black plastic bag.

"I should have never agreed to let you take that job." His father snorted. "Pricks."

Butcher moved away, not wanting to get into another heated battle over past choices. Bullets clinked into a glass jar. Each chunk of twisted metal yanked out of the gaudy headboard with needle nose pliers. On the bed, the bloody remains of a naked man lay tangled in the sheets. Rosalia floated near the bed, her white dress stained with crimson.

"Hell of a way for Gianni to go," his father said. "What I don't understand is that the two others looked like someone took a sledgehammer to them and just ground their bones to bits. Why shoot one and take the time to do that?"

"This is not my son." Rosalia's words echoed in his head like an eerie melody.

"That's not Gianni on the bed." Butcher moved the sheets to expose the body. Bullets had turned the head into mush. He traced a finger along the blood-stained thigh. "He had a scar here from when Salvatore took a heated poker to him. Plus, Gianni's got a tattoo on his ribcage." He turned away and came face-to-face with her. The healthy glow had vanished, replaced with the pallor only stage four cancer could create. Did she torment him because she thought he'd forgotten her final wish? His tongue begged for just a drop of bourbon, but he willed away the temptation.

"Boss. Salvatore Bencivenni's downstairs. He wants to take a look." Jimmy stood in the doorway.

"Send him up, but he's going to be disappointed." His father glanced around the room. "Clean it up, Butcher. We can't let that asshole know he didn't succeed. Make it quick." He held out a large knife, and Butcher took it. With quick efficiency, he sliced into the man's thigh and ribcage, tearing flesh from bone, and further defiled the body. Not even this poor soul's mother could identify his mutilated corpse. The reason his moniker 'Butcher' had stuck. He flipped the knife over and hurled it into the headboard. His gloves would prevent any fingerprints showing up. The alcohol made him The Butcher and the grotesque technique lived on in sobriety.

"I want you to go to the bathroom, son." His father directed him to the general direction. "Help them grind the rest down. I don't want Salvatore to know you're here. Keep your gear up."

Something in his father's tone worried him. All this work seemed to cross a line they never dared tread. In the bathroom, he sliced his hand across his throat to silence the crew before putting a finger to his mask. They nodded. In the bathtub, a soupy mess of human remains slowly cooked down with the help of a special mixture his family concocted. This would dissolve all but the bones. The crematorium would dispose of the rest.

In the other room, Salvatore's voice rose above them all. "Get rid of his body, too. Consider the transfer as good as done. No one will miss him now that Mother is dead. Piece of shit." His footfalls crunched on the broken glass. "I need this place cleaned up for someone special."

"Yes, Salvatore. We'll be finished in a few hours."

"Good."

Why wasn't Gianni here? Butcher wracked his brain for an answer. His release from jail had conditions and leaving his home—beyond the funeral—had to be arranged.

"Is Butcher with you? I have a private matter to discuss with him."

Butcher cursed. His father couldn't be flippant in his answer. Lie, perhaps, but if Salvatore called him out on it, the harm to their reputation would forever damage the family business. Again, he put a finger to his mask. One golden nugget Rosalia had bestowed on him was the layout on the house, including all the hidden areas. She confided in him that she shared her secret with one other person before Butcher. Her son Gianni. He peeled off his gloves and put on a clean pair. He searched along the seam of the tiles by the full length mirror. With a click, the wall slid open. He disappeared inside and closed the passage back up. Cobwebs hung from the high ceiling and the dampness from the lack of proper air circulation wrinkled his nose. What was in the bedroom was more preferable to his senses than this cramped passage. Holding his breath, he heard Salvatore's angry tone order his cousins to pull down their face masks. No way could he leave the passage until that asshole left the premises, and by the sound of it, he'd be here most of the day.

His muscles ached as he tried not to move. Muffled voices waxed and waned on the other side of the wall. Three raps followed by another staccato relaxed his mind. In a few minutes, he'd be free to leave. To be on the safe side, he checked his watch and counted off thirty more minutes. He stripped off the suit and left it in the passage as he emerged. His gun out and ready, he swept the bedroom. Not one drop of blood stained any surface. Three lives wiped from existence as if nothing had happened.

"Where are you, Gianni?" he whispered.

"Behind you." Cold steel pressed against his nape. "Drop it." Butcher complied. "Did my brother send you to finish the job?"

"No. Your mother." The gun cracked alongside his head. More annoying than painful. He cursed. "She sent me to protect you, you little fuck."

"Bullshit."

"I'm going to reach in my jacket and get you the letter she sent me." That earned him another whack.

"Move over to the bed." Guided by the barrel digging into his skull, Butcher shuffled forward, letting his hands stay in Gianni's line of sight. "Take off the jacket slow and toss it to the right." Again, he complied. The gun swung around to the front as Gianni backed near the jacket. The kid had nothing but a t-shirt on. A monitoring bracelet hung from his ankle. By the look of him, Butcher figured he either hadn't slept in a few days since his release or he'd already broken his parole for a little blow. Hair twisted and matted against his head, his irises were wide against the chocolate pigment of his eyes. Paranoia would do that to a man. Years in the yard during a prison stretch would also pack on lean muscle. Butcher tried not to let his mind stray when his captor bent to fish out the letter. Gianni's eyes narrowed as he read. The letter flicked to the floor.

"Why should I believe that?" Gianni gestured to the discarded message.

"Because if you don't, your older brother is going to send more goons to kill you." Butcher pointed to the ankle bracelet. "We need to get rid of that first. My family has a private jet at my disposal."

"You're the fucking cleaners. You don't get involved."

"We do when some little fuck doesn't follow the rules. I'm still on your mother's payroll, God rest her soul. She made me promise to protect you—in blood." He extended his palm to show the deep scar.

"Why?"

"Because whether you want to believe it or not, she loved you and protected you above any other."

"Bullshit. You know what they did to me in there?" The gun wavered toward Butcher again. "Those little fucks? I came here to get ready for the funeral and they were waiting for me." His voice shook as tears streamed down his face. "They killed him in front of me."

A chill ran through Butcher. The body on the bed hadn't been a random hit. The other two bodies were of the assassins. "Who was the man on the bed?"

"I said I'd splatter their bodies with a sledgehammer if I ever got the chance." Gianni sunk to the floor, the gun forgotten as it slipped from his grasp. Butcher lowered his hands.

"We have to go now. If your brother finds out about the other two bodies, he'll be back." If Butcher hadn't been in such a haze when he came through the bedroom door, he would have remembered Gianni was fond of using a sledgehammer to destroy things in a fit of rage. Something his mother often joked about when they talked.

"I can't go anywhere with this bracelet on."

"Leave that to me. Get some clothes on and pack a small bag." Butcher picked Gianni's gun up and extended it to him. "I'm the only chance you got. Unless you think your brother will only send two guys to kill you when he finds you still breathing."

Gianni nodded and took the gun. While he rushed to dress, Butcher retrieved his gun and jacket. Sweat beaded on Gianni's forehead as he sat heavily on the bed. *To even fathom that your own flesh and blood meant you harm.* Butcher shook the thought from his mind and bent to take care of the ankle bracelet. "What I'm going to do is overload it, so to speak. Make it look like it's malfunctioning. The cops take about ten minutes to get here and by then, we'll be gone." The monitor fell to the floor. One minute later, they were on Butcher's bike and on the run.

* * * *

Gianni had recognized the brute in his bedroom right away. Why, after all these years, had they crossed paths again like some sick played-out joke? The torrid night of sex and debauchery in what seemed like eons ago had broken him, though he hadn't known him as Butcher. His moniker had come about a year after their tryst abruptly ended. Alcohol had a way of bringing out a person's true feelings. For all the tough exterior and prowess with women in public, Butcher had hidden what he truly desired just as much as Gianni had.

In a different scenario, he would ask his savior why he'd disappeared from his life. Every hour they shared in bed was in mutual want. Any utterance of the word 'no' stopped any further advancement. Pain flared in his chest over the loss, but he choked it down. The past was the past and his latest boyfriend had been slaughtered.

His judgment had gone haywire. After taking a moment to piss between love sessions, he'd walked into the two prison guards gunning down his lover. Shannon had dispelled some of his sorrow by showering him with the affection he sorely missed. The sledgehammer Gianni had lovingly promised he'd take their heads off with was in his hands before he could think. His blows rained down on them, reducing their flesh to pulp. Crimson madness, coupled with the lines of cocaine, fueled his fury. Afterward, he'd run into the passages, passing out somewhere between the upstairs and the garage entrance.

Shannon had been a constant in his life. No matter how late the night was, he fed Gianni's drug habit. Letting his lover have a measure of control the last time they fucked was his gift to a loyal house guest. So many things in his life had spiraled out of control. The bedroom was his domain and his sanctuary from a family that told him how to live his life. He loved Shannon on a carnal level, and, for that brief moment before his death, loved him madly. Their relationship had been purely based on sexual desire. Finding that unique partnership again would take more time than he was willing to invest.

To see Butcher standing in his bedroom was something out of a dream. His hair was shorter than he remembered, but those piercing blue eyes still cut. How many times had Gianni bent Shannon over and wished that hunk of a man was on the receiving end instead? No matter how many jobs his family did, Gianni could pick out his stiff frame even when they donned their suits to protect from bodily fluids.

As Gianni sat in the plane sipping plain ginger ale, he couldn't keep his eyes off Butcher. His suit hugged every inch of his masculine body. A tailor-made dream he wanted to play out right on the floor of the plane. If the jitters in his body weren't aching for his favorite white powder, the throb in his pants would get some much needed personal affection in the bathroom. Though the thought of whipping out his cock and masturbating in front of Butcher had its own fantasy.

"Where are we headed?" Perhaps a conversation would keep his mind off things. Besides, he loved the deep bass in Butcher's voice.

"Best we don't discuss it here. Far away from your family and a place your mother arranged for me to clean you up." Butcher popped an ice cube in his mouth, furthering the fantasies in Giannis head.

"I don't need any help."

"Those two cops you pulverized? They were on your brother's payroll." Butcher shifted forward in his seat.

"That's only because my mother died. She hired them to protect me." Even as the words left his mouth, Gianni realized the falseness in his conviction. Lies spilled from his mouth on a daily basis to justify his actions.

"Every time you sucked their cock? That was your brother laughing on the other end. He keeps you hooked on cocaine. What better way for you to fuck up again? Next time you violate your parole, you're staying in for a long time. Not even your father's death would save you. "

"What the fuck do you know?" Gianni glanced out the window. Nothing but billowy white clouds breezed past. This flight would violate his parole as it was, unless Butcher had some grand scheme to cover for it.

"You're an addict, Gianni. Sex, drugs, and on a small scale, alcohol, too. That life you had is gone. There's no going back because if you set foot in New York or the States again, you're going to get arrested for breaking your parole, unless my family decides to help out, which isn't a given beyond the plane ride out." Butcher sat back. "I found your stash, by the way. Let me make crystal clear about this trip—no drugs."

Gianni's hands clenched. The need ate at the pit of his stomach, and that bastard had taken his salvation. No matter what was said, Gianni would find a way to get what he craved. What did he know about what he'd endured in the past couple of years? Men could be bought, and he had no problem getting on his knees again to earn his snowy reward. "I'm tired. Does this place have better accommodations than these seats?"

"Follow me."

When he gazed on Butcher's taut ass, Gianni bit his lip. Damn him if he didn't have the best fucking tailor out there. After repositioning his raging hard-on, he followed his protector to the back of the plane. The door opened, and he caught a glimpse of a large bed covered by a plush duvet. Butcher stood off to the side, waiting.

"Are you going to watch me sleep or something?" Gianni sat on the bed.

"No." With a shove, Butcher knocked him back onto the bed and straddled him. "Like I said. You have some issues to work out." Gianni tried to buck him off, but the weight crushed his chest. Cool metal pressed against his wrists and that familiar click of cuffs pinned him to the bed. "This will keep your hands from rubbing your foreskin right off on the ten-hour trip."

Butcher moved off him, and Gianni jerked against the cuffs. "Son of a bitch. Motherfucker. *Fanculo.*"

"It's for your own good, boy."

"Or maybe it's so you're not tempted to watch me jack off."

"Oh, talk dirty to me." Butcher laughed and left the room, slamming the door behind him. Anger seethed inside Gianni, but he didn't miss the tightness in his captor's pants. He screamed in frustration. All his torrid dreams of Butcher moaning his name, and he couldn't relive them without a hand firmly on his shaft. That bastard had played him, yet in some way the act of restraining him to the bed had aroused Butcher. Fucking that prick would be the last thing he'd do while they spent time together. When they landed, he'd find a way to disappear. Fuck going back stateside, he had nothing to go back to now.

* * * *

Back in his seat, Butcher tried to calm his erection. Not one to be a hypocrite, he refused to relieve his tension with a messy palm rub. It took all his will not to strip Gianni down and fuck him while he was tied to the bed. To feel his warm breath on the tip of his cock or the wet inside of his mouth. Rosalia had tried to tell Butcher that Gianni would be good for him. She'd accepted not only Butcher's lifestyle, but her son's. What better way to protect him than to send someone with the loyalty to take a bullet? He had to remember this was a job and not a vacation. Salvatore wouldn't stop until his brother was dead. His father hadn't gotten back to him with the particulars, but he'd asked for silence until they touched down in Switzerland. From there, Butcher would switch to burn phones to hide their movement. One text, and he'd get his information before tossing the phone.

Again, she appeared. A blurry dress covered her head to toe. Clouds drifted across the fabric and the leather seat she lounged in molded to her. In her hand, a crystal champagne glass filled to the brim with effervescent bubbles hovered near her lips, tempting him.

"You should fuck him and get it over with."

"Shut up." He closed his eyes again.

"How long have you loved him? How many men did I catch you with before the cancer worsened?"

"Too many." Real or not, she was right. The first time she'd caught him slamming his cock into the tight rear of a willing man, she had the decency to wait until later on that night to question him. He remembered how she had laughed off his apologies and requests to leave her service. Her gentle kiss on his cheek and the blunt question of whether he used protection. From there on, she provided his entertainment in bed by paying male hookers that knew how to keep their mouths shut. A week later, after a particularly bad round of chemo, she confided her concerns with Gianni. One look at the picture of her youngest son sent shock waves through his system.

"You could love him. Protect him."

Her words held a numbing truth. Five years prior, when Butcher was at the height of his drunkenness, he'd run into Gianni at a nightclub. No doubt the youngest Bencivenni was well under the influence of substances. They'd kissed and fondled each other, fumbling like two virgins in the darkest corner. Butcher had woken up in some hotel room alone with only the soreness of a passionate fuck to soothe the emptiness. He never pursued his one-night stand. His family cleaned up the messes that the Bencivenni caused. That he'd crossed the line with Rosalia was unusual. Perhaps his techniques to dispose of the bodies had crossed the line, too. The methodology removed all traces that a body existed. Dead weight, sheets of plastic, and the middle of the ocean were old school. Too many chances to get caught, and with more and more police taking the moral high ground, Butcher's way of cleaning was more effective.

Standing, he adjusted his jacket before heading to the cockpit. Blue skies above the ground greeted him ahead. "Keep the door locked until we land. I don't trust our guest to do anything."

"You got it, Butcher. Six more hours."

The timeframe gave him plenty to sleep, even if he camped out in one of the chairs. Heading to the back of the plane was too much of a temptation. He trusted in Rosalia's judgment, yet part of him didn't want to open up to Gianni. The end of the road could have them both face down in a ditch. His gaze never left his guest's door. The drone of the plane didn't lull him to sleep. Time faded until the jerk of the wheels on the tarmac. Flipping his phone open, he dialed.

"They know," his father said.

"Cease involvement. I can never come back to the business. Time to sever ties." He'd been prepared for this scenario. Not that never seeing his family appealed to him.

"No. The prick didn't wire the payment. We've informed the company that we can no longer do business until their debt is paid. The asshole hung up on me."

Butcher sat forward. "Are you safe?"

"One company out of more than I can count on my fingers? Stay away regardless. It's going to get messy. I have confirmation that a friend of yours slipped through before lockdown. Keep your eyes open."

Butcher pulled the phone away from his ear. One last message came through before he ended the phone call.

Kill them all. Rain blood, son.

The plane taxied to the private section of the airport. Perks of the family, but ones Salvatore would have access to as well. He grabbed a phone linked to the cockpit and changed their drop-off point. The regular area of the airport would be much more crowded than the select section. Blending in with an expensive suit wouldn't work. Both he and Gianni needed to look like they belonged despite the dark hair. Mustering up his nerve to enter the same space as his guest, Butcher opened the door to the back of the plane. Gianni slept. The angered lines in his face were soft as an angel except for the dark circles from his withdrawal. Getting clean was going to be a fight, one Butcher was all too familiar with. Unbuttoning his jacket, he hung the garment in the closet. Suits weren't his favorite choice to wear, but in order to look the part of a personal guard, he'd donned it. Rosalia had teased him constantly on how uncomfortable he seemed. In truth, he had great range of motion in the well-tailored outfit.

Stripped to his underwear, he rifled through for something more casual and settled for a Henley and jeans. His gun was in the suitcase. No amount of money would get a gun past security in a carry-on. He preferred using his hands when necessary. Hearing Salvatore's bones crunch beneath his palms would bring him a lot of pleasure.

Zipping up his jeans, he glanced over. Gianni was awake. "We're going through the main terminal." He thumbed over to another set of drawers. "There's a change of clothes in there."

"Do you have anything for a headache?"

"Not until we get to the house. I don't carry any of that with me." He leaned over and uncuffed Gianni.

"Why are you doing this?" His voice was ragged. Butcher remained calm. At this stage, Gianni was unpredictable.

"I promised your mother to keep you safe, remember?"

"No." Gianni wiped his eyes, but stayed on the bed. Butcher studied the murky, dull haze in the youngest Bencivenni's gaze. Methodically, he picked a t-shirt and sweater out of the drawers and dressed him. Bruises marred most of his body, attesting to his treatment in prison. His father's reports to prepare him for the job didn't lie. The guards had abused him under the guise of protection. Butcher wouldn't doubt if Salvatore had something to do with it.

Butcher's first line of duty was to get Gianni safe, yet shimmying his sweat-soaked pants off tempted him. The outline of his package was prominent with the drenched briefs. He peeled them away. His parched mouth wished to quench the cock before him. For a whole year he'd tried to forget the slow inferno of his forbidden lover. Alcohol burned away the memories on the surface, yet the subconscious guarded them close. To give in to his desire, to relive those moments lost, would put them both in danger. He had to restrain his urges.

Gianni gripped his neck and forced Butcher's lips to his own. Sweet and salty. He lost control and invaded Gianni's mouth with his tongue. Straddling a leg, he groaned as his guest rubbed a hand along his crotch. He kissed deeper, biting Gianni's lip and tugging before drowning again. His hand folded around his long-ago lover's erection. How he wanted to swallow his cock down to the base until he sated the thirst within. His mouth found Gianni's neck and he sucked hard. A lasting mark to claim him for the days to come.

"I'll do anything you want." Gianni gasped and groaned under his touch. "I just need one more line. I can quit after one more line. I promise."

Butcher froze, but Gianni continued to grind into his hand. What a fool he'd been. Bencivenni's advance had been fueled by his addiction and nothing more. Pulling away, he sat on the corner of the bed to gain composure. How was he going to fix someone who nearly broke him a few years ago?

Rosalia floated in the corner. A single tear rolled down her cheek, sparkling like a falling star.

The hardest thing to resist was the one you desired most. He wanted Gianni, but in the fuck-up world they lived in, they could never be together.

CHAPTER FOUR

With the help of his father's contacts in Switzerland, Butcher managed to move Gianni unscathed through airport security and to a cabin in the mountains, away from anything close to civilization. Supplies would come at random intervals, with a window of five minutes, to let them know the delivery was on the way. Butcher hoped this would give them enough warning if someone followed them up the remote ride. To further protect themselves, he had an underground shelter to lock Gianni in and a station about one hundred yards away equipped with a rifle. He had never attempted a shot longer than that. In his youth, he could run that distance in eleven seconds. With rough terrain and ten more years into the equation, he'd have to figure out in trial runs.

His charge had cursed and pleaded the whole trip up the mountain. By the end, sweat coated his skin and he shivered.

On the couch, wrapped in several blankets, and stripped of all clothing, Gianni slept fitfully. Butcher made sure no drugs, even ones as simple as aspirin, were stashed in the house. While he'd dealt with his addiction through an intense boot camp his father had forced him into, taking his experience to help Gianni was going to be hard. What if he failed Rosalia? Would her ghost haunt him like the many other apparitions from the cleaning jobs in the past? Would they drive him back to the ledge of his apartment complex to jump and end it all?

The probable outcomes to his latest job clouded his mind. Instead of dwelling on any one element, Butcher decided to orientate with his surroundings. The ground floor was one giant room that opened to a decent-sized kitchen. A hearth was the centerpiece on the opposite side. Hidden in the mantle were a few 9mm handguns, along with the ammunition. He ticked off all the invisible areas where a weapon was stashed. Upstairs had a full spa bath nestled between two spacious rooms. Gianni would sleep in the one on the right and he on the left. Hopefully, the space would get the vision of sliding his dick between Gianni's cheeks out of his head. The last thing that boy needed was someone using his body for pleasure.

He remembered how he'd lingered on covering him in the blanket to get a good look at his physique. Too drunk in their past tryst to recollect every inch, he memorized the olive skin. What would one touch cost him?

His phone buzzed on the kitchen counter, taking him away from the growing lewd thoughts in his head. Their supplies would arrive in five minutes. He slipped the phone into his pocket. With a passing glance at Gianni, he scooped him up and carried him upstairs. No one was to see who he had within the isolated house. Whether his father hired these men or not, trust wouldn't be handed out freely. Even within the layer of blankets, the cold chill of Gianni's skin seeped into his. Damn boy had wrecked his body, and for what? His jaw tightened. Had his family not shunned him for his preferred bedmate, addiction wouldn't have taken a firm hold. Their world was nothing but drenched in sin, and if the devil took them in the end, he'd meet him gladly.

Kicking the door open, Butcher held Gianni close. No amount of blankets would banish the demons in his bones. Butcher had been there, entrenched in the throes of addiction, to know the battle ahead. He set him gently on the bed, gazing at the sereneness on his face. Leaning in, his lips touched a cool forehead. "Hang in there." The phone in his jeans buzzed, and he lamented leaving Gianni's side.

Back downstairs, he retrieved one of the guns in the mantle and snapped in a fresh magazine before flipping the safety off. He tucked the piece in the back of his jeans and headed for the front entrance. The door was reinforced with an inner steel core so no bullet would penetrate. Peering out the peephole, he noted two gentlemen on the porch. Both had packages at their feet and their hands were out at their sides and in full view. With a check of the cameras to make sure no one hid to the side, Butcher opened the door.

"On the counter is fine." He gestured to the kitchen.

"I have an envelope for you." One of them tapped on his box after setting it on the counter. "We caught two people at the bottom of the hill snooping around. They claim they've squatted here in the past."

Butcher shook his head. "I highly doubt that, unless they put a lean-to in the back."

"You want to take care of them yourself?"

Again Butcher shook his head. "Blindfold and dump them twenty miles away in the higher regions so while they're sucking for oxygen, some sort of epiphany puts some sense into their heads." He took the envelope and fished two photographs out. He didn't recognize either of the men.

"Mercy from The Butcher." The man grinned.

He didn't smile back. "If I catch them here again, they won't get another warning. You can go."

Without another word, the two left in silence. After securing the door, he placed the weapons back. If need be, he could reach another weapon stashed around the house. Gianni getting ahold of one was more of a danger than anything outside the house. He busied himself with putting the supplies away, but his mind returned to Gianni. The subtle outline of his toned body and the virtual playground it presented.

The weariness of the day gripped him, and he plodded up the stairs. He planned on checking on Gianni one more time before heading to his room. With the creak of the door, he peered in. Gianni shivered on the bed, the blankets a tangled mess on the floor. Butcher's mouth went dry. His gaze traced every contour, memorizing flesh to never forget again. Part of him wanted to wake the sleeping form, the other remembered his duties. Blankets in his hand, he covered Gianni, only to see his guest groan and twist out of his covers.

"I'm going to regret this." Slipping between the sheets, Butcher hugged Gianni close. The chill of his body seeped in before Butcher's heat warmed his skin. He bit his lip as his cock stiffened in desire. The spirit of Rosalia smiled from the shadowed corner before disappearing.

He closed his eyes and willed sleep to come before he did something they both might regret. Gianni's hand smoothed over his, gently tugging the appendage down to his exposed crotch. Butcher should have resisted, yet as his palm touched the hardened shaft, he groaned.

"I was pretty high that night." Gianni softly spoke. "Hell, I've been high most of my adult life." His palm molded to Butcher's hand to encourage him to grab hold. "But I remember you."

"You don't remember shit." Butcher snorted, but didn't pull away. The soft velvet comfort of another's man's cock enticed.

"If my mother sent you, it was for a reason." Gianni arched his back to press Butcher's obvious erection into his ass. "She knew what I was, even if I did parade Tina around at family functions I bothered with." He chuckled. "And fucked Salvatore's wife before their vows."

Butcher stroked the offered cock slowly. "I'm not giving you any drugs." He tugged and covered the tip with the foreskin.

"You fucking me is all I need right now."

Butcher stopped and sat up. "No. I'm here to protect you, nothing more." He trembled, his words ringing false in his ears.

"Touch me again and say that to my face."

He turned. Gianni kneeled on the bed and palmed his cock. "You're lucid."

"Did my mother's instructions say not to fuck me or not to give me any drugs until I sobered up for good?" Each slide along his cock called to Butcher like a deafening command from the heavens. He stood and walked a few steps away, but his gaze stayed with Gianni's cock play. When the youngest Bencivenni left the comfort of the bed and stalked toward him, Butcher stumbled back into the wall.

"Stop me." Gianni's voice held nothing of the slurred speech he witnessed on the plane. Before him was a man seeking the comfort of a lover. Breath close, Butcher didn't stop him when he undid his pants and pulled out his erection.

"Stop me," Gianni repeated. His hand smoothed over Butcher's shaft along with his own. Flesh touched flesh. He groaned, refusing to participate or push his lover away. Their precum mingled, creating a slick surface to pleasure them both. Too long away from the excitement of a male partner, Butcher growled and yanked Gianni to him. His kiss, born of hunger, demanded the same in return. As their tongues intertwined, his cock spent.

"Touch me, Butcher," Gianni mumbled through their passionate kisses. Coated with his cum, Butcher jerked his lover's cock fast and furious. With a cry, Gianni came. Butcher caught him as he nearly collapsed.

"We shouldn't have done that."

Gianni laughed. "The hell we shouldn't have. I'm too tired for anything else."

"I'm supposed to be helping you, not fucking you." Butcher dragged him to the bed and tossed him on it. "Stop tempting me."

"Never." Gianni weakly flopped his flaccid penis at him. "Not until you let me fuck that ass of yours."

"This is the last time we do anything sexual together." Butcher cursed under his breath, buttoning his pants back up. "Go to sleep."

"I'll go to sleep to that lullaby any day, lover."

Fuming, Butcher stormed out of the room. Without Gianni's need for drugs fueling his advance, Butcher had let him break the barrier he tried to maintain.

Rosalia's apparition waited by the stairs. Sadness and decay twisted her features.

Throwing his hands out to sweep the image away, he charged down the stairs. "Enough!" Out on the porch, he strode into the woods for a little solace. How in the hell was he going to keep his distance from Gianni when he remembered their all-too-brief relationship from the past? His cock begged for him to give in and fuck Gianni. His mind remembered when he had to walk away the last time. He couldn't deal with that pain again.

* * * *

Tired, but sated, Gianni stretched on the bed. One of his many fantasies with Butcher hadn't played out to his liking. The sticky residue of his lover still clung to his skin. Not the best for sleeping options to stain the sheets, though the memory would bring a blissful rest. If he gained Butcher's trust enough, maybe he could find a way out of this mountain prison. All he had to do was tempt him enough to give him the fuck of a lifetime. One that would let his guard down for Gianni to slip away. Hearing the front door slam gave him hope he'd have a few moments to explore his surroundings.

He'd recognized this cabin as soon as he'd opened his eyes. Long ago, his mother would take him here on business while his brothers and sister stayed with his father for other family matters. Though his sister was named after their mother, she showed none of the fierce instincts of survival. Her husband—the prick—had her as a cowed housewife with three children each a year apart. His cruel, hard stare always toward Rosalia to fall in line as his little sister did. Gianni grinned at how defiant his mother would be. In the end, she was the neck that guided the serpent. Without her, their family would suffer soon enough. If Butcher watched him, Gianni's family must have broken the pact with the most respected cleaners in the business. That didn't make him feel any safer.

Rising, though his body revolted, Gianni paced his room. Every square inch of him still ached. His first plan was to get Butcher into a routine before planning his escape. Though he knew the cabin, the forest was completely foreign. Survival in the elements wasn't his strong suit, but money would buy anything. Creeping out of the room, he peered over the balcony. No sign of Butcher. He proceeded to the bedroom at the end of the hall. His mother stayed here and whispered all the secrets it held. Inside, Gianni smoothed his hands over the gas fireplace. His fingers pressed into the fluted wood-carved mantle, and a satisfying click answered. Hidden within was all he needed to escape—a fat roll of cash, a 9mm, and a few extra magazines. Closing the casing, a queasiness rose in his stomach. The euphoric state from the simple hand job with Butcher had staved off his unquenchable thirst for cocaine briefly. He needed a fix. His captor had made it clear he'd found everything. How could he have been that proficient when Gianni hid the bulk of his drugs right under the noses of his family?

Back in his room, he rifled through his belongings. "Come on." Shirts flew in the air as he dug farther into the small carryon. He'd been very selective on what he packed. At the bottom, he reached his tailored jacket. His breath lodged in his throat. He'd stuffed a few small bags of white powder in the delicate seams. He cursed Butcher's name. Not for the frayed damage of the jacket but the loss of his cocaine. Nothing remained at the bottom of the suitcase. He frantically poked the exposed seam. Something nicked his fingertips. Blood welled on the pad. Anger seethed as he yanked the fabric apart. A small sheaf of paper taunted him. Scrawled in black ink was a simple message.

Do you think I'm that stupid?

The jacket flew across the room, followed by the suitcase. All he had was gone. The glorious powder that fueled his soul scattered God knows where by that bastard, Butcher. Didn't the asshole realize his lungs would revolt without the sweet ecstasy of fine snow? He snatched up the lamp, intent on smashing it to bits. Chills ran through his veins. His pulse tapped a death march. The smooth wood of the lamp focused his mind. Each delicate detail brought the smiling face of his mother to life. She'd carved the base with quick efficiency on the back porch while he watched in wonder. In it, he saw a piece of dead wood breathing life with every shaving that hit the deck. A masterpiece that showcased her talent in using a knife. He gently placed the lamp on the end table. Crisp air called to him to cleanse the fresh ache filtering into his muscles. His mother would want him to get clean before he ended up in the graveyard with her.

A slight breeze ruffled his hair as he stepped out on the back deck. The boards beneath his feet creaked and bowed. While the interior of the home had been maintained by someone, the outside had become weather-worn. Still, each footfall to the railing didn't send him crashing through. The top of the pines bent back and forth, and the blue sky offset the dark emerald needles. Peaceful as it was, the demon clawing at his battered soul urged him to escape before the devil exacted his payment.

"Are we finished with our little hissy fit?" At the end of the deck, Butcher leaned against the railing, smugness on his face.

"If you're looking for more, forget it. Call it a moment of weakness I won't repeat." Gianni glanced away briefly. Like it or not, he was stuck with the tempting man.

"I believe I made my point on that matter pretty clear." Butcher scraped a knife along a thick chunk of wood. "While you hinted at a repeat performance, so cut the shit, Gianni."

"You're delusional." He gazed out into the woods again, hoping for a clear path down the mountain and away from the hulk of a man who tossed the truth in his face. Too much for his liking.

"The one thing your mother used to say about you was you couldn't stare into the mirror and admit who you are."

"Don't you fucking talk about her." He flared his nostrils. "You don't have the right."

The knife slowed. "I don't have the right?"

Gianni stumbled back as the knife plunked into the wood millimeters from his foot. All amusement had drained from Butcher's face.

"Where were you when she was gasping for breath, trying to hold on in hopes of seeing you again one last time? Oh, that's right. Taking it in the ass from a guard in jail because you can't help but shove that candy up your nose." He jabbed a finger toward Gianni. "The one son she loved the most disappointed her time and time again."

The clang of the truth reverberated in his skull. Every word stabbed at his soul, and Gianni snapped. Ripping the knife out of the wood, he charged Butcher. The beauty of the emerald forest stained garnet as his rage poured out and blurred his vision. He stabbed out. With the jerk of his arm, Butcher twisted him around and slammed him to the deck. His grip on the knife lost, Gianni screamed profanities, yet Butcher never yielded the pressure. He sucked in gasps between each derogatory insult before tears streamed down his face.

Hate consumed him, but not for the man pinning him down. His mother was gone. The soothing words she offered him when out of earshot of the family faded. Her beautiful eyes haunted the edge of his vision. "I can't quit," he choked out.

"Bullshit."

Gianni cried out as Butcher dug his knee into his back while twisting his wrist.

"You don't know what it's like."

His lips brushed Gianni's ear. "Ever wonder why your mother chose me to protect you through all your tantrums? Addiction comes in all forms, Gianni. In the end, you got to want something more. That's the trick."

The weight ceased, but Gianni remained on the deck as Butcher went inside. He couldn't imagine wanting anything more than a quick bump or an all-night party of snorting cocaine off Shannon's beautiful cock. Those days had passed. Nothing survived the aftermath of his brother's rage. Isolated, Gianni curled up and waited for the creeping darkness to take him.

CHAPTER FIVE

How had it come to this point? Mixed emotions tormented Butcher. To deny the attraction with Gianni would be lying to his body. Something deeper probed his conscience, hinting that he craved more than physical. The man Rosalia had described seemed too good to be true, and so far, he saw nothing to belay that. Addiction had taken root and flourished in the younger Bencivenni.

When Butcher became the caretaker for Rosalia, she couldn't beat what was killing her. His comfort had been to ease her suffering with a morphine drip that he regulated so that she'd stay conscious. Even in her moments of weakness, she never begged for more. The calm in her face didn't match the tremor in her hands. She had more strength than he'd ever possess. How could she believe that he could save her youngest son?

"What have you gotten me into, Rosalia?" He snatched the blanket off the couch and headed back outside. Gianni lay on the deck, still unmoving except for the occasional shiver. Night would descend soon and the temperature dropped quickly at this high altitude. A passing thought begged him to leave the whelp where he lay, to teach him what it meant to truly suffer, but Rosalia's spirit scowled at him. He draped the blanket around Gianni. On the ground next to him, Butcher heaved a loud sigh. "I really don't know what your mother saw in this place."

He didn't know how long he lay there with his quarry—at least he tried to think of Gianni as another job—but he re-entered the house with the sleeping prince.

Days blurred into nights. The bedrooms upstairs remained unused for any purpose. Amid the cursing and begging, he spoon-fed Gianni. Withdrawals were ugly on both sides of the fence. Even if he flushed the last of the cocaine out of the younger Bencivenni, the cravings would always linger. To this day, Butcher yearned for a small drop of whiskey to lessen his visions of the dead. When the sun rose and Gianni slept, he practiced his route to the snipe point. He managed a fifteen-second time, but that was with the sun aiding his sight. His night vision goggles would help some, but how much?

While Gianni slumbered on the couch, Butcher stepped outside to watch the sunset. The azure sky faded into ultramarine splash. He waited for the sounds of the night to accent the bitterness in the air. Eerie silence answered him. In such a remote location, that was the last thing he wanted to hear. While the cool air would ease his ache, something itched along his spine. A tick tock warning he never ignored. He headed inside for the monitor hooked to the security cameras. Two in the lower quadrant had gone dark. Toward the middle, two figures moved through the pitch black.

"Fuck."

His father warned him that Salvatore had slipped through, but to find them this fast? Rosalia had never shared the secret of this home to anyone, and only Gianni knew of it. Had the kid talked in one of his drug-filled hazes? In his room, he stripped and changed into something more suited to the dark. Knives slammed into their sheaths along his thighs. At the small of his back, he tucked a 9mm and put goggles on. With a tactical bag strapped to his back, he climbed out the window and sprinted into the darkness. It took fifteen minutes by car to get up the mountain road at a decent pace. He had less than that on foot because the route was more direct. His chest tightened. He ascended the ladder to his hiding spot. Lying prone, he fished out a box of .22 bullets. He slid his rifle over from its resting spot and loaded the chamber with five rounds. His fingers flexed. Gianni would be safe so long as he killed each and every one of them before they reached the house. He trusted his skill, that wasn't in doubt. The dark specters hovering at the corner of his vision, however, were a distraction. Figures moved into his crosshairs, their dark clothing stark against the foliage through his googles. Without a silencer, they'd be able to pick up his location should he miss. Three men, all with AK-47 rifles, spread approximately twenty feet apart. When they were still a significant distance from the house, Butcher slowed his breathing. His finger eased to the trigger as he inhaled deeply. Exhaling, he stilled before firing. Fluid in motion, the next shoot lined up and broke free of the barrel. As he swung to the third target, the man had vanished. Seconds ticked off in Butcher's head. While the house was locked tight, it would only stay that way if Gianni didn't wake from his stupor.

He flexed his fingers searching for the last man. A chill coursed through his spine, and he rolled from the perch to the ladder. Halfway to the ground, he jumped and rolled, ready to sprint to the house. A heavy weight slammed him to the ground. The momentum sent him careening down the slight incline with his assailant holding on tight. Branches dug into his back and tore at his clothing. As he skidded across a rock, he dislodged his attacker, who flew through the air briefly, followed by Butcher. The unmerciful ground knocked the wind from his lungs. Staggering up, he blinked in the darkness. His goggles had broken free during his tumble. In the sparse moonlight streaming through the thick branches, he found the man responsible for his fall. Twisted and mangled, a broken branch impaled his chest. The whites of his eyes glowed in the twilight.

Battered, Butcher winced and scrambled through the brush toward the house. A single light shone like a beacon, but not one of hope. He'd purposely left all the lights off, so if one was on, Gianni had awoken or someone had breached security. He felt dizzy, his legs giving out. He was going to fail the one person who possibly made him feel any kind of emotion beyond regret.

"Don't you dare give up on him now." Rosalia's face formed on the moss clinging to the rocks. His fingertips brushed her cheek. Soft and velvety, the moss tore off, revealing a smear of blood. Droplets fell and her voice resonated in his head again. *"Rain blood, Butcher."*

* * * *

"You little cunt. How far did you think you could run?" Salvatore's fist plowed into Gianni's cheek. When his brother had smashed a window out to gain entry, Gianni had tried to retrieve the gun he'd taken from his mother's old room. Salvatore had reached him first and kicked him back onto the ground. A rain of fists came next. Not enough to break any bones, but to make him bleed like a stuck pig. Salvatore smashed his perfectly polished shoe into his stomach.

"Just kill me and get it over with." Gianni curled into a ball.

"I have plans for you, little brother. I'm going to start cutting things off one by one, but you're not going to die. Oh, no. I'm not going to make it easy on you. I'm going to start with your cock and make you eat it since you seem to like that perverted shit."

A shadow loomed in the broken shards of the window. Another brute to aid his brother in torturing him until his body gave out?

"So fucking worthless." Salvatore leaned over him and yanked Gianni up by the hair. "You could have all the pussy in the world and instead you'd rather have a dick in your ass. I have nice hot poker to curb you of that sick act."

A scream born of rage and violence pierced Gianni's eardrums and Salvatore barreled off him. Rolling, he nearly broke down at the sight of Butcher hammering his fists into his brother. Blood spewed to the sickening wet sound of flesh caving into breaking bones. What was once Salvatore's flawless face was nothing more than a pool of pulverized flesh. Butcher's anger boiled into the crimson staining the floor. His knife whipped out and gouged the skin and cloth protecting his brother's black heart.

Gianni crawled to his gun, the cool steel blurry in his vision. His salvation from the agony tearing through his being. What would stop one of his other siblings from sending another kill squad? He'd end it all with a bullet through his skull. Gun in hand, he rolled to his knees.

Butcher stood, his chest heaving. Blood coated his upper body, giving his dark clothing a wet sheen. Deep cuts crossed his chest. "What the fuck are you doing, Gianni?"

"You heard him." Gianni nuzzled the gun under his chin. "I'm fucking worthless."

Butcher's shoulders dropped. The extent of his injuries from fighting Salvatore's crew on such a big body made Gianni wonder why Salvatore stood there and mocked instead of finishing the job himself. Perhaps if that giant lug hadn't come through the window, he would have eventually, instead of taunting Gianni to do it himself. None of it mattered. The gun pressed against his flesh was his release from a world that didn't want the abomination he was. Staying clean was never going to happen. He had nothing to live for now. He pulled the trigger and gasped.

Nothing greeted his silent farewell, but Butcher stared at him and the click of the gun. He yanked on the trigger again and heard no sweet serenade of a bullet ripping his head apart.

"I removed the striker and firing pin from your mother's gun. It was the only one you'd have access to since the rest were coded to my fingerprints and no one else's."

"You fucking asshole." Gianni broke. Slamming the gun against his forehead, he sobbed. "Just let me die!"

"I can't let you go. Not again."

"You left me!" Gianni sobbed. "Just like everyone else." The gun slipped out of his grasp.

"If I hadn't, we both would have been dead. My father found out we were fooling around." Butcher spread his arms in surrender. "I had no idea who you were, Gianni. We're not supposed to mix. Rule number one for the pact."

"We could have run."

"To where? Your brother found this place. Do you think you're the only one to suffer? You were my first. You set me free. I am never letting you go again."

"I'm not who you think I am."

"You're exactly what I need." Butcher knelt in front of Gianni. Blood smeared on his cheek as Butcher traced his cheekbone. "I'm going to take care of the bodies. Promise me you won't do anything rash."

"Too late for that." He managed a slight smile. "I'm never going to be clean."

"Yeah." Butcher chuckled, getting up. "I said that to your mother about me. Man, did she prove me wrong."

Gianni never let his eyes stray from Butcher as his savior talked quietly on the phone. The man was all business. Tall and strong, he couldn't wait to explore every inch of his taut flesh. His killing Salvatore had more than a tinge of revenge in it. He might be the Butcher, but the brutal reducing his brother to pulp had the same fiery passion as their past love affair. More importantly, he believed him about why he left.

"Why don't you clean up, Gianni? You're not going to like what I do next to Salvatore."

"What's that?"

"Everything the prick said he'd do to you. I only regret he's already dead."

CHAPTER SIX

With plastic strewn in the living room and beyond, Butcher supervised the cleanup of what was left of Salvatore's body, while one of the cleaners stitched the few gashes he received in his tumble. He gave the locations of the other bodies and reluctantly headed outside to be sprayed down with a hose, not that it wasn't necessary with all the blood. His mind was firmly on Gianni, and his need to be with him. Naked, he shook the hands of the crew before heading back into the house. His clothes had to be disposed of, and with his bulk, replacements would have to come from his stash. Several hours had passed, and he hoped Gianni hadn't fallen asleep. Speaking the secret he held for so many years had freed his soul.

Shivering, but clean, he bounded up the steps. The only way he wanted to be warmed was next to Gianni's body. A soft glow radiated from his room. To his delight, Gianni lay sprawled in the middle, fast asleep. Though he itched to wake him, both had a turbulent night. Sliding between the sheets, he wrapped his arm around Gianni's waist.

"I thought you'd never come to bed."

"I was debating moving our location." Tentatively, he kissed Gianni on the cheek. "Get some sleep. We both need it."

Gianni pushed his arm lower. Butcher's hand brushed the rigidness between his thighs. "Sleep is the farthest thing from my mind right now." Butcher tried to protest, but Gianni straddled him. Smoothing his hands over the tight stitches, he smiled. "Better not strain you too much tonight until you heal." Lips gently touched his, slow and steady.

"Oh, fuck the stitches." Butcher grabbed Gianni's hair and deepened the kiss. His tongue searched and explored until his lungs cried out for oxygen. The younger Bencivenni slid down, tasting each nipple. His teeth clamped on the tender flesh before he flicked his tongue on the reddened nub. Underneath the sheets and planted between his legs, the wetness of Gianni's mouth claimed his cock. Butcher groaned. More than he could hope for, the way his newfound love sucked and lapped his shaft left nothing to question on where their relationship would go. Tender care with a rampant hunger, he shivered as his cock disappeared farther and farther down his throat. He almost came when a finger explored his backdoor. Gianni spit and slathered his hole for ease of entry. One digit prodded slowly before another joined.

"Fuck yes. I'm going to come."

"Hold it. As much as I want to taste every inch of you, I plan on riding that cock." Gianni's fingers pumped. "I need lube."

"Shit." The one thing he'd never thought about packing. "Get on your hands and knees."

"But I'm rather having fun doing this."

Butcher growled and fisted the sheets as Gianni quickened the fingering. "Oh, shit. I'm going to come." Clenching his jaw, Butcher tried to stop the overwhelming need to spray his semen. He wanted this moment to last, but his abstaining had hurried his need for release. Gianni, heedless to the warning, bent and sucked on the tip. His tongue twisted along the underbelly before his downward descent matched the ferocity of his finger fuck. Butcher's stitches threatened to pop as each muscle hardened. His cock jerked inside Gianni's beautiful mouth. His puckered hole forgotten, his lover continued to work his balls and shaft until every last drop was swallowed.

"Aww, Johnny. You taste so good."

At the sound of his birth name, Butcher thrust his hips up. "Give me a second and I'm going to fuck you hard and fast."

Gianni shook his head. "Too late. I've already got your ass primed and ready."

Bearing down while lifting his legs, Butcher cursed and moaned as Gianni's cock invaded the space between his cheeks. Smooth, yet forceful, his beloved guest penetrated his ass. Pain flared in his wounds, but with each thrust, it faded to pure pleasure. His vision blurred back to the first night they'd spent together in some cheap motel.

Gianni had bent him in half just like this moment, rubbing his hard cock between his ass cheeks while pouring copious amounts of lube over the area. The beauty of his sweat-drenched skin and the lucid way his eyes had bored into his soul had made him wish the night would never end.

He damned his body for being too broken to ride Gianni, yet the tortuous pace unhinged his thoughts. He screamed out the only name ever to burrow into his heart. "Gianni!"

His lover cried out. Hot semen sprayed inside his ass before Gianni collapsed on top of him, sucking in air. When his cock receded, Butcher rolled him to the side. He explored his flesh one more time. Every defined muscle and twitch of recovery within responded. Tomorrow was another day and their mountain retreat would fade in memory, but not what they shared.

"What now?" Gianni mumbled.

"Sleep and recovery." He licked his partner's ear. "I intend to fuck you hard in the morning, stitches be damned."

"Oh, talk dirty to me."

Butcher gave a weak laugh and let Gianni have that last jab before he drifted to slumber. Their world was shit, but together they could conquer anything that crossed their path.

At the edge of his vision, Rosalia stood in the corner. A red flowing dress, only one of her kind could conjure, billowed in the wind. Her fingers pressed to her ruby lips and she blew a kiss to Butcher. As she faded, he smiled at her farewell. He'd granted her last wish and redeemed more than his soul in the process.

The End.

SLICK

BY

LEA BRONSEN

DEDICATION

To my readers: Thank you infinitely for buying my books. You rock! Some of you I'm overly happy to call my friends. You're always available for a chat, and you're funny, smart, supportive, caring—simply terrific persons. How amazing is it that we connected through my writing! I have even asked a few of you to beta read this story, and your constructive and insightful feedback has been invaluable. Slick is dedicated to all of you.

Special thanks to Jenika for the intro. You are the first erotic romance author I have read, and you are an inspiration. Having your name next to mine on a book cover is the coolest thing evah.

~ Lea

CHAPTER ONE

"Rule number one, no flirting with the customers."

"No, no." Vasilj shakes his bald, moon-shaped head. "I would never, Luke."

"Okay." That's what they told me on my first day in the restaurant. You can do anything you want, or almost, but don't hit on the customers. I don't believe the good-natured Croatian is the kind to hit on anyone. With a round, puffy face, long-lashed deer eyes, and an easy smile, he looks too nice to have sex on his mind. But you never know.

It was the first thing Patrick, the kitchen chef, said to me when he gave me a tour of the offices. Our boss must have thought I was the sex-hungry type and asked him to warn me. I don't know why. Except from having razor sharp eyes, according to the receptionist, I'm an average-looking guy with a normal-built body I like to keep in shape.

Maybe it's my way of looking into people's souls. They usually avert their gazes after a few seconds, while I dig deep to see what they're made of. It makes them uncomfortable. If I wasn't so damn good at cooking and keeping the place clean, I would've had the boss' footprint on my ass ages ago.

Or maybe it's because I've done time behind bars—but it had nothing to do with sex, and nobody here is supposed to know where I was before I landed the job three years ago.

It's my turn to take Vasilj for a tour. Every Monday, I deliver fruit baskets to offices on each of the fourteen floors. I always start my delivery at the kitchen level, the first floor, then work my way up. There are so many offices I need at least one trolley per floor. That's a lot of elevator rides for a Monday morning, when I'm not on top of my game after a weekend of drinking and screwing yet another guy or chick I'll never see again.

"Most people don't even thank us." Vasilj puffs in annoyance as he hits a number on the elevator panel and meets my gaze in a mirror on the back wall. "They think because we work for a service company, we don't deserve respect."

After wheeling the trolley through corridors, open plans, and private offices for an hour, we're a bit sick of deliveries. And the day has just begun. Next, we'll have to help our colleagues prepare the food, make sure things run smoothly during the stressful lunch hours, then clean everything from the utensils to the restaurant tables before switching off the lights long after everyone else has gone home. That's right, we work more hours than the pretty office employees sitting on their asses all day, expecting us to serve them.

Vasilj wants respect?

I raise a brow. "Suck it up." The tone in my voice sends a tiny rush of satisfaction through me. When you're at the bottom of society, you savor having a little power over another person. Like my granddad's status of *kapo* in Buchenwald, earning him a cigarette a day or something for keeping order among the prisoners. He loathed imprisonment, but being allowed to command his peers saved his life.

There's always a hierarchy among workers, especially in a restaurant. Who dominates who depends on seniority and the position one is given. It can depend on your personality, too, as in my case. I may have the lowest position and arrived last before Vasilj, but I don't let anyone step on my toes. I demand that my colleagues treat me equally, and at the slightest hint of injustice, I bark. Except not when the boss is around. If I lose my job, I'm back in the gutter, which is sure to send me back to the hole. Never-fucking-more.

Vasilj scrunches his brows in the mirror. "Why do I have to suck it up?"

He doesn't know. I grin, the white scar on my chin stretching beneath my brown goatee. Fourteen floors takes a while to climb, and I enjoy every opportunity to give a naïve employee a lesson about the way things are run in this place. "You and I are *workers*, right?"

"Yeah?"

"In case you haven't been told, this building houses managerial companies. They represent powerful firms, from industry to construction to service to infrastructure and so forth. You following me?"

"Um…yeah?"

He looks a bit lost, but I want to make sure he gets it. "So, they have lobbyists pleading their case to politicians on one hand, and they have lawyers stepping on workers' rights on the other. You know what that means?"

"No?"

"It means cockroaches like you and me are kept at the bottom of the social ladder. They'll fight so we don't get raises. They'll tweak the law so we have as little vacation or sick leave as possible, and they'll sack us for the smallest mistake."

His look darkens.

Welcome to my world, pal.

The elevator stops, and aluminum doors slide open to a vast land of desks and busy office workers.

I lean closer to his bald head and whisper, "That's why you shut the fuck up."

* * * *

At lunch hour, the restaurant buzzed with low conversation and *clinks* of cutlery and glasses.

Roman hunched over the table. His neck and shoulders ached. A headache hovered, threatening to cripple his mind for the rest of the day. Work always piled high this time of year, but today, his secretary, Cindy, stayed at home with a sick child, so he had more on his desk than he could handle. It didn't help that his kids had a day off from school, and since Jen, their mother, attended an important meeting, he brought them to his office. Well, *it didn't help* in the sense that the kids were high and low, exploring, asking questions, taking up his time. But they were sweet and good-hearted, and he loved them more than life itself. If he had to sacrifice something for them—anything—he would not hesitate a second.

Time to go. Impatience made him sizzle. So much to do. At the end of the day, after Jen picked up the kids, he had two meetings to attend. One with representatives from a construction firm, and the other with his company's board members.

He drew a deep, relaxing breath and looked at his kids. Usually, it took little Lily ages to finish her meal, but now she ate like a trooper. Maybe she sensed daddy carried a load of stress and she decided to be nice. As for Nick, he went to and from the kitchen twice to refill his plate with meatballs and fries. He dreamed of becoming a famous soccer player, so he ate huge servings to grow big and strong.

Roman smiled. "C'mon." He stood from his seat and took his tray. "Let's go put this in the dishwasher and—"

"They have a dishwasher?" Nick asked, his clear blue eyes big. "I thought they had people to clean stuff for us."

Roman raised a brow. "Who told you that?"

"Mom."

He held back a groan. Jen was such a snob. How typical of her to think floor-level employees had to do the dirty jobs for others. They disagreed on a number of issues. Their ongoing divorce wasn't solely due to her finding a new man. He had loved her fiercely for years, but nowadays, he grew tired of her. "No, it would be too much work for them. Just imagine, there are about a thousand people in this building. How would the kitchen workers be able to wash a thousand plates and...?"

Nick smiled, exposing a couple of missing front teeth. "The plates would pile *aaall* the way to the roof."

"Exactly. So they have a really big dishwasher in the back of the kitchen. A monster of a dishwasher."

"Oh," Lily exclaimed, her baby-girl voice full of wonder. "Can we see it?"

"Sure."

Both kids hurried up from their seats and, trays in hand, steered to the kitchen with Roman in tow.

Behind the counter, uniformed workers moved back and forth. He was usually too lost in thought to pay attention to them, but his kids' questions had him take in the scene. At the front, two guys helped people unload their trays. One of them, big and bald with Slavic features, and the other, younger, much fitter, and with a hard, angular face, a goatee, and strikingly piercing green eyes.

Roman blinked, amused. It was strange how people could work in the same building for years—actually spending more time there than they did with their families—and never interacted, simply remained anonymous.

* * * *

Vasilj and I work our asses off in the steamy kitchen's washing station, sharp clattering and clinking filling our ears. It's his first time, and his stress is evident from a stream of sweat rolling down his temples. We have to act fast. A constant line of customers stops at the counter separating us from the restaurant to put their dirty dishes, glasses, and cutlery into their respective boxes. A shelf is placed at head level for the trays, barring our view of people's faces. All we see is fluttering hands moving things around.

Though the line proceeds at snail-speed, the boxes fill quickly, making our job behind the counter hectic. When a box is full, we set it aside and replace it with an empty one. Then, since these asses don't bother to do anything right, we rearrange the first box's content and spray everything with hot water to remove food remains they've neglected to wipe into the bins. Apparently, they believe the dishwasher—or we, the assistants—will do every single thing for them, just like their mothers or wives do at home. They have no respect or understanding for the way a kitchen works. They don't even take a second to look at us and say, "Hi," or, "Thanks for the great job you're doing." Our work is what it is, but we do it well, yet they treat us like we're part of the décor, a practical necessity. *We* must always be polite. That goes with the job, whereas they strictly don't need to have manners.

Two pairs of small hands appear in front of me, carrying trays with dirty plates and glasses. That's surprising. Employees seldom bring their children to work, unless it's a holiday and they couldn't find someone to care for them.

Happy to be pulled out of my monotonousness, I bend to see beneath the tray shelf.

Two kiddos look back, a boy of about seven and a sweet, blonde girl of about five, both a bit disoriented by the fuss and the noise.

"Hey, guys." I smile, gazing from one to the other. "Helping someone at work today, are we?"

The girl nods, while the boy stares at my goatee and points to his own chin. "How did you get this scar?" he asks bluntly, like only a child can.

He doesn't need to know the terrible history of that wound, so I tell him my usual lie: "My shaving machine and I had a disagreement."

At my side, Vasilj chuckles. He doesn't know the truth. No one here does.

"Does it hurt?" the boy asks.

"Nope." I shake my head like a goofy cartoon superhero. I may dislike the adult workers in this building, but I'll always be nice to their kids. "Here, I'll help you. You put your plate in this box"—I point to the one containing dirty plates—"and then…"

"I know." He hurries to place his plate, cutlery, and glass in their respective boxes, before dropping his balled napkin into the bin.

"Of course you do." I laugh from his eagerness. "You're a smart boy."

He looks up to me with a gaze full of pride and expectation.

I reach him a fist over the space between us.

He smiles, flashing a row of teeth with a hole in the front, and fist-bumps me like a street champ.

It's the little girl's turn. She's so small she needs help, so I take the items from her tray and put them in the right boxes. When I'm done, I slide a gentle finger along her cheek. "Thanks for your help. You're amazing."

She giggles and squirms from my touch, looking at me as if I were Santa himself.

Warmth fills me. This kind of interaction is so rare at work—or any place at all—it not only pulls me out of my haze of boredom, it gives me something nice to live for and replay again and again for days.

I've spent twelve years in jail, so you can't exactly blame me for savoring a little humanity. Before that, when I was too small to remember, my mother died of a drug overdose. She didn't know who my father was. My granddad, who had survived extermination in WWII, swore he would keep me off the street. I still ended up behind bars at the age of fifteen.

The little girl asks, "Where's the monster?"

"The monster? Is there a monster in here?" I turn to sweep the busy kitchen behind me. Patrick, the chef, stands in the back eyeing us. We're taking too long. I ignore him.

"The dishwasher." Grinning, the boy points to the gigantic brushed-aluminum machine alongside a wall.

"Ah, that one. Well, it's not a *bad* monster. But it did swallow my colleague's hair once."

As the kids stare wide-eyed at Vasilj, he runs a hand over his bare scalp and laughs.

I send him a wink. It's important to use humor in our kind of dirty work.

"Move on, now," a tall man next to the kids tells them, voice low and soft. "We don't want to stop the line." Their father?

They obey, throwing Vasilj and me a last look of wonder before leaving the station and turning a corner.

The guy may be a loving dad when he addresses his kids, but when he turns to unload his tray, he takes in everything and everyone around him simultaneously with sharp, black eyes that gleam of shrewdness. Startling.

I don't remember seeing him before, but then most of the office renters are anonymous to us kitchen workers. They come and go, usually looking down to avoid any interaction. As for us, we're too busy doing our tasks efficiently to stop and *see* our customers. At the end of the day, several hundred people, maybe a thousand, have visited the restaurant, and I don't remember a single face.

He sure stands out. A short, neatly trimmed beard and mustache frame aristocratic sun-licked features that match his black gelled hair. To strengthen the impression of elegance and high social standing, his custom-tailored clothes seem to be made of some expensive fabric a thug like me would never know. His hands look so neat and fine they must be manicured, one of them wearing a large dual metal wedding ring. All of this combined, he exudes wealth and power, and with the black pirate eyes of a slick business fucker, he's the kind to have a suite on the top floor, the kind to profit on others less fortunate, the kind to despise low-paid workers like Vasilj and me.

Such arrogance. I swear on my mother's grave, he needs to be put in his place, and though I'm not a beast, I'd like to see him visit prison for a few days. I know a pedophile or two who would have a field day with him, teach him a little respect.

Better yet, I could fuck this slick shithead myself right here on his turf, at the top of our power tower. And when I say fuck, I mean bend him over his million-dollar mahogany desk and slide my thick, hard cock into his million-dollar anus for the whole city at our feet to see.

CHAPTER TWO

Most workers have gone home. Both the ones sitting on their asses in a pretty office all day, and those spending that day working their asses off in the kitchen. The only people left in the building are the lowest of the low who don't have a life, like me, and the ones at the very top, too busy screwing the world to want to have a life.

One task left for me: wipe the tables clean. I don't mind working late, don't have anything better to do anyway, other than chain-smoking in my tiny, stinking room on the other side of town and watching TV 'til I fall asleep.

I wet a cloth and go into the low-lit restaurant. In a corner, three suits sit around a table, discussing. Nothing out of the ordinary, except one is the guy who brought his kids to lunch earlier, the one I've thought of as *Slick* since. He's lit my curiosity. Who is he, and what fucked-up business does he do for a living?

Moving between tables, I wipe dirty surface after another, and eavesdrop.

"Who cares about the renters," one of the strangers says, leaning back and crossing his arms over his monogramed shirt so his opulent belly protrudes underneath.

The second suit nods. "You took the words out of my mouth. They're all drunk or drugged." He fidgets a fat leg over the other, revealing dark brown leather shoes that look handmade. "Get 'em out, that's what I say."

"No." Slick gives a small shake of his head. "I'm not asking the City to kick these families out. They don't have the resources to find new homes. You know it as well as I do."

Pretending not to listen, I move closer and clean tables like a robot.

He turns to me. "They'll end up on the street."

Wiping cloth in hand, I pause and stare.

Our eyes connect, and he squints, indicating recognition. "They have kids. I'm not doing it."

"You can't mix ethics into this," the first suit grumbles.

Slick's sharp black gaze wanders back to him. "You can build elsewhere. It's perfectly possible."

"*If…*" The second suit leans over the table. "We're being sentimental in this business…"

"We lose projects." The first nods. "Turnover drops."

"And *boom!*" The second one slams his palm flat on the table, the slap resonating in the empty restaurant. "We sail into bankruptcy land. We fire people. We lose competence. The banks refuse to fund new investments. But *you*"—he points a thick finger at Slick—"you have the connections to do something about it."

"That's your assignment," says the first.

Slick frowns. "There's vacant, very attractive land all around the city border. If you prefer in-town housing, building higher is the new trend. Architects will jump on any occasion to design taller buildings or add floors to existent ones."

The second shakes his head. "You know who to talk to. And considering our company is one of your biggest members, you should—"

"With all due respect." Slick lowers his voice. "I'm not going to kick these people out of their homes." He stands abruptly, forcing the two others to look up to him. "Now, if you'll excuse me, I have a board meeting to prepare."

Ha, if these two suits are affiliated to his company, he has some nerve. I'm impressed. Having finished wiping the tables, I'm heading back to the kitchen when he walks over to me. The other men put their coats on and pick up their suitcases.

Despite lines of fatigue on his forehead and dark patches beneath his eyes, Slick looks young, maybe in his early thirties. Yet deep black, scrutinizing pupils that seem to have an endless depth and centuries of wisdom suggest otherwise. "Have you finished your work for the day?"

"Yeah." I hold his gaze.

"I have a meeting in a half hour and would need some coffee. I forgot to tell my secretary to make the booking last week." Behind him, the suits leave.

"No problem. I can bring you coffee. How many guests?"

"Seven."

"Anything else? Cookies?"

"Anything you have will do. And thanks." He gives a tired smile.

Pleased by his good manners, I ask, "Where should I bring the tray?"

"I'll come with you."

"Okay. I'll get everything." I'm not too happy about serving a slick suit after hours, but my boss expects that much. He wants his employees to be service minded, which entails leaving my disdain behind and doing what it takes to maintain our good reputation.

We go to the kitchen. The food section is closed, but the coffee machine is always on. Swiftly, I grab two cans, fill them with hot coffee, put them on a trolley, and add cups and teaspoons.

Slick throws his watch a glance. He's in a hurry, and here I am making him wait.

"I'm sorry it's taking a little time." I give him an apologetic smile. *Always be polite with the customers.* "I'll just get the cookies."

He nods and checks his smartphone, which looks to be made of titanium. *Slick.*

I find a pack of cookies in a cupboard, dispose them into a bowl, and place it on the trolley with some napkins.

We hurry out of the kitchen, he thumbing his phone, and I wheeling the trolley, coffee cups clattering. The elevator doors are already open. He flashes his ID on the panel board and hits number fourteen. The top floor, as I thought. As the doors slide shut, we study each other over the trolley.

"What's your name?" he asks.

"Luke."

"Sorry I'm asking you to do this, Luke. My secretary had to stay home with her little girl today because she's sick."

His concern for me is surprising. And he accepted that an employee took a day off because of a sick child? I've heard of people losing their jobs for smaller infractions.

"Are they paying you for extra hours?" he asks.

"It's not a problem. I'm happy to help." The truth is I won't be paid for something a customer hasn't booked in advance, but I don't want to tell him that. His kindness earns my goodwill.

"You have a family to go home to?"

"No." When I was sentenced to jail, whatever I had that I could call family stopped talking to me, including Granddad, who died while I was inside. He was too ashamed. He may have served time, but as a prisoner of war, not a criminal. "Where are your kids?"

"Their mother picked them up earlier." His phone rings. "Speaking of which." He answers on a deep sigh. "Hi, Jen." A silence. The elevator dings and the doors open. He hurries out. "I have a board meeting in fifteen minutes. Can this wait?"

I follow him, wheeling the trolley out into an empty, open land. From the mess of papers on scattered desks and cabinets, you'd think a blizzard had hit and everyone evacuated.

Phone to his ear, he strolls to a private office section a few desks down. A long corridor with aligned doors on each side stretches to the other end of the building. I struggle to keep up the pace. The carpet absorbs the sounds of our shoes. At the bottom, he turns a corner and leads me past more offices to a door that has a plate with the words *Associated Builders* engraved on it.

He unlocks and opens the door to a vast conference room. The lights are already on. It's the kind of work place where you never turn them off, for some stupid reason. A wide, oval chestnut table stands in the middle, flanked by a dozen executive chairs. Abstract paintings adorn the white walls. A gigantic floor-to-ceiling window overlooks the city, allowing the low afternoon sunlight to flow in.

"I need to change," he whispers to me. "I stink." Sending me a wink, he goes to an adjacent room.

Heh. I smile. I haven't noticed any perspiration smell, but I guess these guys can afford changing clothes several times a day.

"Your lawyer said *what?*" he shouts into the phone. "Son of a bitch!"

Minding my own business, I close the main door and place the coffee cans and the cookie bowl on the table.

"Hey, Luke?" A different tone.

"Yeah." I walk to the other room, a corner office made of huge, perpendicular windows. Two black wood desks stand opposite each other in the center.

Slick paces along one of the glass panes with the phone to his ear, a deep line on his forehead. On the biggest desk between us, a laptop, piles of documents, pens, and empty coffee cups elbow for space. A photo of his lovely kids stands on a corner, with a smiling blonde looking over their shoulders.

Moves hurried, he walks over, stretches his free arm out, and whispers, "Can you undo this for me?"

Ah, the sleeve buttons. "Sure." While he listens intently on the phone, I unbutton both of his cuffs, help him pull one sleeve off his arm, wait for him to take the phone with his other hand, and pull the other sleeve off.

Wow, fucking *wow*. His body is impressive. I stand with his shirt in my fist staring, almost frozen. Damp heat oozes from his naked, well-built torso. He has the long, lean, and firm muscles of a swimmer or a runner, and a mass of black hair covering his chest and arms. Not too much, just enough to be...*sexy*. I've seen all kinds of muscular torsos in jail, but this guy is clean, neat, and combined with his handsome looks and attentive behavior...he intrigues me.

"Thanks," he whispers, before walking to a tall cabinet along a wall, opening it, and displaying a row of hanging shirts and ties. "No, you can't do this to me!" he tells his wife. Frowning, he grabs a shirt, bumps the door closed with his hip, and hangs the shirt on the back of his executive chair.

He needs to be alone. I fold his dirty shirt on the table and prepare to leave, but the sound of a new cabinet opening piques my curiosity.

Phone to his ear, he picks a bottle from a generous selection and spins to show it to me, lifting his brows as if to offer me a drink. The bottle has the rich gold-orange color of a bourbon.

Is he crazy? I don't drink at work. I shake my head and walk out to give him some space. It was a nice gesture, though, making a point of treating me like his equal. I had no idea such an important person, a managerial director, apparently, could be so thoughtful. I'm too used to their looking down at me.

I arrange the coffee cups around the conference table, wheel the empty trolley to a corner, and go to the large window to have a look. Fourteen floors separate me from the ground, and rooftops of varying heights stretch into the horizon. Feels like the building is swaying.

This is power. You can drink alcohol in your work hours, come and go when you want, and have the most luxurious office on the top of the city.

Still, I may be a cockroach living in a dump on the lugubrious side of town, I wouldn't trade my miserable life for Slick's privileges.

"No! They're my kids, too!" A yell from the door, followed by a *bang* and the sound of shattering glass.

A shiver runs through me. I freeze and strain to hear.

Gasps.

Should I help him? He probably wants to deal with his personal issues on his own. When I have problems, I sure don't want anyone to interfere.

Silence. So fucking quiet, I can hear the blood pulsing in my temples.

Alarm shoots through me. Broken glass and anger don't do well together.

I swivel and hurry into the adjacent room.

Slick sits on the edge of the desk with a hand covering his ashen face and the other arm across his naked chest. His phone lies next to him. On one of the walls, a brown splatter narrows to a streak gliding down to the carpet, with sharp shards of glass at the bottom reflecting light.

"You okay?" I ask.

He nods, but doesn't look at me. He seems petrified. Maybe the phone call was the drop that made the vase spill over, and he can't handle the overload. Or maybe he's ashamed of letting his anger get the better of him. Powerful people want to be in control, they don't explode and destroy things. That's what thugs like me do.

I circle his desk, find a trash bin, and squat in front of the pile of shards to help pick them up.

At last, he pushes from the table and kneels in front of me. He says something I don't get because heat from his naked torso brushes me like the sensuous caress of a whore, and an ensnaring scent of musk mixed with cologne sneaks into the dark parts of my brain. Turning to mush, my head buzzing, I use my thick fingertips to pull the biggest shards out of the carpet slowly, placing them in the bin with exaggerated care to prolong the time I can be near him. This moment will be over too soon.

He puts a hand on mine, his fingers radiating heat.

Fuck, I can't stand the intimacy. As if burned by fire, I retract my hand from underneath his.

He growls, "I said, be careful. You're going to cut yourself."

I suck in a breath. He's referring to my trembling? My callused hands always tremble in every situation. It's something I developed in prison. But he doesn't know it's normal for me. Maybe he thinks I'm a bundle of nerves and that the sight of broken glass shocked me. If he knew the things I've seen! Holding back a chuckle, I focus on the difficult task. Now that I've picked the bigger pieces of glass, miniature ones are revealed beneath, lodged between the carpet fibers.

"Didn't you hear me?" From the hard tone in his voice, he's used to giving orders.

For a while there, I forgot he's a customer—thus the boss—and I the employee, the one who has to bow and give thanks for having a job at all.

Trembling hand mid-air, I gaze up into his stare and swim in the storm of emotions in his black, strained eyes, framed by long lashes. I can't resist glancing downward, to his mustache, full lips, and bearded jaw.

Everything about him makes me sizzle. The vulnerability exposed by his ex's phone call, dueling with the toughness he showed dealing with the suits earlier. His perfect muscles playing underneath tanned skin and a mat of manly hair. The very basic human way he kneels before a pile of glass shards, proving he's mortal like the rest of us, while wearing one of the most expensive pant fabrics I've seen in my lifetime, in a luxurious office on the rooftop of the corporate-finance part of the city.

A tick runs through his features. "I would never do that," he tells me, dark eyes shimmering.

"What?"

"Keep the kids from her. Use them to bargain for what she wants. That's so—" He bites his lip and muffles a guttural sound deep in his throat.

"Amoral? Unethical?"

He nods.

My, my. How many times have I witnessed him sticking to ethics today? He may be wealthy and have fought his way to the top with means unknown, but he seems to be an honest person, not as shrewd and slick as I thought. Every moment I spend with this guy, I like him better.

He returns the stare with something akin to recognition, as if reading my thoughts and agreeing.

A rap on the door breaks the spell between us.

"Would you mind letting them in?" Groaning, he gets up and goes to his chair. "I need to put my shirt on."

"Sure." A bit dizzy, I stand and walk to the conference room scratching my head. What a strange day.

I open the door, and a bunch of fat suits try to push in, not bothering to give me a look.

These morons are the association's board members? Ha. Well, I'm too son-of-a-bitch to let them in just like that. I *loathe* abuse of power. Slick is cool enough and treats me like a fellow human being, but these fuckheads... I stand in the doorway blocking their entry with my beefed-up arms crossed. I have the build of a bodyguard, and if I wasn't wearing my stupid kitchen uniform, I'd pass as one. "You have an invitation?" I ask, using my most lethal thug voice.

Maybe what I'm really doing is protecting Slick, buying him time. But why do I feel the need to cover for him? He has proved he's more than capable of handling pressure in business affairs. But the personal vulnerability he allowed me to see moments ago is etched into my mind. He's not as tough as he wants the rest of the world to believe.

One suit with the hanging cheeks of a bulldog presses between the others and looks me up and down. "We have a board meeting with Mr. Spencer. He in?"

I make a point of looking the bulldog up and down, too, before giving a level stare with my nose in the air, as if he's annoying the living daylights out of me.

He squints.

"Who's that?" someone grumbles behind him.

Satisfied, I take a step back and leave the door open.

Several sleazy fuckers enter one after the other and spread around the table, noisily pulling chairs back and throwing their document cases on the table.

My work is done. I head for the main door.

"Luke?"

Now what? I spin.

Slick walks over with a clean shirt on, looking amazingly handsome compared to his board members. He extends a hand with dollar bills in it. "For your extra hour."

He thinks I want his dirty money? I give him a cold look.

From the change of color in his eyes, he understands I have a problem with his offer. But he doesn't know why. He has no idea how deep my despise of his power world runs. Maybe he thinks I'm just being modest.

He keeps his hand proffered to me. "At least let me pay for the coffee."

I snicker. "We don't accept money under the table." How bold. What happened to the politeness mantra? I don't know, but his standing there representing the self-important managerial companies pisses me off. Minutes ago, he showed me who he was beneath his slick businessman layers. We connected on a personal level. Now, waving dollar bills in front of my nose, he's treating me like a lousy bottom-of-the-ladder worker again, someone below his status.

His eyes flash before he regains his cool and pockets the money. "What do you need? A written order confirmation?"

"Yep."

He nods, gaze hard. "I'll get it to you tomorrow. I have to start the meeting. Thanks for your help." He closes the door on me.

I turn on my heel, chuckling to myself. The sleazebag thinks he owns the world. Someday, I'll be back in this luxurious office on top of the mightiest building and impale him.

CHAPTER THREE

The next day, an inhuman workload had Roman pushing his lunch break numerous times. He checked his watch every now and then, and his stomach growled several warnings as half the day passed—the kitchen downstairs would close soon—but it was only when a sharp ray of sunshine slipped past the blinds of his office and landed on his arm that he rose, his body ankylosed. It was ten to one, and if he didn't hurry to the restaurant, he might as well drop the whole lunch idea altogether and stick to caffeine for the rest of the day.

Grumbling in annoyance, he logged off the computer, put his phone in his pants pocket, and left the office. From the intensity of the high sun outside, he *knew* he was missing out on something, working hour after hour in the shade like a maniac. He loved his job. Being the managing director of a construction oversight company gave him plenty of challenges and fit his personality like a glove, but sometimes the amount of work was just too much for one man. New cases kept coming in, old documents piled on his desk, and he struggled to keep up. His associates expected him to solve every business issue they encountered, and wanted him to perform lobbying miracles. They were crazy.

In the elevator, he breathed deeply and stared at his reflection in the mirror. He had dark patches under his eyes and his mouth made a straight line. The divorce weighed on him. After seven years of marriage to his best friend and the most beautiful woman in the country, he learned she had fallen for a younger partner in her law firm. Why she thought their affair stood a better chance at a *forever after* than the one she'd promised Roman, he couldn't understand. They'd made two children, for God's sake. Surely, it had to mean something.

The doors slid open to a practically empty restaurant. His gaze swept the vast, open space. In a corner, the kitchen employees had lunch together at one of the long tables, chatting and laughing. It'd be nice to join them. Whenever he travelled alone, he aimed to meet real people instead of going to fancy restaurants reserved for rich tourists. Jen wouldn't have it. She demanded luxury. It was she who had pushed him to buy a mansion on the residential side of town, cruise in an expensive car, and wear that high-end watch. Maybe now that they split, he could go back to enjoying the simple life and connect with people on the ground.

Where was Luke? He turned to check out the kitchen. They got off on the wrong foot yesterday, and since Luke had been so kind to help with coffee, he wanted to make up. He didn't know why the offer to pay for Luke's extra hour had vexed they guy. It was a natural thing to do, for him, at least. Everything was measurable and had a price, even a kitchen assistant's time.

Speaking of the devil—Luke appeared from behind a counter, wearing his gray uniform and carrying a tray with a sandwich and a glass of water. His features resembled those of a Viking—strong and angular, his slicked-back hair a mix of blond and brown slashes. Formidable. His striking green eyes focused on Roman, but showed no sign of recognition.

"Hey." Roman raised a hand. "I was going outside. Want to join me?" His heart jumped. What the hell was he doing? He hadn't intended to go out *or* invite anyone to eat with him. He needed time alone to think about the divorce.

Luke paused, seemed to consider the invitation, then nodded. He glanced at Roman's empty hands. "You're not eating?"

"Um…I'm not hungry." Another lie.

Luke grinned. "Yeah, right." Tray in hand, he spun and said over his shoulder, "I'll getcha something."

A minute later, he reappeared holding two wrapped sandwiches and a water bottle. "I need to get some sun, too." He waved to his colleagues in the corner and led the way out of the restaurant.

Roman followed him, head dizzy and stomach slightly nauseous. It had to be the caffeine overdose. Or his starved bowels. He'd skipped breakfast again.

As Luke walked before him, he couldn't help noticing his easy, smooth step. He seemed to glide over the floor with the grace and virility of a wild animal, his large shoulders straight and head held high. Intriguing, for a kitchen assistant.

They passed security and exited the building without a word. The high sun shone intensely, blinding and stopping them in their tracks. Roman pulled his sunglasses out of his chest pocket and put them on, giving his eyes relief. He'd spent too much time in his cool, dark office.

Luke didn't have sunglasses. Squinting, he walked on.

They crossed the street, then a parking lot, and reached an open park. Their shoes crushed gravel and the scent of warm grass and dirt snuck into Roman's nostrils. He took deep breaths. Birds sang of happiness. It was spring, his favorite time of the year. Renewal. How fitting, now that he was embarking on a new journey in his life.

A row of tall chestnut trees cast shadows on an elderly couple on a bench. They had their eyes closed as if they, too, listened to nature coming to life. On the next bench, a teenage girl in pink sportswear hunched over her smartphone, head bobbing to music. She didn't even look up when Luke passed her and slumped on a third bench with his legs spread in a very manly manner. He put the water bottle in the middle and handed out one of the sandwiches.

Roman sat and accepted the gift. "Thanks." He closed his eyes and leaned back for a moment, molding his spine to the hard wooden boards and sinking into pause mode. He should do this more often. With Cindy gone for a couple of days, he would never be able to catch up on the workload. "My secretary is on leave today, too," he said on a sigh. But a sick child was a sick child.

"You banging her?"

"Huh?" He opened his eyes.

Luke rolled back the sleeves of his gray kitchen uniform and unwrapped his sandwich. His forearms were pumped in a hard, chiseled way. The kind you got working out in a gym. Prominent veins and white scars zigzagged across clumsily drawn tattoos. Every move made muscles ripple beneath his pale skin. What else did his clothes conceal? He had the tough look of a boxer, a thug, someone you'd see in a mugshot.

Roman's head drained of blood. A mugshot? How long exactly had Luke worked in the restaurant? He could have been there for years and Roman didn't notice. Maybe he had started out a construction worker. They were a special breed. Roman should know; he represented their employers.

Luke turned to him, eyes gleaming. "Are you banging her?"

"Who?"

He chuckled. "Your secretary."

"Of course not." Roman huffed. What an insinuation. He had always been faithful to Jen. Not once had he considered cheating. He couldn't say that much about *her*. The affair with her young firm partner had lasted a year. Roman suspected something was up when she no longer wanted sex. She looked exquisite and filled the house with her sensuous-woman perfume and cheery laughter, but it wasn't for him.

He tore a piece off the aluminum foil around his sandwich. The smell of fresh bread, ham, and cheese seeped out, but…no, he'd lost his appetite.

The sun moved, sending rays of diffuse light through the tree leaves. Something gave off a white-golden glow on his hand. His wedding ring. Why was he still wearing it? When was an appropriate time to take it off? After Jen's lawyer advised her to claim custody of the kids, Roman didn't want to have anything to do with her. They were over. His chest tightened with renewed pain, and he ached to go back to his office. That's what was nice about having so much work—it helped distance him from his emotional turmoil.

How did their relationship turn bad like this? Unlike most couples, they'd been best friends since their childhood, then married and became parents. First to Nick, a chubby mini-Roman, then Lily, the sweetest baby girl on the planet. Life was perfect. He couldn't ask for more. For seven years, he and Jen shared everything and more. They were meant to be together forever.

Now she was willing to destroy all they'd built and cherished. For what? Cheap orgasms with a younger guy? How crazy was that? Worse, she wanted to take his most valuable possession—his kids.

Hot tears sprang to his eyes, as if someone had turned on a tap. He blinked to clear his vision.

Goddammit, she was not only crazy, she was mean. He had never expected her to change and become such an evil woman.

A tear rolled down his cheek. He put the sandwich on his lap and pulled at the ring. It slid off his finger easier than he thought, as if mirroring the ease with which she had split their loving family.

At thirty-one, Roman was a divorced man.

* * * *

Until now, I wondered what the fuck I was doing in the park with the slick douche. When he invited me to join him, lines of fatigue in his face said he needed a break, and it didn't cost me much to accept lunch with him. But then, as we sat on the bench, his fine clothes, shiny shoes, and movie-star sunglasses reminded me of who he was: a representative of those who profit on others. It didn't help that he refused to eat the food I gave him, as if it wasn't worthy of him or something.

And, now—the curtain fell. He took off his wedding ring and pocketed it. Just like that. In public.

I stop munching my sandwich and stare at him.

He avoids me and wipes a cheek with the back of his sleeve. Is he crying? He must be at a crossroads.

I don't know what to say. As much as I despise the world he belongs to, his fragile sensitivity gets through to me like an arrow traversing my heart. In prison, whenever someone broke down, inmates and jailers alike would look the other way, but I would be touched and try to give a little humanity. That's one of the few good traits I inherited from my late granddad.

"You all right?" I resist putting a hand on his arm. We're not exactly fraternal, Slick and I.

He shrugs, fixing the sandwich in his lap. "If I can give you a piece of advice…"

"Yeah?"

"Don't ever tie the knot."

"Oh, no worries there." I chortle. Sex partners come and go, and I never see them twice. "I don't want a stable relationship."

He fiddles with the aluminum foil.

One-handed, I reach for the water bottle and unscrew it. My hand trembles as I lift it to my mouth. I'm used to adjusting my movements and not missing a thing, but in the corner of my vision, Slick eyes me. He must think I'm a wuss. He doesn't know shit. I swallow delicious gulps of cold water, rinsing my throat, and turn to him. "Ask me something."

"What?"

"Anything."

He hesitates. "Okay… Tell me something about you that I'd never guess."

"When I get off, I don't make a sound." A trick I learned in jail.

He leaves his mouth agape.

I chuckle. "You asked."

His face breaks into a grin. Good, humor always works.

"Now, your turn." I screw the bottle and put it on the bench between us. "Tell me something about you."

He draws a breath and stretches his legs, the material of his satin-looking pants tightening over long, firm muscles. Does he run? I wonder what he looks like underneath these fine clothes. If his lower body is as good as the upper I saw yesterday… My cock stirs at the thought of peeling everything off layer by layer and uncovering the goodies.

"I don't know where to begin," he says on a sigh, taking off his sunglasses, his gaze following a squirrel that chases another up a tree. Spring means love in the air. "There's so much to tell."

"How about you tell me your name, for starters."

"I haven't told you?"

"No."

"I'm Roman."

"*Roman.*" I taste the name on my tongue. "A fitting name."

"How so?"

"There's something Italian about you." I unashamedly take in his black gelled hair, dark brows, raven-colored pupils in a frame of long, feminine lashes, and neatly bearded cheeks. He's so devilishly handsome. If I met him in a club one night, I'd bring him home and do his sweet butt until the rise of dawn.

"Oh." He gives a half-smile. "Well, that's not very surprising. I have Italian blood on my mother's side."

No shit.

He holds my gaze for a moment. Or is it me holding his? A bit longer than what is appropriate for two men of our statuses.

The warning *'Don't flirt with the customers'* comes back to me.

Yeah. Step back, boy.

I lean against the bench and put my sandwich to my mouth. Fuck me if that little interlude didn't make my cock stiffen. Usually, roughness, a bold remark, or a daring stare will turn me on. Roman is more. He's not only tough, he's smart, he looks better than your average movie star, he's not afraid of showing his feelings, and he's available. He just took off his wedding ring.

The sun shifts in the sky. Through a hole in the trees, a serpent of fire reaches down and lick bits of my exposed skin. With the job I have, I hardly get out, seldom did in jail either, so whenever I feel the burn, I savor each little ray of sun and store its heat in my cells for darker days.

Last sandwich bite. I crush the aluminum wrap, throw the ball into a bin on my side of the bench, and fish out a pack of cigarettes and a lighter from my pocket. Since Roman doesn't eat, he won't mind the smoke. My fingers tremble as I pull a cigarette out of the pack.

"You don't need to be nervous," he says. "I'm tough in business, but..."

He's funny. Chuckling, I turn to him. "You think I'm nervous?" He's a powerful man, but mentally, he can't touch me. I'll always be stronger, nastier, more determined. I tilt my head and whisper, voice cunning. "No one makes me nervous."

He gives me a steady look. Maybe he thinks I'm naïve, that I don't comprehend the power he possesses. He can use his corrupt lobbyist connections and sleazy businessman techniques to get me fired. But he doesn't know the things I've seen and done, where I come from, what I've endured.

I stare at his perfectly handsome face. So arrogant, so fucking self-important. He needs to be put in his place. *Now.*

I lean over the space between us, bring my free hand to his neck, and kiss him, my lips hard and firm on his. I want to show I have power over him, too. I can affect him, provoke his reaction.

Eyes wide, he jerks back.

Are you kidding me? I hold his neck firmly and press my lips to his a second longer, just for show, before releasing him and sitting back.

Ha ha. Now I can light the cigarette, my trembling hands no longer a subject for conversation.

In the corner of my eye, his chest heaves, and quicker breaths sound in my ears. A moment passes, the thudding of my heart increasing with each second. I'm aroused, my cock pressing painfully against the fly, but I've trespassed. What is he going to do about it? Waiting, I roll the trigger and drag on my cigarette to light it.

He wipes his palms on his pants. Is he sweating? Did I cause it? After a while, he turns to me. "Look at me." His voice sounds choked. "*Look at me.*"

Exhaling a long chain of smoke, I turn to him, my head pounding with a sudden ache. Too much blood pulsing in there, and it's not the nicotine.

He looks tense. A vein beats in his neck. A thin layer of sweat covers his shiny face in the sun. His features are hard, and his black eyes deep and vibrating with emotion as he glares at me. I don't know what stops me from kissing him again.

"I'm not gay," he whispers.

Coldness invades me, then heat, then coldness again, a sweat breaking out all over. He's telling me he thinks I want something to happen between us, but he can't accept it because he prefers women. Even so, he's not scolding me for kissing him. He's not angry, vexed, or disgusted. I don't know what to think. If he hadn't liked the kiss, he could easily have wrestled out of my grip, screamed rape. He didn't, so he's using this lame excuse to cover up he can't accept me because of who I am? It's not about his sexual preference. It's about him being powerful and wealthy, and me a mere kitchen assistant, right?

"I'm not gay, either." I have another drag and blink as smoke tickles my eyes.

He makes a guttural sound.

After letting my reply sit for a few moments, I add, puffing with each word, "I'm bi. I like fucking girls' pussies *and* guys' butt holes." I glance at my watch. "Time's up. Have a good day." I get up and leave, passing him, the pink-dressed girl, and the couple of elderlies one after the other, not offering either a single look.

CHAPTER FOUR

After the episode in the park, Roman had been unable to find peace of mind for the rest of that day, or any sleep the following night.

Wednesday morning, he was *beyond* exhausted as he dragged his feet through the maze of corridors, burning coffee in hand, and distributed feeble greetings to the colleagues on his floor. When he reached his office, he put the cup on his desk, sank into the leather chair, and ran a hand over his face.

As if he didn't have enough problems with Jen claiming custody of the kids, with Cindy calling in to say she'd caught her daughter's disease so she would probably stay at home for the rest of the week, with the endless work calls, texts, and emails he had no chance of handling anytime soon... His mind was stuck on Luke and their awkward kiss like a CD-player choking on a broken disc.

Roman had never been kissed by a man. Though *that* wasn't the problem—using the "I'm not gay" card was just an excuse to bolt when things got a little heated. He didn't see a relationship with another man as problematic. Gay couples were increasingly frequent and accepted in his social milieu.

The problem was the kiss itself. And even though he *knew* from the gleam in Luke's eyes he'd only done it to make a point, he couldn't wrap his mind around the provocative gesture and take it in a cool, relaxed way. He couldn't rationalize it or put it into perspective, the way he needed to treat every issue in his life.

The kiss bothered the hell out of him. Mentally, it *haunted* him like a recurring nightmare that never gave respite, and physically, lit something hot and fierce in him. Years had passed since the last time he'd felt this kind of reaction to someone. A need had awoken, a hunger, an urge even more difficult to tame or ignore than the psychological impact. It involved caressing skin, exploring sweaty body parts, teasing with his tongue, sticking his erection into wet holes, pumping, ascending to a climax, shooting cum, screaming.

His brain reproduced images of Luke. His rock-hard face, high cheekbones, piercing eyes the color of emerald, and full lips breaking into an easy grin. The scar across his chin that he concealed with a goatee, and his slicked-back blond/brown hair.

Conjuring up Luke's features was wrong. Dammit, *all* the consequences from what happened in the park were wrong, yet Roman was too tired to think of the reasons why he thought so. Simply labeling the situation as wrong would have to do until he got some sleep, calmed the fuck down, and put some distance between all of this.

Right, who the hell was he fooling? They worked in the same building. They had common denominators. "Lunch." "Coffee." "Fruit delivery." "Elevator." The list went on. They may never have known about one another for years, but he was willing to bet a month's salary that from now on fate would have them run into each other day after day—mere coincidences, of course.

He gave a sardonic chuckle. Roman, the pragmatic, man of logic, business magnate, was reasoning like a simpleton.

Truth was, if he didn't handle this situation very well, very soon, he was heading for a disaster. What exactly he meant by that, he had no idea, for he was blabbering.

He took a sip from his searing hot coffee. The first of many cups today.

Now what?

At the very least, he needed to do some risk assessment. That's how he rolled, how he became an executive at a young age, and how he intended to continue controlling all facets of his life.

In this case, risk assessment meant doing a background check on Luke. The more information he uncovered, the more cards he'd have in hand to figure out how to deal.

Sudden eagerness and purpose pulling him out of his torpor, he got up from his chair. He knew exactly how to acquire that information. Luke's boss, the restaurant manager, also had an office in this building, and they'd connected during an in-house Christmas dinner last year. If Roman excelled at something in his line of work, it was exploiting connections.

* * * *

I'm sweating gallons and loving it. Working out in the afternoon, when all my daily tasks are finished, invigorates me and relaxes my tired muscles. Thank fuck there's a gym in the building, under the reception, and it's free of charge for employees.

The damp place stinks of testosterones, rubber, metal, and machine oil. After a half hour on the running mill and a half hour lifting weights, a hot shower will bring me back on my feet. Maybe I'll even jack off a little, since I'm the only one here today. Usually, people exercise a bit before hitting the road. Maybe the nice weather convinced them not to go down the labyrinth of corridors in the basement to the most remote, chilly room of the building.

Well, I'm not complaining. I'll seize any opportunity to get off. I've used my right hand a lot lately. Even in my sleep, coming in silence while I spread my pulsating spunk all over the sheets.

It's Roman's fault. I loathe everything he represents and spit on his slick business world, yet, on a personal level he's so attractive I let him seep into my mind like a poison and fantasize about fucking his brains out. Over and over.

He'll never know. We won't talk again. But he'll be there in my dreams, the crack in his butt open for me and my hard cock ready to pump.

Speaking of pumping, it's time. All beefed-up and sweaty, blood speeding in my bulging veins, I leave the weights section and steer toward the showers.

I'm tearing my soaked t-shirt off when a door handle clonks behind me.

"There you are!" a familiar voice calls.

Roman.

What the hell? Wiping my face and chest with the t-shirt, I spin.

It is him, by the door, dark and handsome. What's he doing here?

He strides toward me with a deep line between his eyebrows. "I've been looking for you."

He has? I gape, my heart doing a triple somersault.

He stops a few feet away, black eyes flaring as if he wants to kill me. His chest heaves. What the fuck? Then for the slightest moment, his hard gaze descends to my torso before trailing up again and stopping at my eyes.

So, he has seen my scars, my tats, the history of my life. And what does that tell him?

He steps forward and growls, "You've done time."

The tone in his voice and the audacity of his question hit me like a slap. I blink, trying to compose myself. "How do you know?"

He gives me a level look.

I shake my head, unable to believe what's happening to me or comprehend the consequences. I haven't prepared for this. Not a single soul is supposed to know about my years in jail. Anger boils inside, heat rushing straight to my brain. "Jesus fucking christ! Who told you?"

He keeps his lips closed, face impassible.

An image of slick suits putting their heads together flashes before me. It's all about connections, talking to the right people. People of power. But Roman had no right to ask about me, and whoever he asked had no right to answer.

I leap forward and grab his shirt collar. "It's *strictly confi-fucking-dential,* you asshat!"

His dark pupils light with alarm, but he stays calm, too calm, assessing me. So he must know: they released me four years early for good conduct. They also told me the smallest mishap would send me straight back into the hole.

I'm not letting that happen. Nope. Never. At least not over some fucking sleazebag like him. Fighting to rein it in, I release his collar but stay in his face, so close his warm breaths brush my lips.

"Why did they put you away?" he asks, holding my glare. "What did you do?"

I snicker. "They omitted the details?"

"All I know is you did twelve years. That's a lot. If they let you out at three fourths of your time, you had sixteen. Few crimes will get you that much."

"You had no right to—"

"You can't expect us to be friends if you're not being honest with me."

"*Friends?*"

"Yes. I gotta know who I'm dealing with."

"Who you're dealing with? What does my past have anything to do with... Jesus, cut me some fucking slack." My head drains of blood, as if I'm about to faint. I take a step back to demonstrate my refusal to go where he wants to lead me, but I also need space to think.

He's gone to great lengths to learn more about me. He's asked someone, or several someones, to break the strict rules of confidentiality. Why? What's his motivation?

It hits me. He's telling me he wants to be close. He wants whatever we've developed in the past days to have a chance. He calls it a friendship, but I'm not so sure... Maybe my kissing him in the park has something to do with his conduct. Is there something he's not saying?

My heart thuds in my chest, and I'm mollifying, I can't help it. "I've been trying very hard to put it behind me," I wheeze. How can he ask me to dive back into the past and bring all that darkness up to the light again? I already *live* with the guilt, hand-in-hand, like a partner. *That* sentence is for life.

He nods. "It's all about weighing the risks. I'd never have made it to where I am if I didn't go by risk assessment."

"All the time?"

"Yeah."

"In your personal life, too?"

"That's how I roll, man. If you can't be honest with me..."

"That's why you married the woman who's now divorcing you?" As soon as the sarcasm leaves my mouth, I regret it. I don't know why I let him push me to attack. I'm not the defensive type.

He closes and reopens his eyes a bit slower than a blink, and when he refocuses on me, they shine of unimaginable pain.

Angry voices shout in my head. I step forward and put a hand on his arm. He flinches.

"I'm sorry," I croak, retreating as if touching fire. "I didn't mean to hurt you."

He clenches his teeth, small muscles popping in his jaw, and takes several deep breaths. "Tell me what you did, or this conversation is over."

What he asks is too much. "Roman, I'm already living with my past every single day of my life. There doesn't go a minute that I don't regret what I did. Isn't that punishment enough?"

He stares.

I stare back.

He looks down. A small gesture telling me he's giving up. He's going to leave and never talk to me. I know the kind he is. Once he's made up his mind, there's no going back.

Okay. I reach out again, grab the back of his head, and pull him to me so our foreheads connect, bone-to-bone. A few inches of heated air separate the rest of our bodies. "Look at me."

Once he raises his black eyes and holds my stare, I tell him my story. "I killed a boy. He was gonna hurt me. I pulled out a knife to scare him, but he threw himself at me and the knife went in. I never meant for it to happen. Never." I swallow to keep the pain at bay and clench my teeth. "At the trial, I begged his parents to forgive me, but they refused."

My eyes bleed. The pain from my clenching jaw becomes unbearable. I release the back of Roman's head and turn from him to hide.

Shame races through me, ruthless. How can I be such a pussy? I never cried in jail, never showed any feelings. I hardened so fast in there.

Now that the guy who has given me wet dreams recently is demanding the truth, it's difficult to hold back. He's asking for my honesty. He wants to see my heart, my soul. He wants to know what I'm made of, what has turned me into who I am. Again, I can't help but question his motivation. Why does he want to know me? Where does he want to take us?

Voice softer, he asks, "How old were you?"

"Fifteen." Tears rush to my burning eyes. I grimace and hurry to put my fingers to them and stop the tears. My jaw trembles and my lips quiver. With the other hand, I cover my mouth and press. I still can't stop a muffled gasp from escaping my throat. It's very telling. Though all Roman could see was my hands flying to my face, he must know what I'm doing and—

Strong arms enclose me from behind, startling me. I'm not used to having a man's arms wrapped around me, except in fights where I'm quick to disentangle from the opponent and throw him off. But this is Roman and so I let him hug me.

He locks his arms over my chest and brings me closer against his broad torso, the back of my legs meeting his muscular thighs and my ass molding to his warm crotch.

His empathy causes more hurt to rush through me, and I barely hold back a howl. Tears press through my closed eyes and around my fingers. My hurting torso heaves with sobs, violent as hiccups. I can't stop the pain, it's like a rolling avalanche. Another gasp evades the depth of my throat, then a plaint, the sound resembling the wailing of a hurt animal. For the first time since I was a little child, I'm tempted to let the tears run.

Roman rests his chin on top of my shoulder and holds me tightly without a word. His cologne invades my space and the warm skin of his cheek brushes my ear. With this hug, he tells me he sees me and believes me and understands my pain.

I've never experienced such an exchange of kindness from one grown man to another. But this can't go on. Tightening my body to the extreme and breathing evenly, I concentrate on getting my feelings under control. I swallow to force the pain down my throat, rub my eyes with my knuckles, and clear my throat. "Okay, I've got it."

"Hmm." He doesn't release me yet, his hold so brotherly and genuinely kind it boggles my mind.

With an immense boost of emotion coursing through my chest, I spin in his embrace. My lips find his. I wrap my arms around his firm waist, want to melt into him. He's the only one who can provide comfort and help me get away. Forget.

Mouth-to-mouth, he lingers for a few seconds as if accepting my intimacy. Then loosens from my grip and steps back with a determined shake of his head. "I told you, Luke. I'm not gay."

CHAPTER FIVE

Two days later, it's Friday, and I'm drained, aching all over. Rolling my shoulders, I wheel the tea-and-coffee trolley back into the kitchen. One more task on my weekly to-do list is done. I've emptied, cleaned, and refilled all coffee machines on fourteen floors. That's two hours up and down from the kitchen. In and out of elevators. Through doors, through hallways. Each time beeping my ID on security panels. I'm sick of my job, but it's been good to have something mechanical to do. Working like a robot, focusing on a manual task helps get my head off the murder I committed.

Following my breakdown in the gym, hair-raising nightmares have interrupted my nights, and in the daytime, I'm bordering on depression, unable to enjoy a thing. Diving back into the past is taking its toll. I keep replaying the moment of no return. Every available minute, I flash the episode before my eyes as though it's happening again and, helpless, horrified, I watch my knife slide into the kid's guts.

He slumped over me after, sending both of us to the ground so I didn't see blood gushing out of his wound, his mouth forming a surprised, *"Oh!"* or his eyes widening as he realized he was going to die. But I imagine all of that too easily.

I'm conscious it was an accident, and I don't know what I could have done differently in order not to be killed since he was charging me with his own knife. Even so, I cannot accept having the death of another on my conscience. A kid killing another kid is not in the order of things.

How I coped with the crippling guilt all these years in jail is a mystery. I guess I was on survival mode, tricking my brain to be content with saying a mental apology whenever I thought of the boy I stabbed. *"I'm sorry."* It was enough to surf on life then, but today? I'm struggling to keep my head above water. There are moments when I'd be willing to swap with him. My life for his.

I know nothing about him, but I do know this: if the accident hadn't happened, he would be about my age, probably have a wife, children, and a job, and I wouldn't be living this fucking nightmare for the rest of my miserable days. If only there was something I could do to bring him back!

The kitchen reeks of fried fish, a warm, greasy steam drifting out of the ovens. It's sickening. This shit looks good adorned on a plate, but out here… Holding my breath, I park the trolley next to another in a corner.

I deserve another kind of steam—a smoke—and my colleagues know I do after my endless tours up and down the building. No need to apologize for taking a break. Usually, I'll invite one of them out with me, but now, I'd rather have a quiet moment alone. I get my jacket in the personnel room, stride through the busy kitchen with a, "Having a smoke," over my shoulder, and steer to the elevators. No one bothered to reply.

The restaurant is emptying after lunch. Fat, slick suits walk back and forth between tables, crowding like ants. At least none are waiting for an elevator. I click on the "Down" button for the umpteenth time today, my foot tapping an impatient rhythm.

A *ding,* and one of the doors slide open.

There's a shadow inside. Not in the mood to interact with anyone, I keep my eyes low. As I walk in, my gaze lands on shiny leather shoes. My heart jumps. I have a feeling they belong to Roman. Just a feeling, because the building is full of sleazebags and they all have shoes like these. But it would be just my luck, wouldn't it?

"Hi, Luke."

Fuck. His voice. The hairs on my neck rise.

Work has helped get *him* off my mind, too. It's been a duel between the dead kid and this slick but oh-so-hot employer representative, a sordid game of who would be plaguing me more. I haven't had respite since the last time we met. Whenever I managed to leave my stabbing accident behind for a minute, Roman was there to make my head spin and my body throb with need. I would never have thought a guy of his standing—the complete opposite of my social status—could attract me the way he does. There have been moments late at night when I consider quitting my job just to make sure I'd never run into him again. But it's not realistic. Not with my background.

The doors close, and I must look up to acknowledge him. Being rude and not saying hello would be typical of a thug. That's not really me. Granddad raised me to be a good boy, and I landed in prison over a stupid, stupid accident.

I gaze into Roman's charcoal eyes and give a curt nod. Nothing more.

Features tight, he shakes his head. "Why do I keep seeing you?" His voice is hard, but not too hard, as if he doesn't really want to be mean.

"You don't," I retort, turning to hit number one on the panel. "Not in the past two days."

"Nice to hear you're keeping track."

Heat shoots to my brain. What the fuck does he think, that I'm infatuated with him? I turn back to glare.

He tilts his head with a smile full of warmth, telling me he was teasing. "I meant to say, with my family splitting and all, I'm glad to know at least one person cares. Where are you going?"

"Out for a smoke."

"Hmm. Long day, huh?"

His kindness touches me. I'm simple like that. Influenceable. The pull from him is too strong. Though I know we can never engage in anything, I want to lean into him and feel his humane warmth enveloping me. It's crazy. I ask, "Wanna join me…?" and immediately regret it, but it's too late.

"I don't smoke."

Chest tightening, I give one, slow nod, looking down because each time he refuses my advances, I'm disappointed. Who am I fooling anyway? I just reckoned we can never have a relationship.

The elevator opens to the basement. We head out into a corridor, he first, and me in tow, fishing for my cigarettes in a jacket pocket. After passing a couple of emergency exits, he pushes open a heavy aluminum door and enters the low-ceiling, gasoline-reeking car park. Our footfalls resonate in the wide space. Without a word or a look back, he steers to what must be his car, a huge silver BMW whose polish screams, *Look at me, I'm a symbol of wealth!* Damn, that steel monster looks as slick as he does, and I hate him all the more for owning it. Fucking snob.

I jut my chin in the air and head to the personnel door, next to the large car door. A big engine roars to life behind me, its growl echoing between walls. I snort. The guys on the top sure know how to display their power.

Outside, the sun blinds me. I turn away to light my cigarette and inhale the first drag of harsh smoke. So good.

Who cares about Roman? He must despise me. Especially now that he knows I've done time for murder. He only smiled because he was playing nice, pitying me. And fuck knows I *loathe* pity.

Blowing out round puffs of smoke, I sit on a concrete slab alongside the building wall. The garage door opens, gliding upward and folding into the ceiling while Roman's vehicle pokes its nose out. What a huge thing, so shiny it casts sunlight back to the sky as it passes me.

I look in another direction and suck on my cigarette. Soon Roman will disappear behind the building and out of my life.

* * * *

Roman drove past Luke, then stopped, put the car in reverse, and backed to where he sat. Motor idling, he pulled the window down and stared at him across the passenger seat.

Luke studied the glowing tip of his cigarette.

Why did he pretend not to see him? They were closer than Roman had ever been to anyone since his wife. Luke had kissed him *twice*.

Roman wasn't a fool. The first time Luke's eyes gleamed with defiance, as if he was making a point, and two days ago, he sought comfort in a moment of deep sorrow. A cool, proud, and hardened street guy had no genuine interest in a white-collar like Roman. His advances had nothing to do with love or whatever Roman dreamt of, crushing on him like an inexperienced teenager. Roman was in an emotional and sexual vacuum because of his divorce, that was all, starving for the slightest consideration from another person. It happened to be Luke, but it could be anyone else. Once the ordeal was behind him, he would drop this childish infatuation and start focusing on the *real* matters of his life, such as his children and his job.

Maybe Luke was vexed because Roman didn't pursue their conversation in the garage. But how could he stay and talk, when every time he did, his body heated and sizzled with desire? Dammit, he couldn't look Luke in the eye without growing all kinds of mushy. It was nonsense, really. But he didn't mean to vex him, couldn't leave him like this. They needed to talk. And for that to happen, he needed for Luke to look at him. But he refused, the stubborn hot-head.

Growling a, "Fuck him," Roman released his seat belt, opened his door, and jumped out. It took him two seconds to circle the trunk and reach Luke—who still wouldn't acknowledge him.

Impatience tore at him. He didn't know what to do, or what he was already doing, standing at another guy's feet with his hands clenching and unclenching and needing to make bodily contact with him, make him see him. He wanted Luke's piercing green eyes to look into his and tell him he liked him. Lusted for him, even.

Since Luke refused to, he bent forward, grabbed the arms of his jacket, and pulled him up on his feet. Luke got up willingly, but stared over his shoulder. How strange to be face-to-face with this guy who drove him crazy. The same height, the same mental strength. Equals.

Then, slowly, Luke moved his gaze to him with a *"There's not one thing you can do that I haven't already seen"* look. What Roman read—strength, endurance, defiance, and animalistic power—cut through him like glacial fear. For a moment, he'd forgotten Luke had spent years behind bars with ruthless criminals.

Defeated, he released Luke's jacket and lowered his hands.

Luke tilted his head and whispered, mouth near so the stench of cigarette filled Roman's space, "Watch your moves. There are cameras everywhere." He nodded upward, and Roman didn't need to follow his look to know they were being watched. This building was one of the most secure in town.

He was cornered, but the urge to settle their issue overwhelmed him. Just not here. "Come with me. We have to talk."

Luke smirked. "What about?"

"Don't make it so difficult."

"Hey. You gotta earn my goodwill."

"Just get in the car."

"In that fancy snob thing?" Luke sent a nod to the BMW.

"Yes. And don't be an ass about it."

Cackling, Luke went past him, cigarette in hand. Cocky.

"No smoking," Roman said.

Luke turned with a questioning brow.

"For my kids."

"Okay. For *them*." Luke dropped the burning butt to the ground and crushed it. "So, where do you wanna go, Slick Boy?"

Roman swallowed the insult as he climbed back into his seat. "I don't know."

Luke slammed his door shut with a *bang*.

"Careful with the door!"

"I know, I know. It's a very expensive car. Listen, I only have a few minutes. You slick suits have all the time in the world, but I can be sacked for being five seconds late." He took in the interior with a fake look of admiration and sniffed the air, frowning, as if to say it smelled of money.

"Since you're asking," Roman grumbled, "I'm exhausted so I took a half day off to go home, but home isn't what it used to be, so I might as well go back to the office."

His life was coming apart. Mood darkening by the second, he pursed his lips and drove around the block aimlessly.

Luke's fingers drummed a beat on the door side, the other hand in his lap, trembling again. Those nervous ticks seemed to come and go.

They turned a corner and stopped at a red light. Traffic sped across the street in a long line, roaring engines filling the silence.

Luke tapped a faster beat. "I gotta get back to the kitchen."

Roman glanced at the hand on his thighs. "What's that trembling?"

"A disease I caught in the hole."

A disease?

"It's green." Luke nodded ahead. "The light."

"Fuck." Roman hit the pedal, sending the powerful car forward, and turned another corner.

"The prison doctor said it was psychosomatic."

"Is that where you got the scar on your chin, too?" Roman purposely omitted the other scars on Luke's body, and the clumsy tattoos.

"It's a souvenir from the kiddo I stabbed. He cut me first, made sure I'd never forget him." He looked away. "As if."

"Good God." Roman's chest tightened. They were back at the office building, and he stopped in front of the car park. "He cut you first?"

"He did. I thought he was gonna kill me, so, like I told you, I pulled out my knife, too. It was instinctive."

"So it was self-defense."

"Try telling that to the prosecution. My blade went in. He died."

Shaking his head, Roman pulled his window down, flashed his ID to a panel on the wall, and waited for the wide aluminum door to slide up.

"I have this, too." While the engine idled, Luke grabbed Roman's right hand and led it to his head. Now what? Gelled-back hair slid along Roman's finger as Luke guided it to a dent in his hard skull.

"Jesus." He grimaced. Disgust sent a shudder through him. He retreated his hand. As the door folded into the ceiling, he pulled the window up, eased the car inside the garage, and zigzagged his way between parked vehicles. "How the hell did you get that? Someone hit you with a bar?"

"No. A cop came to the scene. I got up and ran. I panicked. I was a kid. The only way to stop me was to shoot at me. They're supposed to hit a leg or an arm, right, but he missed. A bullet grazed my head."

Roman bit his lip to hold back a curse and drove nose first into his parking spot.

Luke had been through too much. He would never recover from his physical wounds. Could he heal from his mental ones?

A foot from the wall, he killed the motor.

An ugly thought popped into his mind. Maybe he shouldn't ask the question, but he needed to know. "Were you raped in jail?"

Luke sent him a black look. "I don't know. I was knocked unconscious a few times, so maybe." He shrugged as if to diminish the importance. "If it happened, it didn't kill me."

Roman wanted to ask, *"Did you rape anyone?"* but he already knew Luke hadn't. He was a victim. He didn't have a criminal mind.

Nausea shot up Roman's throat. Head spinning, he pulled the window down again and inhaled deeply. The garage air reeked of gasoline and concrete dust, which didn't help.

Luke's pain was mountainous, and Roman didn't know how to help him overcome it. It wasn't strictly his task to comfort him, yet against all odds, he was falling for him, and taking care of him felt natural. They had developed a tiny, fragile bond. The prospect of making this bond grow scared him. What would it lead to? He wasn't ready for a new relationship in the midst of his divorce. And what would people say when they saw Luke?

He was too much to absorb. His pumped-up, scarred, and tattooed chest the other day in the gym was the perfect image for his mental state. If Roman let him into his life, he had to let in all of his past, too, plus his current misery. Gigantic baggage. Did he have enough room in his heart?

Tears rushed to his eyes. He pinched his lip. He didn't want to cry for Luke, but couldn't help it. This tough, independent, yet oh-so-vulnerable former prisoner had gotten under his skin, and he didn't know how to handle anything anymore.

Grumbling a low, "I can't fucking believe this," Luke unsnapped his seat belt and turned to him.

"I..." Roman pressed his fingers to his wet eyes.

"I don't want your stupid pity. You can stick it up your—"

"It's not pity. It's...sadness." Shaking his head, Roman asked on a whisper, "What do you want?"

"Huh?"

"I said, what do you want? Is there anything I can do to help you?"

"I wanna move the fuck on." Luke grabbed Roman's chin with a couple of fingers and forced him to face him. "And no one's gonna stop me." Luke leaned over the space between them, approached his gorgeous and determined-looking face, and pressed warm, firm lips to his.

Roman gasped, but Luke held him in place while slipping his wet tongue into his mouth, bringing in the taste of tobacco. He slid the other hand down Roman's chest, past his belt, and over his crotch, grabbing a handful of dick.

Need shot through Roman like a wild flame. He groaned. "D-didn't you have to go back to the kitchen?"

"They can wait another minute."

Roman rarely allowed another person to be in command, but for once, he let Luke. It was crucial they didn't separate on a bad argument. If they didn't seize the chance to adjust the situation, they would never see each other again. Luke would pretend not to see him, like he did earlier. In the restaurant. In the elevators. In the garage. Outside, at his favorite smoking spot. He was too proud. Once he made up his mind, he would never budge.

Luke released his lips and moved down. He unbuckled Roman's belt, unzipped his pants, and took his hardening cock in his hot, wet mouth.

"Oh..." Roman moaned while Luke pumped him, expert tongue licking, exploring, roaming around the shaft. He leaned back into his seat and closed his eyes. It had been months since he'd masturbated, and Luke knew what he was doing. This blowjob felt so good, everything faded and Roman's sole focus was on Luke's hungry mouth sucking him to an imminent release. The intensity in his balls increased. He climbed higher and higher until he had to spray all of that burning seed out of his cock. A little more, and the pressure became intolerable. He arched his back as heat traversed his length and semen spurted into Luke's steamy mouth. He gritted his teeth and tried not to groan too loud, recalling what Luke had told him about being quiet when he came.

After Luke let his cock slip out of his mouth and raised his head, Roman pushed him back into the passenger seat. A little mean and ungrateful, maybe, but he needed space. His head spun. Their relationship escalated way out of control. What had they done? What had they become?

He was to blame. He'd invited Luke into his car.

Without a word, Luke wiped his lips with the back of a hand and stared out his side window. His chest heaved and a bulge in his crotch threatened to pop his pants open.

Gulping air, Roman tucked his still-hard, still-dripping cock into his briefs. It was his turn to have shaking hands. He zipped up. "Fuck."

"Exactly." Luke opened his door and slipped out of the car like a shadow.

Chilly air snuck in, brushing Roman's sweaty, overheated body. "Wait." He leaned over the passenger seat and reached out to stop Luke. He didn't know what to do about him and the situation they'd put themselves in, but he wasn't used to leaving issues unresolved. His brain was trained to untick tasks on a to-do list. When he encountered problems, he solved them and attacked the next. On and on, never leaving anything unsettled.

Luke turned to him, his eyes a dark, smoldering green.

"Um…" Roman sucked in a breath. "What time do you finish work?"

"About five."

"Come to my office then. I'll have the booking confirmation ready for you."

"The what?"

"Don't you remember? You brought me coffee on Monday."

Luke gave a slight nod and left.

CHAPTER SIX

At last, Friday afternoon.

Vasilj takes off his uniform and gives me a high-five. "Careful with the women, Luke. Save some energy for Monday."

I laugh and wave my bald friend off. What a long and eventful week it's been. I don't know what to make of everything.

After my other colleagues have exchanged goodbyes and leave for their respective families, I get my jacket, switch off the lights, and take an elevator to the fourteenth floor.

On my way up, I glance at my reflection in the mirror and fake a smile. I'm a lost soul, lonely as shit and dragging a pretty heavy load, but I'm used to it.

In a few minutes, I'll see Roman again. My body sizzles. It's not the usual trembling, it's nervousness. Or annoyance? I'm not necessarily happy to see him. We're a mess. I like him a lot more than I've liked any of the people I've had fleeting relationships with, but I can't stand his upper social position. Snobbism gives me the creeps. Power stinks. Manipulating those of lesser social position and stepping on their rights is a downright crime.

Besides, after I sucked his dick in the car, he pushed me away—again—so who am I kidding? Did I believe he would return my feelings because my story touched him? Geez, I'm so naïve. Why would he have the slightest interest in an ex-con?

Well, I may be a low-life in his eyes, but I have a certain pride. You don't get to reject me too many times. If he thinks I'm going to make another advance, he can rethink that. I'm done with him. Once I get his goddamn coffee confirmation, I'll go home and find someone else to fuck for the weekend. End of story.

The elevator doors slide open to an unusual scene on the highest floor. Smiling ear-to-ear, party dressed people flutter around, decorating walls and moving furniture. Disco music blasts from computer speakers in a corner. Bottles stand on one desk and bowls of crisps and cookies on another.

I pass through the semi-chaos, minding my own business, when a curvaceous blonde stops me in my tracks.

"Hey, there." With heavy make-up, a mini-mini skirt, and a tight, see-through blouse revealing black lace that struggles to contain a pair of magnificent boobies, she's a sight for starved eyes. "How're you doin'?" she asks, inching closer, sensual smile at her mouth, hips swaying. Her flowery perfume sneaks into my nostrils.

I cross my arms and lean against a desk. "I'm good. What's goin' on?"

Her kitty eyes run me up and down, pausing at all the right places, the blunt invitation making my cock jump to life. "The whole floor is invited to a party. Wanna join us? The more, the merrier, as they say."

"Why not." I drink her in. She could well be the one I choose to bring home. After I get that damn document in Roman's office. "I need to talk to someone first."

She tilts her head, a brow raised. "Someone on this floor?"

"Yup."

"Should I be jealous?" Her glistening red lips form a pout.

I grin, having always liked an up-front chick.

"Who is it, if I may ask? We're a big family up here."

I bet they are. Slick fuckheads, the whole bunch. All the more a reason to screw her. My ultimate vengeance. If I can't fulfill my fantasy of fucking Roman on his desk, I'll do this doll against one of those gigantic windows instead. Leave the trace of her sweaty tits on the glass for the whole city to see.

Cock throbbing in my pants, I push from the desk. Dammit, I've had blue balls since I feasted on Roman's dick earlier. "Just a minute."

"Wait." She follows me down the corridor. "It would be really cool if you joined the party."

Why such insistence? Is she afraid I won't come back? I turn a corner and continue in direction of Roman's office.

Behind me, her high-heels make muffled *clunks* on the carpet. "I was home with a sick child this week, and tonight is my first get-out, in like, ages. I can't wait to have a drink and dance and…"

The rest of her sentence is more than clear. But she needn't worry. As soon as I'm back, the drinks better be ready for me, and she better have found us a room.

* * * *

Roman gaped.

When Luke entered his office with Cindy in tow, he wasn't surprised. She'd told him she felt better and would attend the party on the same floor, while Roman had refused the invitation, blaming a headache and the stress caused by his divorce. Since he'd asked Luke to come here, he almost expected them to run into each other. But when the two stood in front of Roman's desk and Cindy's flirtatious gaze roamed all over Luke, he nearly fell out of his chair.

He tightened his jaw until a muscle popped, then stood, fuming.

Cindy was single and had every right to choose whomever she wanted, which she clearly intended to do, anyway, considering she'd dressed like a cheap slut. Her opulent breasts spilled out of her bra. He'd never seen them, never *wanted* to see them. He didn't even want to know what she did in her private life, whether she stuck cucumbers up her ass or fucked her dog.

As for Luke, he didn't know if he was single, but since he'd made some rather intimate advances on Roman, there was reason to believe he was. Or, at least, he didn't have a serious relationship.

But. He. Was. *His.*

Roman would never tolerate that Luke went for someone other than him in the whole building, especially not his own secretary.

While Luke read the confirmation he'd handed him, Roman circled the desk and stood in Cindy's face, towering, intimidating her. He had never treated her like this, always respected her like a fellow colleague, but today…today, she pushed him to be the arrogant boss he'd refused to be.

She shrunk and stepped back, her kitty made-up eyes widening with fear.

"I'm having a meeting," he growled. "I won't need your services."

Her face paled to such a whiteness he thought she would pass out.

"Besides," he continued, sarcasm lathering his voice, "you look dressed for another occasion."

"Y-yes." Voice squeaky, she crawled backward like a terrified animal.

He didn't care. This wasn't a matter of him abusing of his authority, of him being a chief and she his subordinate. No, this was happening on a different level. A maleness level. She was on *his turf* and she hit on *his prize.* Simple as that.

For another boss, seeing a secretary dressed like a whore in his office would be a good enough reason to fire her. But Roman wouldn't. He didn't have it in him. Still, right fucking now, she had to go, and he had to claim back what was his.

Features decomposed, she muttered a meek, "I'm sorry," and turned on her heel.

He followed her scantily clad ass to the exit and slammed the door shut with a *bang* so loud it shook on its hinges. She wouldn't dare come back before Monday morning at eight am sharp.

* * * *

I laugh. "That was quite a show you pulled there."

Roman spins like a whirlwind of anger and glares at me.

Fuck, he's something. Looking devilishly handsome in his white shirt and slacks, with the dark hair, night-black eyes, and matching beard and mustache strengthening the aura of hot, sexual danger. What a turn-on. Forget about that silly bimbo. Who needs big boobs and a waxed cunt when you have such a virile specimen of manhood in the same room? I don't know what stops me from tearing off his clothes.

Ha. He was so infuriated, he was willing to breach his own barriers of social conduct and dig deep into some dark side of him to bring out raw masculinity and strength. I love it. Not only because his power display proves he's more than man enough to handle me, but because he did it *for* me. He was jealous. I laugh again, the situation too incredible.

Normally, I despise authoritative behavior, but in Roman's case, I don't believe he behaves like this very often, and his secretary deserved to be put in her place. She's too damn cheap. Good thing he interfered so I didn't end up with my dick in her.

He walks over, nostrils flaring and eyes like black diamonds, and stops inches from me. His warm breaths pulsate against my lips, ensnaring my cock to press against the fly, and I have to fight not to rearrange it in my pants. He doesn't touch me, just stares. I don't move. Heat oozes from him like an invitation and makes me lightheaded. He wants me, it's more than evident. If he doesn't make up his mind soon, I'm going to kiss him or something, provoke him to act. But I have to wait. It's his call.

After a lengthy stare-down, he draws a deep breath and asks, voice strangled, "What are you doing to me?"

"I don't know what you're talking about." Wanting to tease him, I pretend to make a side move and leave.

He puts a hand on my chest. "Stay."

Boom, I win. "What if I don't want to?" Face placid, I make another move.

He pushes me back against the desk. "Stay!"

How rousing. I like that he plays the dominant when we're equally tough. I put my hands on the desk behind me, lean my ass to it, and snicker. "Are you holding me here against my will?"

"I wouldn't insult your obvious superiority in strength by insinuating you wouldn't be here if you didn't want to."

I chuckle. He makes the same comparisons as me. "Obvious superiority," I tease, "says the representative of a managerial company to a kitchen employee."

"Since you're not listening, I'll repeat that you wouldn't be here if you didn't want to. Ergo, you want to. You want me."

"Your head is so big you don't see your arrogance."

"You gave me a blow job."

"And then you rejected me. *Again.*"

His eyes droop. "Listen. It's not that easy. I'm in the middle of a divorce. I can't just…"

"What? Accept my advances? 'Cause of my past? I'm not good enough for you?" I don't need to fake the searing anger. It's right under the surface. Always will be.

"Luke, it doesn't have anything to do with you."

"Yes, it clearly does, and you've blown your chances, stupid." I pretend to push from the desk, but he pins me to it.

"Is that why you came in here with my secretary drooling all over you? To make a point?"

Instead of replying the simple truth—that she followed me—I want to press him and see how genuine his feelings are. "It's 'cause *you* don't make the cut."

My words seem to hit home. He pales and drops his arms to his sides. Black pupils glimmering, he whispers, "So, that's what it's about. I had a feeling. Earlier, you called me Slick Boy. You called my car a fancy snob thing. You said, *"You slick suits,"* or something. Is that how you see me?"

I gaze into his eyes and see a bared soul. He's showing me the real him, telling me my insinuations are wrong. But I'm not done pushing his buttons. "Isn't it true?"

"You really think I'm a rich, self-satisfied guy who enjoys power and expensive things?"

"*Isn't* it true? Aren't you an executive?"

"I am, but that doesn't mean—"

"Don't you own a big house on a nice, quiet side of town?"

"Yes. But it's much too big. Jen wanted it. I'd do with less."

"Now you're gonna tell me she wanted the BMW, too."

"In fact, she did."

"And that watch." I nod to his arm. "And that titanium smartphone. And those hand-tailored clothes and shiny Italian shoes."

"Goes with the job."

I chuckle. He's sincere, and his willingness to convince and satisfy me touches a chord within, but I enjoy this game far too much. For once, the tables are turned. A man of power is begging a subordinate. "Well, that dirt don't work for me, Roman. I don't want any of it in my life."

* * * *

Roman's blood boiled. Luke was being a complete asshole, questioning his moral position and affirming all he cared about was money and power. He didn't know *shit*.

"For God's sake. Before you came here, I was on the phone with my lawyer. I asked him to make Jen an offer. I'm willing to concede both our house and our car to her if she gives me the legal right to keep the kids fifty percent of the time."

Luke raised a brow. "You're willing to trade all that for a partial custody?"

"It's not a matter of money. I love Nick and Lily more than anything. What else do I have to do to prove I don't care about these goddamn materialistic things? Can't you just look past them and see who I am?"

"You mean, can I look past your slick big-boss attitude, high-society status, and—"

Roman threw his hands in the air. "If you hate me so much, why did you blow me?"

"It was a mistake. I'm not doing well up here." Calmly, Luke tapped a finger to his temple.

"Bull."

"Yeah?"

"I'm used to calling bluff."

"I know. You gotta be slick to recognize slick."

Fuck, Luke was pushing too hard. Roman wanted to punch him in the face, wake him. But he needed to swallow his anger and find an intelligent way of showing he was an honest, hardworking, and moral person. How? He was already giving away his house and car. What else could he strip of, that Luke despised so intensely?

The son of a bitch stared, unfazed.

Okay. Hands shaking, Roman took off his Rolex watch and put it on the desk beside Luke. Then he unbuttoned his shirt so fast he nearly tore off the buttons before he shoved it into Luke's hands.

Luke caught the shirt and lowered his gaze to Roman's chest. "What are you doing?"

Teeth gritting, Roman unbuckled his belt, unzipped his pants, and pushed them down his legs. The pants folded into a pile at his feet, leaving him half-nude for the city to see. The blinds were up because he liked to let the low afternoon sun in. He refrained from checking out the two perpendicular floor-to-ceiling windows that made the corner of his office. The sun probably reflected on the glass panes, so whatever he did wasn't visible from the outside. Still, it *was* possible someone in a building on the other side of the streets saw him, identified him, and contacted the chairman of his board. He didn't care. The cost of losing his job was lesser than the cost of losing Luke.

"I'm just a guy," he said through a growl, glaring at Luke. "It's just me, Roman. A simple guy." He bent to take a shoe off and threw it in a pile of documents on his desk so papers flew to all sides. "I *love* like everybody else." He did the same thing with the other shoe, sending it crashing into more papers. "I *make love* like everybody else." Moves quick and hard, he removed his socks and pulled the other clothes off his legs—his briefs, too—before straightening stark naked in front of Luke. "What more do you want?"

With a small grin, Luke brought Roman's shirt to his nose and sniffed. "Do you have lube?"

CHAPTER SEVEN

I couldn't be more satisfied. I'm leaning against Roman's desk with his intoxicating scent in my nose and a raging hard-on tenting my pants. I've led Mr. Powerful to where I want to have him: naked in his office and very eager to please me. He stands before me seething, pumped-up, fists clenched at his sides, hairy chest and stomach heaving.

How such a smart guy could let me play him like that boggles my mind. Either he's suffering from temporary loss of intelligence or he really, really likes me. Maybe it's his small head doing the thinking. It would seem so, for as I glance down his perfect, sexy body, his dick lengthens and thickens.

I'm dying to reach for him, spin him toward the desk behind me, flatten him on top of it with his legs spread, and do his sweet ass while the whole world outside the tall windows watches. Now on his rich man turf, I can show him I ignore our difference in social position and take command. Where he dominates me in the material world, I've got the upper hand when it comes to our human relation.

That was the idea, but the situation is inversed. He offers himself willingly as my lover. I no longer need to prove I'm his equal. I've won. I'm the king of the mightiest building in town.

Now what? We both know what's going to happen, but apparently, neither knows how or wants to make the first move. Maybe he thinks it's my turn, because he's done everything in his might to show me his submission. But I want more. I've always been the one to make sexual advances, now it's up to him.

Why is he stalling, simply staring, desire evident in his smoldering gaze and his cock growing for me?

Oh, I forget. It's his first time with a man.

Not wanting to wait another minute, I put his shirt on the desk and push forward. His eyes widen as I meet him full front, chests colliding, punching a little air out of his lungs. I'm a beast like that. Hungry and determined, no one standing in my way.

We might have all evening, but I don't have any patience. Not after lusting for this hunk for a week. Lips clamping on his, I run my hands along his warm waist to the small of his back and down to his firm, round ass, pulling him to me so our erections touch, only separated by my jeans. He shudders. I focus on his mouth, and, with the tip of my tongue, lick the seam of his lips, then demand entrance. I want to explore him, claim him as mine. When he gasps, I dive in and seek his tongue, swirl mine around it, lick the wet inside of his mouth, his hard teeth one by one, and again, his swollen lips. I love feasting on him like the most delicious dish, my mouth watering with each ensnaring taste.

To my delight, he opens to me and kisses me back in a rough manner, too, clashing our teeth and rolling his tongue around mine. Not only has his anger worn off, he's showing me he's one hell of a kisser and more than worth me. My dick goes rock hard and pushes into him, right next to his long and thin one standing commando. Too fucking tempting. I move my hands from his ass to his groin, one hand fisting him and the other grabbing his sac. Moving back a little to allow space, I stroke his perfect cock from the base of the shaft nesting in a bush of pubic hair to the thick, velvety head, and I finger the wet slit on the tip. All the while massaging his balls. He groans, his tongue a dagger in my mouth.

I don't know what I want most, to have him thrust inside me, or to be the one banging him until I explode. I enjoy being both a top and a bottom, and I have a feeling he'll also be okay with both. We're equals, one as strong as the other.

The more we kiss and fondle, the more the air between us heats, and the afternoon sun slamming into the office bathes us in light, makes me boil in my clothes. Sweat beads all over. I release Roman's lips and ass and take a small step back. "Why don't you...uh, help me here. It's too hot."

A thin layer of perspiration coats his handsome features. Cheeks flushed, look hazy, he reaches for the hem of my t-shirt and pulls it up over my stomach and chest. The fabric sticks to my clammy skin. I lift my arms to help him, damp heat drifting from my armpits. From the lust in his eyes, I half-expect him to lean forward and lick me, tease my nipples, gently nibble my flesh, but he hesitates. Of course, he's never been intimate with a man. How can I think he'll behave like a gay? I smile to tell him it's okay.

Regaining confidence, he finishes pulling my t-shirt over my head and arms, ruffling my hair, and sends it flying somewhere behind me. Again, like in the gym, his gaze roams over my naked torso, studying the tats and the scars. He runs a finger along some of them, his touch warm and ticklish on my skin. "One day," he whispers, "you'll tell me their history."

"Yeah, but if you don't mind, I have more pressing matters now."

A grin grows on his mouth. "I don't know if I'll be able to sate you."

"Somebody down here has been waiting all week."

He reaches for my belt, unbuckles it, and pauses.

What is it, he's afraid of my cock? I chuckle. It's thick, all right, making the front of my pants protrude, but it's not a monster. I move my hands over his and force his fingers to pop the button through the hole and unzip my pants. I push my boxers down, under my balls. My cock uncurls into his hands like a large snake.

"Take it," I tell him, tone urgent. His warm hand closes around the base of my shaft and strokes upward. I hold my breath and savor the amazing feeling. There's nothing like it, except pushing past a ring of muscles and diving into a tight, hot depth. I groan, "You know where I want to put it."

He releases my dick and looks down, as if ashamed of something. "You know, I've never…"

"I know. I promise I won't hurt you. I'm not a brute."

"I never thought you were."

I swipe a finger across his lips, and though my hard-on demands immediate relief, I take my time to be kind. "You're a very handsome guy."

His eyes flutter up again and search mine.

I smile. "I like everything about you. Your sexy beard." Cupping his face with my hands, I lean forward and nibble at the neatly trimmed hair from his jaw to his ear, the short stubble grazing my lips like miniature darts. "Your high cheek bones. Your dark brows. Your Italian eyes." I place a kiss over each of his eyes, on the soft flesh beneath his brows. "Your roman nose, so fitting." I run my lips along the strong, straight bone of his nose, then do a small leap down to his lips, nibbling at the lowest one. "And these. My fucking God, so full and tantalizing. I wish I had time to devour them, but…"

A smile curves the corners of his mouth, his gaze warm and trusting.

Impatient, I retreat, let my pants and boxers drop to my feet, and step out of them. I put my hands on his shoulders, and gently, but firmly, push him down to his knees. I'm careful to go down with him, too, so we're always at the same level and he doesn't feel I'm dominating him. It's important he's with me all the way, that he doesn't think I'm forcing him to accept anything.

When we're both kneeling on the carpet with our erect cocks poking between us, I lean forward and kiss him again, our lips melting together. His tongue meets mine and curls around it, making me want him even more. Sweat rolls down my chest muscles. I'm so hot for him, I want to pin him to the floor and enter his sweet hole right away. Fluid leaks from the tip of my cock. But I have to wait a little more. There's one thing I need to set straight.

It takes all of my will strength to pull back once more and simply look at him, my chest heaving and body trembling, aching for a sexual release. "I have a confession to make."

He nods. "Okay."

"All week I've been dreaming of screwing you on your desk and wiping that rich-fuckhead arrogance off your face."

His brows shoot upward.

"But now…"

"Now what?" he hisses, as if what I'm about to say has immense importance.

"Things have changed completely. I don't know what you've done to me, but you've turned everything upside down, and all I can think about is making love to you."

"Oh." His face breaks into a cute smile.

"It's true." I tilt my head. "I've got the hots for you, you fool." I have no idea what the future holds for us, but at least I've told him how I feel, and it's up to him to decide what to make of it.

Just not now. I reach for his shoulders and push him further down, onto his side, while I lay next to him on the soft carpet and enlace him with my arms and legs.

He lets me maneuver him, features calm. If he didn't want to be in this situation, he wouldn't. He's not the kind to let anyone boss him around.

I stroke his back, the firm mounds of his ass, the soft crevice between his butt cheeks. "I wanted to do it here, in your office, with the whole city at our feet, so everyone could see you being fucked over by a simple street punk."

He frowns. "You're far from a punk."

"My past defines me. I can't run from it."

He shakes his head, but I refuse to argue. I've had blue balls for days, and the moment has come to savor him. I move my longest finger to the puckered crack in his ass and play with it, circling the hole and applying light pressure. "I take it you don't have lube."

He gives a shy chuckle.

"Okay. Maybe she does." Swiftly, I get up on my knees again, move over to Cindy's desk, and open its drawers. Among all kinds of office items and chick stuff, there's a tube of hand lotion. That'll do. I gather my jeans on the floor, find a rubber pack in a pocket, and get back to Roman. "Turn onto your back."

He stares at the lotion and the condom in my hands, the white in his eyes visible.

"Hey, I'm not gonna force ya. If you don't wanna do this, I'll just jerk off in your mouth." I grin and teasingly stick out my tongue.

His features smoothen. After a little hesitation, he obeys and spreads his legs for me, his erection lying amid black hair on his belly.

My cock goes straight up and heat rushes through it, more pre-cum leaking from the tip. My balls are so full I'm about to burst. Won't need much friction to come. Gritting my teeth to rein in, I roll the condom over my length and smear a handful of creamy lavender-smelling lotion on it. I kneel between Roman's legs, pour lotion over his dark, puckered hole, then on my hand, and insert my greasy index finger into his tight hotness. I proceed slowly, smoothly. Don't want him to feel violated. He gasps, but I push on, deeper, curling my finger upward and stroking the flesh inside.

He bucks and shouts out, his pelvis lifting in the air.

I grin.

"Fuck." He exhales air, lowering to the floor again. "What—what the hell was *that*?"

"Your prostate."

"Ha! I thought I was coming."

I laugh. "It's one of the strongest erogenous zones in your body. Few people know." After inserting a second finger and scissoring them for a bit to stretch his ring muscles, I pull out and lower myself over him on an elbow, one hand fisting my cock and guiding the tip to his crack. I'm going to come so hard this time. I'm going to be blown away.

* * * *

When Luke's thick, hard cock penetrated his hole, Roman thought the sensitive flesh would tear apart beyond repair. He'd never felt so stretched down there. But the sting of hurt subsided, replaced by a strange sensation of fullness and contentment. It wasn't as dirty as he'd feared either. On the contrary, this physical connection with Luke felt right, the same way it had been with his wife. The in and outward gliding of Luke's oiled shaft inside him strangely natural. Suddenly, it no longer mattered whether it happened in a pussy or an asshole. What mattered was the giving and taking between two people making love.

Luke lay on top of him, resting on his elbows, handsome face inches from Roman's. He would probably not last long. Sweat pebbled on his forehead and ran alongside his temples. Panting heavily through parted lips, features contracted, he thrust in and out at a quick, rhythmic pace, chasing his orgasm. Each rough movement pushed Roman a little on the soft carpet.

What an amazing turn on. Roman would have rubbed his own erection if he could and tried to climax at the same time as Luke, but his cock was squished, trapped underneath Luke's muscular belly. He turned his head and glanced at the big windows overlooking the city. If anyone in the opposite buildings had a chance of looking in, it had to be one hell of a sight. He didn't care. He was with his lover, happy, insanely aroused, and the rest of the world could screw themselves.

Luke arched his back and opened his mouth, but no other sound than ragged breaths came out of it. He had taught himself to be quiet.

Roman urged, "Don't hold back! I wanna hear you."

Moving fast, grimacing, Luke closed his eyes. A groan erupted deep in his throat and grew with each thrust, ending as the growl of a lion in heat. He jerked and squirmed, back and forth, pounding into Roman, growling. His intense orgasm seemed to last and last, as if he'd waited not just a week, but years.

Roman had never seen anything like this. When Luke fell on top of him, in a sweat, breathless, then eased out and rolled onto the floor, Roman laughed. Now, he would play. He followed him and put a leg across his muscular thighs.

"Wait!" Hands shaking, Luke peeled off the condom.

As soon as he'd tied it and thrown it into a bin under the desk, Roman moved up to his large shoulders and straddled him. High on eroticism and aching for release, he wrapped a hand around his hard cock, brought it to Luke's sweaty, grinning face, and ran the head over his parted lips, circling them like a caress.

It was Luke's turn to laugh. He stuck his tongue out and with a mischievous gleam in his green pupils licked the underside of Roman's shaft, along the thick, apparent vein.

Delight shot through Roman. Mechanically, he rubbed base-to-tip with long, urgent strokes, building his orgasm, eyes locked on Luke's intense gaze. Their connection was insane. He couldn't imagine living a day without him. Though they belonged to different worlds, Luke brought out the best in him. And the most erotic. And the most raw, real, down-to-earth, basic. There were not two men like Luke.

After a minute of rough, purposely pumping, Roman came, the sharp pleasure shooting through his length making him cry out. He ejaculated hot semen on Luke's lips, nose, cheeks…all over his face, telling whoever was watching from the outside that this guy here was *his*.

It was his strongest orgasm in a long time. Not because of the tension and fatigue he'd accumulated lately, or because he'd had a nice, thick cock gliding inside his ass moments before, or because Luke was exceptionally sexy—all of which was true—but because amorous feelings were involved.

EPILOGUE

"Luke?"

"Mm?" I jump awake in a foreign bed, nude under soft sheets, my feet sticking out. A glance at an open door reminds me of where I am.

The hottest male I've seen in a lifetime stands in the doorway. Roman and I have spent the night together in a bedroom down the corridor from his office. It's a small, sparingly decorated room without windows, reserved for overnight workers. Light from the hall shines through his black hair and caresses the tanned skin of his face. He's dressed, but images from last night come back to me, of sweaty, naked skin and intense fucking. Just recalling that has my cock jerk to life and tent the bedsheets.

"Hey, Sweetheart." With a gorgeous smile, he approaches the bed, bringing a whiff of his cologne, and bends to kiss me. His lips are full and warm, and I have to fight not to reach for my cock and stroke it.

"*Sweetheart,*" I huff instead, pretending to be vexed. I've never been called anything sweet. But he's cute, and he makes my heart sing like those birds did in the park.

He points to my phone on a bedtable. "Someone called earlier. You were passed out, so I told her you'd call back."

"Her?" Frowning, I sit up against the bedhead, grab my phone, and stare at the screen. It shows a list of answered calls. On top, a number I don't recognize. A woman? I've had many in the years following my release from jail.

"She said her name was Marilyn something. Ring a bell?"

"No? Should I know her?"

He shrugs. "Call her."

"She didn't say what it was about?"

He gives an exaggerated sigh and turns on his heel. "Call her!"

"Would you mind getting me a coffee?"

"You forgot *please*."

"I didn't."

Laughing, he goes out the door.

I hit the number on my phone screen.

It dials, and after a couple of rings, a young, feminine voice replies. "Hello."

"Hi, I'm Luke Vance. You called earlier?"

"Yes. I'm Marilyn Hill. Thanks for getting back to me. "

"What is it about?"

She hesitates. "Well, it's a long story. And it wasn't easy to find you. There're like, a zillion guys with your name out there." She giggles, the sound making me picture a teenager. "The Bureau of Prisons refused to give me information."

Ice cold dread rushes through me. The Bureau of Prisons? My old life is coming back at me, or fate, whichever, a full-circle thing about to unfold and hit me in the fucking face. Blood pulses in my temples, giving me a sudden headache.

"...So I had to play detective. At least I had your name from my mother."

"Okay." I suck in a mouthful of air and wince from the pain in my head. "Go on."

"Fifteen years ago, an accident happened to my dad, and he died. He was very young, but my mom was already pregnant. Since he had known I was on the way, she told me about him while I grew up. She said he loved me and that he was watching me from Heaven. So I've got a fond memory of him. I miss him, of course, but in a good way."

Fuck me. She's the daughter of the kid I stabbed? He was expecting a baby at the time? I can barely believe it. Petrified, I stutter, "W-why are you telling me this?"

"Well, my family refused to talk to me about the guy who killed him. It was taboo. But I wanted to meet him. Not because I wanted a vengeance or anything, but because I felt sorry for him. You see, I've seen tapes from the trial, where he was crying and pleading my family to forgive him. They refused, and I thought it was very heartless of them to send him to prison without giving him the chance to apologize and redeem himself. I mean, everybody knows it was an accident."

I hold my breath. I'm dreaming this phone call. This girl can't be real.

"So," she continues. "I want to make things good again. It's taken me a long time to find you and even longer to work up the nerve to call you, but I'd like to..."

She talks on, but I'm only half-listening, half-understanding her words. My throat chokes with a fierce emotion, a very dark one that has lasted half my life, strangled the smallest flames of joy, and, at times, provoked thoughts of suicide.

When she's finished, I'm too messed-up to say anything intelligible, except, "I-I would love to. Thank you." And then I hang up and bring my fingers to my burning eyes to stop the tears, but fail.

The mattress moves. "What's going on?" Roman's voice. And the smell of hot, roasted coffee.

With a groan, I remove my hands and glimpse at the only person who has *really* listened to me since the accident.

He sits on the bedside, gorgeous and all, two coffee cups in hand, his black eyes filled with concern. "Who was it?"

"His daughter. He has a daughter. And she wants to take me to his grave." More tears roll down my cheeks.

"You mean the guy you—?" Mouth gaping in astonishment, he puts the cups on a bedtable before extending his arms to me.

Marilyn's offer is so fresh I can't possibly have comprehended all that it means to me yet. When its full importance dawns on me, I'm going to hit a wall. I bite my lip until it hurts and bow my head, sobbing. "I've never had a grave to go to." I wipe one wet eye after the other, but the tears keep coming.

Roman catches me in his strong arms and gives me the soothing hug I should've had many years ago. I wrap my arms around his warm, firm torso, my trembling chin on top of his shoulder, and use him for comfort. He presses me to him, molds us to each other. We're an amazing match. A team.

"When will you meet her?" he asks, stroking my back.

"At noon. I didn't see any reason to delay it. I've already waited fifteen years." Sniffing, I glance over his shoulder. A lamp in the hall casts a diffuse white light on us. If I didn't know better, I'd think we were attending a ceremony in some sacred place.

"Where?"

"About an hour's drive from here."

"Can I go with you?"

Unable to believe his words, I release him and look into his eyes. Inches from my face, he smiles, honest gaze telling me he's serious. He wants to be there for me. No one has ever wanted to, no one has cared. Indescribable warmth fills me. I see only good things in this man, and he couldn't be farther from the slick impression I had of him the first time we met.

"And after that," he continues, turning to grab the two coffee cups, "we can go pick up the kids."

"Jen accepted your offer?"

Smiling from ear-to-ear, he hands me one of the cups. "My lawyer called earlier. I'm having them for the weekend."

"What? That's fabulous news. Congrats." I raise my cup in a toast. "But it does make you wonder what kind of a mother she is, to prefer having expensive material things rather than the full custody of her children."

He shrugs. "Believe me, I've thought about it more times than what's good for my sanity. For instance, how could I marry her in the first place? But regardless of the selfish person she is, I've had to accept that fathers don't have the same rights as mothers, and I'm just happy I can have my kids at all. Then…" He slides his free arm around my waist, bringing us closer and his fantastic scent of maleness into my space. "Since it's Saturday, I thought I'd take them apartment hunting. I need a new place to live, right? And I want you to come with us."

"Me?" I widen my eyes. "Why—"

He laughs and kisses me, lips soft and so, so fucking enticing. My cock stiffens again. "It's not up for discussion. As soon as I got the news from my lawyer, I called the kids and told them I was with you and we'd go looking for a new home. They were ecstatic and they said it was, I quote, *"Awesome,"* that I'm seeing that cool guy from the kitchen."

"But—"

"Correction. Lily said you were cute, and Nick said you were cool."

My head spins from the wealth of information. One thing sticks out, though. "Wait, did you tell them you were *seeing* me? As in *dating?*"

Roman grins, his gorgeous black eyes twinkling, and reaches for my hard-on under the sheet.

The End.

ADDICTIONS

BY

R. BRENNAN

DEDICATION

Dedicated to devastating dimples.

~ R. Brennan

Alexis set her backpack on the stone bench and leaned against the retaining wall of the university campus center. Her head ached in time with her pulse. Wincing, she took a long draught from the Styrofoam cup in her hand and prayed the shot of caffeine would appease the headache gods. With a sigh, she settled in to wait.

Wouldn't be long. Exams started next week, so desperate customers would be coming out of the woodwork. If they weren't looking for anything they could get to stay awake, they were looking for a bit of pot to use to de-stress. She'd sell out by noon, easy, and the sooner she ran out of product, the sooner she could square up with Billy, and score something to take care of her own needs. She was usually better about making sure she had enough supply to get through, but she'd had to up her dosage recently just to get by. Not a good sign.

"Hey, Lexi. How's things?"

She quirked a brow in her first customer's direction. "I'd complain, but who'd care?" Her shoulders lifted in a shrug. "So, how'd you like that BC bud? Killer, right?"

Brian swiped at the rust colored fringe of hair hanging in his face and grinned. "You know it. Chuck and I enjoyed quite a bender on that bag." He shoved his hands into his front pockets. "But, uh...we were kinda wondering—"

She had him. Lexi grinned. The eyes always gave them away. "What else I can score? Maybe something a little stronger?" She grabbed her backpack from the bench beside her. "What's your pleasure? Do you snort, shoot? Like pills? If I don't have it now, I'll be able to get it. Just need to know what you're looking for."

His eyes widened. "Oh, wow...uhm, cool. Well, we were talking. You know, Chuck and me. And we were hoping we could score some X, maybe, but I'd be up for a little blotter if you had that, too."

Easy pickins. "I have the X on me. Single stacks and doubles. I'll have to catch up with you on the acid. Don't get much call for that, so I don't carry it on me. Have it at my place, though."

Brian's crooked smile returned. He'd actually be cute if his eyes weren't just a bit too close together and he didn't have quite so many freckles. "Sweet. A half dozen rolls of the double stack should do for now. Thanks, Lexi."

"No problem. It's what I'm here for." She unzipped the top pocket of her bag and pulled out a small black film canister. With a wink, she stepped in close and lifted on her toes. She whispered in his ear. "Ninety bucks, stud." She slyly deposited the film canister in his hoodie pocket and stepped back.

Cheeks red, Brian withdrew the money from his pocket and handed it over. "Thanks again."

She gave the bills a quick count before sticking them in another pocket of her backpack. "If you come by tomorrow, I'll have the paper."

"Cool." He bobbed his head. "Okay. I should go. Got class across the quad in ten. See ya."

Lexi tossed her thick chocolate braid back over her shoulder and returned to leaning against the stone wall. "Yeah. See ya."

Her prediction for the morning turned out to be pretty accurate. By one thirty, she'd exhausted her stash and headed across campus with a satchel full of cash. A quick stop at Billy's, and she'd have what she needed to take care of the throbbing in her skull and the ever-present ache in her left knee.

As she worked her way through a chattering crowd of students intent on making their next class on time, a small part of her wanted to turn and follow them. To go back to who she used to be. One of them again. Her soul ached to return to the time she'd been a star on the university volleyball team with a bright future, a 3.7 GPA, and no pain. Before the injury and lost scholarship. Before her whole world was shredded along with her fucking weak–ass ACL.

A growl pushed past her lips as she thrust the bitterness aside. *Woulda, coulda, shoulda.*

* * * *

Lexi gave Billy's front door a quick double knock and pushed her way in. People came and went from his place at all hours of the day and night. Besides, Billy knew her better than anyone. He'd be expecting her.

He wasn't in the main room of the one-bedroom apartment. That left the bedroom or the bathroom. Her gaze shifted to the right. The bathroom door lay open.

"Billy?" she called. "It's Lex. Drag your ass out of bed and get it out here."

The bedroom door swung open to reveal Billy, clad in a long, tattered bathrobe, flannel pants, and a stained white T-shirt. His thick black hair was tousled and jutted from his skull in every conceivable direction.

"You're looking particularly haggard this afternoon." Lexi dropped onto the sofa and set her backpack beside her. "Big party last night?"

Billy ran his fingers through his hair, only managing to make matters worse, and shuffled into the kitchenette of the tiny apartment. He grabbed a mug from the counter and filled it with cold coffee from the pot. "Nothing out of the ordinary. Just feeling lazy today." After sticking the mug into the microwave and punching at the buttons, he faced her and grinned. "Did you bring me presents?"

Lexi shook her head and laughed. "Yeah, I guess you could say that." She withdrew a stack of money from her pack and set it on the coffee table beside a cluster of empty beer cans. "Three grand. That should square us and leave me a bit left over."

Billy pulled the steaming cup of coffee from the microwave and joined her in the living area. He reached out and grabbed the stack of money before settling on the sofa next to her. He took a swig from the mug and placed it where the cash had been. "Did you want change? Or did you have something else in mind?" He counted, folded, and stuffed the bills into his robe pocket.

"Very funny. You know damned well what I have in mind."

"Yeah. I just like fucking with you." He withdrew a bottle of pills from his other pocket and dropped it onto her lap. "You're running out faster lately. Everything all right?"

Despite Billy's chosen occupation, he'd been a good friend to Lexi since her injury. He'd given her a place to stay when she'd been forced to drop out of school after the university pulled her scholarship, and he was one of the few people who'd visited her in the hospital after the ACL surgery. And when she got hooked on the pain killers, Billy was the one to make sure she didn't run out.

"Yeah. You know me. Living the dream." Lexi manufactured a smile.

Billy's brow furrowed. "You know we're friends, right? That I genuinely care about you, and that's why I ask? You're one of my best salesmen, not to mention the sexiest by far. I worry about you."

Lexi shifted on the sofa, cheeks heating under his scrutiny. "Yeah. I know, but I'm fine. Really." She cast him a sidelong glance. "Why? What have you heard?"

He laughed. "Nothing. Just being proactive. Looking after my best girl. You know me."

"Yep." She let the tension seep from her shoulders. "You're a saint, Billy."

"I just hope you remember that when it comes time to forgive me."

Lexi eyed him. "Forgive you? For what?"

"This."

Before she knew what was happening, Billy was on her, pushing her back into the sofa, his weight pinning her arms to her chest.

She squirmed beneath him, trying to free herself, confusion clouding her thoughts. "Get off me!"

"I swear this is for your own good," Billy whispered.

Lexi felt a sharp prick on the side of her neck an instant before the heat started to spread. "What the fuck"— Spots floated in her field of vision. — "did you do?" The words were heavy on her tongue. She fought against the drooping of her eyelids.

Billy's weight left her and Lexi struggled to sit up. She couldn't make her limbs move.

His face hovered above her, expression filled with concern.

The black abyss swallowed her.

* * * *

Lexi groaned and rolled onto her back. Her aching head and sluggish muscles protested. Tentatively, she cracked a weary eye open to reveal an unfamiliar white tiled ceiling. She scoured her murky memory for clues.

Billy. She'd been with Billy. At his place. Sitting on the couch. Paying him.

She bolted upright, her fingers curling into the blankets.

He fucking drugged me!

She frowned as cool air caressed her torso.

And I'm fucking naked!

She clawed through her recollection for details, but came up woefully empty. Her frantic gaze scanned the room, hoping for clues.

There wasn't much to see. Empty space beyond the bed she woke up in and a tall oak dresser across from her. No pictures adorned the plain walls. No décor or personal items on the dresser. Nothing but the bed, the dresser, and her.

Where the fuck am I? How had Billy gotten her out of his apartment? And what did he do with her clothes?

She glanced at the door.

"Yeah. Time to go." Lexi tossed back the covers and swung her feet over the side of the bed.

The sound of a chain rattling echoed through the empty room. Her left leg, heavier than her right. Dumbfounded, Lexi glanced at her feet. A steel manacle encircled her ankle.

"What the—?"

She drew her tethered foot up and rested her heel on the edge of the mattress. Her fingers wrapped around the cold metal encircling her ankle and gave it a yank, but the manacle didn't budge. Brow furrowed, she slid the metal around, hunting for some kind of release clasp. She noticed the keyhole.

Growling, she began gathering the length of connected chain, pulling the slack into her lap. The other end was attached to the wall at the foot of the bed. She dropped the length of chain and pushed up from the mattress, intent on getting to the loop of metal affixed to the wall.

"It's good to see you up and about."

The rich masculine voice startled her, and she swung about, eyes wide.

No one was there.

"Up here," the voice said.

Her gaze darted upward. Positioned near the ceiling in the corner of the room was a small white camera. Her heart hammered against her ribs. While the voice was almost familiar, she knew it wasn't Billy's. But who?

She glared into the lens, hands balled at her sides. "What the fuck is going on?"

The voice in the ceiling tsked. "Such a nasty mouth."

Anger churned in her stomach. Who the hell did this guy think he was? "If you don't like it, come do something about it, asshole." She bent and grabbed hold of the chain and tried to jerk it free of the wall.

"It's no use. You're only going to hurt yourself trying."

She swung her attention back to the camera. "You need to get the fuck in here and unlock this ankle cuff before I lose my shit."

His thick laughter grated on her nerves and sent a strange, almost electric shudder through her limbs. "While the act of you losing your shit, as you call it, holds a certain intrigue, I have other plans for you, my dear Alexis."

He knew her name. His voice and manner of speech tickled at her subconscious, urging her to identify him. Maybe if she kept him talking, she'd be able to place him.

"What kind of plans?" She walked the length of the chain, coming a few feet shy of the room's door, the tether just short enough to keep her from reaching the handle.

"I plan to save you from yourself."

It was Lexi's turn to laugh. "How very gallant of you, sir." She wiggled her chained foot. "But as you can see, the only thing I seem to need saving from at the moment, is you. Whoever you are."

"Mmm… I like when you call me sir, Alexis. Would you really feel better about being my guest if you knew who I was?"

Not really, no. "Yes. Along with knowing why you have me chained up." She folded her arms over her breasts, suddenly aware of her nudity. "And what the fuck you did with my clothes." She pulled the sheet from the bed with a grunt, wrapped it around her body, and tossed a glare at the camera.

After a few moments of silence, the handle on the door clicked, drawing her startled gaze. She held her breath as the door slowly swung wide.

He stood in the opening, the light at his back casting him in an intimidating shadow. "Hello, Alexis. I trust you remember me?"

Confusion muddled her thoughts. "Professor Foster?"

Her captor hadn't changed much in the two years since she'd last seen him. His hair had grown a little longer maybe, the dark curls her fingers had always ached to play with hanging lower on his brow. Overall, he seemed a bit more unkempt. But his eyes. Those penetrating gray eyes Lexi swore could see into her very soul had not changed at all. They pinned her now, and she squirmed. Her chest tightened. "Y-yes, I remember you."

"Good." He stepped into the room, his broad, muscled shoulders filling the small space.

She took a hesitant step backward, thoughts racing. "I-I don't understand. Why am I here?" She frowned. "Where's Billy?"

A smile stretched his firm lips, exposing a row of white teeth, and flashing the adorable right cheek dimple she recalled quite fondly. God, how many times had she tossed out ridiculous one-liners in his Western Civ. class just for the chance at eliciting that dimple's heart stopping appearance?

"You're here because I brought you here. You're chained because that's how I want you to be. And Billy isn't here because I didn't invite him." He took another step closer, and she held her breath. "Sensing a theme?"

Lexi swallowed the lump in her throat, and her grip on the sheet tightened. "Yeah, I get it. You're in charge." She lifted her chin. "Still don't understand why."

He folded his strong hands before him, the picture of scholarly grace. "You will." He studied her from tip to toe. "When did you last use?"

Her heartbeat skipped. "W-what?" She backed up until her calves pressed against the cool metal bed frame. She hadn't had a chance to take any of the pills she scored from Billy, wherever they were. How long ago had that been? Her new prison had no windows, so she had no way to know how much time had passed since Billy gave her the shot. "How long have I been here? I don't even know what day it is."

"You were out about four hours. Not very long." He folded his arms over his chest, expression darkening. "I will repeat myself just once, Alexis. I am not in the habit of doing so with my slaves. When was the last time you used?"

His what? "Slave? What are you talking about?"

Angry sparks flashed in his eyes, sending a jolt of fear through her limbs. This wasn't the professor she remembered, crushed on for the better part of a year.

"This morning," she supplied, not willing to risk his ire while chained to a wall and protected by a sheet. Not until she knew why he brought her here. And what the hell he meant by *slave*. "I crushed and snorted my last two pills this morning before hitting the campus center." Annoyance overruled intelligence and spurred her next words. "Why? You got something in your pocket to take the edge off?"

He closed the space between them in an instant. His fingers tangled in her hair, tilting her head until her wide-eyed gaze locked with his. "Do not for a second misunderstand the gravity of your situation. You have lost control over your life, Alexis. I have taken that from you. From here on out, I will decide when you eat, when you sleep, and when you go to the bathroom. I will tell you what to wear and what I expect of you. It will be up to me, and me alone, to decide what you are allowed to put on or in your body. My body. You are done abusing yourself." His grin chilled her blood. "Now, it's my turn."

She was acutely aware of his pure male hardness pressed against her, separated from her flesh by a thin strip of cotton. The frantic racing of her heart increased.

He abruptly released her.

She stumbled backward and dropped to her bottom onto the mattress.

"I wager you will be much more willing to hear reason in a few more hours. I'll be back then." He turned and stalked away, movements stiff. Without a glance back, Professor Foster left the room and closed the door. The grating sound of metal against metal rang in her ears. Instinct told her what it meant.

He'd just locked her in. As if the chain around her ankle wasn't enough.

* * * *

Alexis wasn't sure how long she stared at the closed door. Her mind tumbled and churned over her predicament. What had Professor Foster meant? He spoke as if there were others. Other students? Other junkies? Had he kidnapped them, too? Where were they? She glanced at the camera hovering in the corner.

Why me?

Professor Foster wouldn't hurt her. Despite her situation, being chained and locked away, she would be safe there. He had a job, a reputation. Surely he wouldn't risk all that because of her. Right?

Nothing made sense. Why would he jeopardize his position at the university to take her? She'd never have believed him capable of kidnapping. But, she wouldn't have ever guessed Billy to betray her the way he had either, so she really wasn't the best judge of character. The more she tried to make sense of things, the more her head pounded.

She rubbed her throbbing temples and pretended she didn't recognize the signs. Soon the shakes would start, and the sweating, followed by nausea, vomiting, and the return of the pain. She sat upright, twisting her fingers in the sheet. She needed a fix.

A quick scan of the sparse room confirmed what she already knew. There wasn't a fix to be had. Not there. Unsure on how to keep the obsessive thoughts away, she paced the length of her ankle tether, keeping the bedsheet tied off above her breasts. Her agitation increased with each lap, until she had worked herself into a mental frenzy. How long did he plan to leave her locked in a room? Was he ever coming back?

Anger bubbled to the surface and spilled over. She spun on her heel and glared at the camera. "Let me the fuck out of here, you bastard! You have no right to keep me here against my will."

She glanced at the door. Waited.

The knob didn't move.

Was he even watching? Listening? Where else would he be? Frustrated, she swung about, stalked to the end of the bed, bent, and yanked at the chain with all of her strength. After a few jerks proved futile, she gave up, dropped the chain, and sat on the cold floor with a *harrumph*. "What sort of twisted fucking game is this?"

"My game." Foster's stern voice vibrated down her spine.

Startled, she jumped to her feet and came about, gripping the sheet tightly to her chest as if it were made of steel.

His intense gaze burned into hers, melting her where she stood. "W-what happens if I don't want to play?" She cringed at the quiver in her voice.

The smile he awarded her was affable, more in line with the kind professor she remembered from history class, but his expression held an intensity that captivated her. "You will." He crossed the space and covered her hands with his warm ones. "You're trembling."

She swallowed a surge of embarrassment and glanced down at his knuckles. "It's going to get worse."

He leaned in close. His fragrance, rich and all male, danced across her nostrils. His lips seared her forehead with a paternal kiss before he moved away, taking his intoxicating scent with him. "Then we should get started." He left the room and disappeared into the corridor.

She frowned, confused.

Get started with what?

Was her heart racing from the escalating Vicodin withdrawal or his enthralling proximity? Lexi didn't have long to consider the question before he returned to the room carrying a pint glass of what appeared to be water.

He crossed to the dresser across from the bed and set the glass down, then reached into his pocket. He set a round white pill beside the water and pivoted to face her. "The first thing I expect of you is for you to get clean. You are done with Vicodin. You will get no more." He thumbed over his shoulder. "I have no desire to see you suffer"—his lip twitched—"needlessly, so I offer an alternative." He flashed his devilish dimple. "One you will have to earn."

Lexi glanced at the pill on the dresser.

Methadone.

It would alleviate the withdrawal symptoms without offering the high her Vicodin offered. With regular doses, she could be clean in a few weeks without the agony normally associated with the process. Did he really intend to keep her chained up that long? "Earn it how, Professor Foster?" She wasn't sure she wanted to know the answer, but couldn't stop from asking.

"First off, call me Mark. I'm not your professor anymore, and I think the intimacy of our new relationship warrants more familiarity. As to how, we'll start simple. I want you to kiss me."

Lexi swallowed back her trepidation and forced herself to look at him. A mistake. Heated blood rushed through her limbs. "W-what?" She folded her arms protectively around her waist.

"Kiss me, Alexis." His voice arrived husky, softly commanding. "Like you want to."

Her cheeks burned. What kind of game was he playing? Did he really intend to keep her here like some kind of sex slave? For how long? To what end? Her sobriety? Why did he even give a shit? "And if I refuse? Demand that you release me?"

His wide shoulders lifted in a shrug. "Then I leave you to suffer your addiction and self-abuse in solitude. But, understand one thing. No matter what you decide with respect to your therapy, I will not be releasing you."

"You're crazy. You can't just keep me here. It's illegal."

"So is dealing drugs. Consider this a citizen's arrest."

As the irony of her situation hit her full force, an unsteady laugh burst from her throat. She should be enraged by his actions. Furious. She was chained to the wall, for Christ's sake. But anger wasn't anything close to what she felt at his demand for a kiss. In truth, what Profess—err, Mark offered was something Lexi had fantasized about since freshman year. Her crush on her history professor, fodder for her most erotic dreams. She'd thought about kissing his firm lips more times then she could count, teased herself to orgasm while she imagined his intense gray eyes hovering above her, her quivering body pinned to the bed by his thrusting hips…

Alexis gave herself a mental shake and did her best to slow her racing pulse. "I kiss you and I get the pill? What happens when it's time for another dose? What will you expect me to do for that one?"

"All recovery comes in steps, sweet Alexis. Let's get through this one first, shall we?"

Tension knotted her shoulders as she took a step closer to him. She glanced at his sensual lips with the next step, the weight of the chain tethering her ankle a harsh reminder of her situation. She gathered courage and took the final step, closing the distance separating them.

His masculine scent, a spicy mix of forest freshness and Old Spice, assaulted her. Knees quivering, she raised on her toes and lifted her chin. Concentration still on his mouth, pulse pounding in her ears, she pressed her lips to his.

At the moment of contact, a jolt of electricity shot through her and sent Mark into his action. His arms snaked around her waist and he pulled her pliant body against his hard one.

Her eyes flew open.

"Like you mean it. Remember?"

Swallowing down her shock, she slipped her hands up his glorious chest to encircle his neck. She moved in. Her pliant, open mouth pressed to his, and her eager tongue danced along his waiting lips.

Mark's grip on her tightened and he opened to her exploration. His tongue seared hers as he took control. Her fingers twined in the hair at his nape of their own will as he nipped at the corner of her mouth. She swallowed a whimper.

He drew his lips from hers and his arms fell away, leaving her breathless and shivering, her body instantly missing the heat of his. "Take your pill. I'll return shortly." He turned and, without a second glance, left the room.

* * * *

Shortly turned out to be hours later. While Lexi had no real way of knowing, her growing impatience with her solitary confinement told her it had to be at least three. She lay stretched out on the bed, the bedsheet toga wrapped tightly about her, staring at the ceiling, when her prison door swung open.

Mark came in carrying a food laden tray. A bottle of water jutted from his left pocket. He set the tray on the dresser and put the bottle beside it before pivoting to face her. "Do you need to use the bathroom yet?"

"Yes!" Lexi scrambled from the bed like it was on fire, the toga slipping from its moorings. She grabbed frantically at the makeshift covering, jerking it back into place, but not before Mark got an eyeful of her twin Cs. She straightened, fingers curled tightly around the sheet. Her cheeks burned. "Very much so."

His rich laughter warmed the rest of her body to the temperature of her face. "I guess so." A dark grin teased the corner of his mouth. "I'll take you to the bathroom before you eat, but the sheets belong on the bed, not your delectable curves, so it stays here."

Her jaw dropped. "W-what?"

"You heard me perfectly clear, Alexis. I'm not sure why you insist on making me repeat myself."

"And if I refuse?"

"Then I don't unchain your ankle, and you don't go. I'll bring you a chamber pot for the corner. You can use that instead. Rather humiliating, I'd imagine. Not much help for the modesty hang-up you seem to have either, but I'm all for offering choices."

She wanted nothing more than to wipe the smirk from his face, but had very few options for doing so. The darkness in his gaze left little doubt about the truth of his words. He wasn't bluffing.

You can do this.

Steeling her spine, she lifted her chin and released her stranglehold on the sheet. The white cotton slid down her body to pool at her feet. She resisted the urge to look away. He'd not see her cower. Her fingers tried to curl to fists at her sides, but she forced them to remain relaxed, let the tension seep from her shoulders. But there was nothing to be done for the frenzied butterflies wreaking havoc with her stomach. She raised her chin, defiant. "Whenever you're ready then."

Mark's smoldering gray eyes held hers as he reached into his pocket and withdrew the silver key. He swallowed the distance between them. She held her breath as he bent before her slowly enough she imagined he took in every inch of her nudity on the way. Senses on high alert, her skin tingled where his knuckles grazed her calf.

With a click, the lock broke open, releasing her ankle from its imprisonment.

He came to his feet again, took a step back, and inclined his head toward the door with a nonchalance that annoyed her traitorous pulse. "After you. Bathroom is to the right. First door on the left."

Of course. How could he fully enjoy her humiliation if he led the way?

Lexi folded her arms over her breasts, anxious to deny him something, anything, and stalked to the bathroom. Once inside, she turned and shoved the door closed. There was no lock to keep him at bay, but that didn't diminish the pleasure she took in the fleeting moment of solitude. No smoldering eyes bearing down on her, no cameras watching her every move, and no chain wrapped around her ankle. She took a deep breath and let it out slowly.

There wasn't much to the bathroom beyond the necessities. A white porcelain toilet and small pedestal sink the room's only décor. At least it was clean. She glanced at the mirror perched above the sink.

Medicine cabinet?

She drifted across the small room, her palms itching. Surely, he'd have cleaned it out before allowing her to use the toilet. Mark was a college professor, for fuck's sake. He was too smart to leave anything good behind. Wasn't he?

The methadone he'd given her would take care of any withdrawal, but it wasn't going to give her a buzz, and what she really needed at that moment, was a strong, mind numbing buzz.

Sending a fervent wish to the heavens, she jerked the cabinet open. While she wasn't surprised to find the small shelves empty, disappointment still jabbed at her chest as she pushed the little door closed again.

She looked at her reflection. She barely recognized the bloodshot green eyes staring at her from the other side of the mirror. Dark smudges nestled beneath them, as if she'd spent ten hours sleeping off a bender while in full theatrical makeup.

She was sober less than twenty-four hours and already a mess. She shook her head. Why was Mark even wasting his time? What did he stand to gain from bothering with her? Where was the benefit to him? If she'd taken anything from her short education at the University, it was one simple lesson. Nobody did anything for nothing. Everything, and everyone had a price. An ulterior motive. So what was Mark's?

Grunting, she turned from the mirror and sat on the toilet.

Did he really think he could force her to get clean? Even if he could, he couldn't make her stay that way. What was to stop her from using again as soon as he released her? Assuming he ever planned to let her go. He had to eventually. Didn't he?

While Lexi's mom wasn't going to win a mother-of-the-year award anytime soon, she still called. Sooner or later, she would tire of getting no response from her ungrateful daughter and come looking.

A sardonic laugh bubbled to the surface. Which could, and probably would, take months. In the meantime, Lexi was completely at the professor's mercy. She sighed. Why did the prospect thrill and scare the shit out of her at the same time?

Because you're fucking sick in the head.

Lexi got up, flushed, and washed her hands. Before she opened the door, she took a moment to run her fingers through her tangled mess of thick hair and pinch some color onto her sallow cheeks.

Yep, fucking sick.

Only someone who's lost their grip with reality primped for their kidnapper.

As expected, when she pulled the door open, Mark waited for her, leaning against the wall, shirtsleeves rolled up to his elbows, hands tucked harmlessly in his front pockets. He pushed upright as she exited the bathroom. "Better?"

"Much." She offered a shy smile.

"Good. Let's get you back to your room then. Your dinner is getting cold." He inclined his head toward the hallway. "I'm sure you know the way."

Lexi headed back to *her* room. As she stepped over the threshold, she immediately noticed two things. First, Mark had apparently brought steak for dinner. Its succulent aroma filled the small space and set Lexi's mouth salivating. Second, and far more disturbing to her churning stomach, the bedsheet she'd dropped on the floor before going to the bathroom had disappeared, along with the bed's solitary pillow.

She spun on him, anger lacing her words. "I did what you asked. Why did you take my sheet and pillow away?"

He quirked a brow. "My?" His hands slid from his pockets. He held the key to her ankle cuff in the right.

"The."

"I took away *my* sheet, because if I had wanted you to cover yourself, I would have given you clothes to wear. And before you ask, I took *my* pillow away because I felt like it."

Lexi sputtered as her mind tossed a volley of curses in his direction. "How am I supposed to sleep without a pillow? Even prison inmates get a pillow."

"Not in my prison they don't." Mark bent and fastened the metal collar around her ankle.

As the weight of her tether returned, Lexi cringed.

Standing, he slipped the key into his pocket and smiled. "Have something to eat and get some rest. You're going to need it. We begin in the morning."

She frowned. "Begin? Begin what?"

Mark left the room without answering, leaving her alone in her cell to fume, and consider all the devious possibilities her drug ravaged imagination could conjure.

* * * *

Lexi woke to the sound of a lock springing open. She bolted upright on the bed, eyes wide.

Mark stood over her, imposing, silent, probing her very soul. The steel manacle hung from his hand.

How long had he been there? A shiver of pleasure danced down her spine at the thought of him watching her sleep, leaving her unsettled.

He tossed the chain aside and extended a hand in her direction.

Heart hammering, she placed her palm against his.

He drew her to her feet. "It's time for your first therapy appointment."

"Therapy? For what?"

"You and I both know I can feed you methadone all day long, but unless we deal with the reasons behind your addiction, you're doomed to repeat the same bad habits as soon as you're given the chance. Is that really what you want for yourself, Alexis? For your life?"

While his concern seemed sincere, and her stomach, and parts lower, warmed as her brain absorbed that fact, warning bells still clanged in her skull. Her eyes narrowed. "What does it matter to you what I want?"

He shook his head, disappointment evident in his expression. "Looks like you have a lot of work ahead of you."

Lexi barked a laugh. "So you sent for a therapist to cure me? Save me from myself?"

"Not exactly." Mark left the room and returned a few moments later, carrying a large black duffel. He set it on the floor beside the bed. The disarming smile returned. "I'm your new therapist."

Her brow furrowed. "You have degrees in History *and* Psychiatry?"

Chuckling, Mark bent and unzipped the bag. He reached into the opening and withdrew a riding crop. "It's not that kind of therapy, Alexis."

She took a step back. "That looks a lot more like punishment than therapy."

"It's just a tool. One of many I carry in my medical bag." He tapped the business end of the crop on his open palm. "Now, turn around and put your hands on the bed."

Lexi shot a glance at the open door.

"You'll never make it." His grin widened. "But by all means. Give it a try."

"What does beating me have to do with therapy?"

"At your core, you're a masochist. A misguided and untrained one, granted, but a masochist all the same. I'm about to show you how to feed those instinctual desires without using drugs to do it. As you probably know, the methadone won't give you the euphoric feeling your Vicodin did." He motioned a circle in the air with the end of the crop. "But I promise I can. Now, don't be such a coward. Turn around and do as you're told."

The challenge in his words was unmistakable. Lexi would admit to being many things, but a coward wasn't among them. Despite the screaming protests of her thoughts, she spun around and put her hands on the mattress. Her knees quivered, forcing her to accept that a part of her was curious to see what came next. She focused on keeping her breathing even, calm, as if she hadn't a care or worry in the world. He wouldn't know the turmoil churning her insides.

His palm caressed her hip. She jumped, startled by the gentle contact.

"Easy, girl." His fingers trailed down her outer thigh. "Just relax and remain as you are. Stay still and let me have a proper look at you."

She bit down on her lower lip. Fire burned her cheeks. She closed her eyes. If she didn't see it coming, maybe she wouldn't flinch.

Mark's hand left her side a heartbeat before his belt buckle pressed against the crack of her ass. The fabric of his shirt caressed her back as he bent over her. His hands found her breasts.

She gasped, jerking back, her knee-jerk revolt stopped short by his hard chest.

"Don't move." His words were a whispered command, one that weakened her knees.

Her fingertips dug into the mattress. "I-I'm trying."

"Well, try harder, Alexis." Mark weighed her dangling orbs in his warm palms, gave them a soft squeeze. His thumb and forefinger found her tightening nipples. "Like little diamonds. I think they are enjoying this." His hot breath rustled her hair.

Then he was gone, cold air rushing in to take his place, raising gooseflesh on her arms. Lexi turned her head slightly to see where he'd gone.

Swoosh!

The riding crop came down hard across her bottom.

She squealed and bucked, tears blurring her vision.

"I said stay still. I mean it."

A stinging burn heated the right side of her ass. She resisted the urge to rub the pain away. "Sorry," she muttered.

"Sorry what?"

"Sorry…sir?" Her stomach performed a little flip-flop.

"Good girl."

She sensed the smile in his voice, and a jolt of pride shuddered through her. She marveled at the feeling. Proud of what? Avoiding another whack from the crop he'd just blistered her with?

Mark's hands returned to her skin, fingertips trailing down her back from shoulder to hip, scattering her thoughts. He traced a digit over the source of the heat.

Air left her lungs in the form of a sigh.

"You're beautiful, Alexis." His warm lips replaced his hand on the raised flesh of her ass before he moved away again.

Disappointment taunted her.

"Stand up straight and turn around."

Pulse racing, Lexi did as told. She studied the floor.

"How do you feel?"

The question took her by surprise. How did she feel? She tried to get her brain to form thoughts again. Helpless. Nervous. Aroused, but she had no intention of saying so. "Embarrassed."

He grinned. "Why? Because you're naked? Because I'm caressing you? Administering discipline if you disobey me? Or embarrassed because you know you're enjoying it?"

Lexi looked up at him. A mistake. Her stomach tightened and her breath caught. She swallowed hard and all the excuses she'd scrambled to come up with flittered away. "All of those."

Mark closed the distance separating them, his proximity drawing the air from her lungs. "Honesty is so sexy." His fingers tangled in her hair and thick waves, drawing her head to the side. His mouth crushed hers in a breath-stealing kiss.

As if drawn by a magnetic force, her body molded against his, but before she could explore the hard planes of his chest with her eager hands, he broke the tantalizing contact and drew away.

"Lock your fingers over your head and spread your feet."

"Am I under arrest?" *Cavity search?*

Mark lashed out with the crop. The swooshing sound cut the air again. The leather tip bit into her thigh.

She sucked her breath between gritted teeth.

"Now."

Lexi laced her fingers on top of her head and slid her left foot out until her feet were a little wider than shoulder's width apart. Being exposed and vulnerable, at his mercy, kindled an odd fire in her belly, one that smoldered low and warm, but threatened to burst free and consume her.

He moved around her, scanning up and down her naked body. When he'd made one complete circle, he reached out with the crop and traced the underside of her breast.

Her nipple puckered in response.

"Tell me, Alexis. How long has it been since you started crushing your Vicodin and sucking it up that cute as a button nose of yours?" He traced a tightened nub of her left breast with the crop's end.

The question caught her off guard. The effects of the attention he paid to her body occupied the majority of her concentration, so it took her a few moments to give a response.

Apparently a bit too long for Mark's taste. The crop drew back and snapped at her right nipple, sending a shockwave of electricity straight to her pussy.

She squealed and jerked, earning a second surge of current from the crop's impact on the left side. "Fuck!"

"You're very bad at the don't move game, Alexis. Seems you and the end of this crop are going to become well acquainted by the time we're done. Now, answer the question."

Gray steel held her mesmerized. "Uhh…" She glanced at the crop resting harmlessly against his pant leg. "I started crushing last summer, so about eight months now."

"Why?"

Lexi shrugged. "I guess that's when I finally realized my college days and my volleyball career were over, and I was never getting my scholarship back."

In a blur of motion, the unforgiving crop struck her flank.

She sucked in a breath. "What was that for?"

"Shrugs count as moving."

Fuck!

"I don't see what difference it really makes when I took the big leap off *Fuck It Point*, I did. Just like I took the jump off *Sell Your Soul Mountain* by hooking up with Billy and agreeing to sell on campus for him. Let's just say there's been a long line of bad choices over the last two years."

Mark nodded. "Fair enough." He lifted the end of the crop again, sliding it down Lexi's body in a leisurely trail, from her collarbone to the landing strip of curls at the apex of her thighs. "As to the difference it makes, understanding why we do what we do is the first step in the long process of changing unwanted behaviors."

He flicked the end of the crop against her pelvic bone over and over until Lexi squirmed and dodged the onslaught of shocking pleasure rippling through her body.

Her reaction earned a pair of stinging strikes on her backside.

Heart pounding against her ribcage, body singing with desire, Lexi resumed her previous pose, making sure to keep her fingers locked tight above her head. Her chin notched upward.

Mark awarded her with a smile. "You have a very expressive face, Alexis. Are you aware of that?"

Her brow furrowed. "What?"

The end of the crop traced her hip. "Your eyes sparkle when your stubborn kicks in, for example." He watched her intently as he slid the crop upward. "And they turn to molten emerald when you're aroused."

Her breath hitched, but she remained still despite the trail of tingling flesh his ministrations elicited. Her nipples ached for his touch and her pussy throbbed like a chasm of desolation, desperate to be filled. Could he read all that in her expression? Her cheeks flamed.

Mark dropped the crop to his side and returned to the black duffel. He deposited the crop into the bag and reached inside. He straightened, a pair of nylon cuffs dangling from his fingertips.

A surge of fear jettisoned through her bloodstream. "What are those for?"

He moved in, stealing her view of anything but his broad shoulders. "For you, silly girl." His aftershave tickled her nose with its masculine spice. He wrapped one of her wrists with the cuff and pressed the Velcro strip running its length into place, and repeated the process on the other wrist. "You can put your hands down now."

He stepped back, and Lexi released a breath she didn't know she held. She lowered her arms, the tether connecting them settling just above her pelvis.

"Lay down on the bed." His voice held a grit she hadn't noticed before.

She cast a quick glance behind her before turning his way. "And if I say no?"

He took a step toward her, earning one of hers in retreat. "You don't get to say no."

The urge to flee rocketed through her, but the knot in her stomach anchored her somehow, keeping her feet rooted to the floor. The challenge in Mark's expression was unmistakable, but what she couldn't be sure of, was whether he challenged her to refuse him, or if he was fully aware of his effect on her and merely challenged her to refuse herself.

Lexi had no interest in denying him. Desire singing through her veins, she sat on the mattress, shifted, and lay back. Her cuffed wrists settled on her stomach.

Mark moved to the head of the bed. He held out a hand. "Wrists, please."

She lifted her arms, setting the tether in his waiting palm.

"Good girl." He arced her hands downward, affixing the cuff to something under the bed frame. Something clicked, like a lock. She tested the restraint, finding only a few inches of movement before her arms stopped short. Her heartbeat jumped into a faster pace.

Mark squatted beside his bag and set to searching through it. He placed a few things on the floor to his side, but she couldn't see from her prone position.

"I told you I could replicate the high your drugs give you with something that wouldn't destroy you." Mark straightened, hovering over her, intense, penetrating. He traced his fingers through the tendrils of her hair fanning the mattress. "We've arrived at the time where I prove I can." His lips twitched, but no smile came. Instead, he winked. "So relax and enjoy the ride, my sweet Alexis." He produced a blindfold, affixing it over her eyes, plunging her into darkness.

Lexi let out a nervous laugh, flexed and curled her fingers. "Relax, he says." Body stiff, skin prickling in anticipation of his silent touch, she took a deep breath and let it out slowly.

The first whisper of a caress came across her middle. Just a tickle of sensation dancing over her stomach, around her belly button, and higher to circle each of her breasts.

A feather?

The tension seeped from her body as her nipples tightened in reaction to the gentle touch. She squirmed as she imagined his hands replacing the achingly soft tease of the feather. Heat flushed her cheeks, while gooseflesh rose on her arms. The leisurely trail ended abruptly, leaving her straining to hear him, and determine where the next sensation would come.

Shuffling sounds reached her. He was by the duffel again.

She licked moisture onto her dry lips, pulse racing in anticipation.

Mark's thumb and forefinger closed over her right nipple. He rolled the hardened nub, sending jolts of shocking pleasure through her. A soft gasp escaped her as his other hand joined the game, taking hold of the neglected needy peak. He teased the twin pleasure points in unison, kindling the ball of smoldering heat in her stomach into an inferno. Warm palms closed over her breasts. He kneaded the soft flesh with gentle fingers.

Lexi swallowed the urge to purr in satisfaction while the churning fire in her stomach tracked lower.

His hands left her again, but were replaced almost instantly when his mouth closed over her left nipple. His tongue traced the outer edge of her areola before he sucked lightly on the raised nub.

Lexi jerked against the wrist restraints, and sucked air through clenched teeth.

His mouth abandoned her.

A pang of regret stabbed at her chest.

"So reactive," he whispered. "So very beautiful."

Mark's soft words washed over her. She luxuriated in them, her fingers itching to reach out and draw him back to her aching breast.

As if he could hear her thoughts, his fingertips returned, teasing her nipple back to a hardened peak. He placed something over it, and let go, but the pulling sensation remained. He flicked the source of the suction.

Shivers of pleasure shot from her nipple.

Mark repeated the process on the other breast, and gave the nipple cover a matching flick, eliciting a tortured groan from her.

"What are you doing to me?" Her words arrived hoarse, laced with breathless desire.

"Showing you the way."

Emptiness swooped in as he stepped away.

"Open your legs for me." He'd moved the foot of the bed.

Without hesitation, she slid her legs apart until her ankles slipped over the edge of the mattress.

Warm fingers wrapped around her calf and lifted. A cuff, like the ones encircling her wrists, surrounded her ankle.

Her stomach twisted with nervous excitement as he fastened her leg to the bed with a click. "More restraints?"

A soft chuckle caressed her ear as his presence moved to the other side of the bed. "Does that worry you?"

"Worried wouldn't be the term I would use to describe how I am feeling right now, no." Her cheeks burned

"Good." Mark surrounded her other ankle with a cuff and drew her leg back down to the bed. Another loud click. He moved back to the head of the bed, giving each of the unseen nipple attachments a flick on his way.

Lexi imagined him assessing her. She was completely exposed and at his mercy. Her clit reacted to the thought by throbbing in approval. She bit down on her lower lip. Was he aroused, too? Or was he merely playing with her?

"How do you feel?" His breath caressed her right cheek.

Instinctively, she turned her head toward his voice.

His mouth captured hers. Light exploded behind her blindfold. His tongue traced the outline of her lips, coaxing them to part and allow him entry. He swallowed her whimper as she opened to him, her mouth molding to his. Eager for a taste, her tongue reached out to join the erotic dance he'd begun.

Disappointment needled her. She squirmed against her restraints and heaved a sigh. "Abandoned. I feel needy and abandoned."

When he pulled his delicious mouth away, a soothing hand settled at her waist, stilling her. "Poor girl." He stroked a trail over her hip and down the outside of her leg before sliding his palm over her kneecap and caressing along the more sensitive skin of the inside of her thigh, inching his fingertips ever closer to her aching mound. "What can I do to help?" Humor laced his tone.

Lexi wanted her blindfold gone, needed to see him standing over her, touching her. "Let me see you?"

Mark clucked in response. "That isn't an option available to you at the moment." A fingernail traced through the landing strip of hair at the apex of her thighs. "Was there anything else?" His hand continued its path, his touch leaving her aching, so very empty pussy to tease a line down the inside of her other leg.

Her fingers curled to frustrated fists. Her nipples burned with the exquisite stinging heat of whatever he'd left attached to them. Her entire body thrummed with desire. "Please…"

His hand stopped moving, his palm searing her inner thigh where it lay. "Did you think of something, sweet Alexis? Do tell."

He knew damned well what he did to her. What she wanted. Needed. Lexi growled, the sound coming from deep in her throat. "Please, touch me."

"But I am touching you."

She arched her back and pressed her bottom into the mattress. "You missed a spot." Her voice held more petulance than she'd planned. She gnawed the inside of her cheek, chastising herself for letting her desperation show. "I mean…"

Mark's fingertip found her opening and tickled her clit. "You mean you want me to touch you here?"

Lexi groaned and lifted her hips, pushing her center against his hand. "God, yes. There. Please touch me there."

His hand slipped lower, slowly, until an exploring finger pushed inside her slick folds. "Like this?"

She drew a ragged breath. "Please…yes."

Mark dipped two fingers inside her. "Please what, Alexis?" His free hand released the suction on her nipples, first the right, then the left, letting loose a surge of stinging tingles in her breasts, while his plunging fingers wreaked havoc on her desire soaked pussy.

Lexi writhed beneath his ministrations, her head tossing side-to-side as she strained at the tethers holding her in place. "Please, sir!" She lifted her hips to drive his probe deeper. Heat coiled in her stomach and radiated outward. Pressure built in her center.

Mark pushed his fingers deep, the base of his hand pressed tight against her pelvic bone. "What do you want?" He teased her engorged clitoris with his thumb. "Tell me."

Lexi moaned in response. Her pussy contracted around his waiting fingers in time with her heartbeat. "Please don't stop."

Mark drew his hand back and added a third finger on the next thrust.

"God, yes. More." She rolled her hips against his hand, wantonness overruling any sense of embarrassment she might have left. Her thoughts, her senses, were consumed by him, what he did between her legs.

As his fingers pumped into her, Mark teased her clit with his free hand, pushing Lexi closer to the edge of bliss with each stroke. Her body answered his pace of its own accord, her hips lifting to meet each thrust. She gasped for breath and climbed higher, her nerve endings singing with pleasure.

He increased his pace. "Do you want to come for me?" His voice took on a gravelly tone that made Lexi's heart soar. A sign of his desire, proof he was as caught up in the moment as she.

The knowledge pushed her over the edge of oblivion. Her muscles tensed. "Yes!" She arched her back and pressed her head against the pillow. "Oh, God!"

She crashed over the precipice of desire, her pussy pulsing around his fingers, throbbing out her orgasm. She rode the wave of her explosion, breathing ragged, until the quivering in her limbs subsided. A soft moan slipped past her lips as she relaxed into the soft mattress.

Mark withdrew his hand, drawing a forlorn whimper from her. "You didn't wait for me to give you permission, my greedy girl, but since this is our first therapy session, I can forgive the misstep."

It took a few moments for his words to penetrate her bliss-addled skull. *Misstep?*

Had he expected her to hold back? She recalled the feeling of his fingers inside her. No way in hell could she have stopped her orgasm. Not when he so expertly teased her into a frenzy. Who could? Had the other girls done so? "For real?"

He released her ankles from their restraints, came around to the top of the bed and untethered her wrists. When he slipped the blindfold from her head, the dimmed light of the room stabbed at her eyelids. She blinked, squinting beneath the onslaught.

Mark stood over the bed, his arms folded, expression stoic. Where had the longing she heard in his voice gone? Had this really been some twisted kind of therapy? Had she only imagined his desire for her?

Lexi pushed to a sitting position, mind spinning.

"I'll be back shortly with breakfast and your medication." Without another word, he grabbed his duffel bag, turned, and left the room, locking the door behind him.

She heaved a sigh. He'd forgone reattaching her ankle tether, but she remained his prisoner. Self-doubt washed over her. Hugging herself, she curled up on the mattress, confused.

What the fuck am I doing here?

If she wasn't there because Mark desired her, why had he stopped? Why hadn't he fucked her? Surely that wasn't really part of his attempt to cure her of her addictions. But, he left. Without so much as a blow job. Could he be mad because she came? She thought that would have been the point. Show her pleasure without drugs. But, he just left…

"Who does that?"

He was human. Like all humans, he had to have some motive for going through all the trouble of tracking her down. Finding out who she sold for, then working out a deal with Billy. Everyone had ulterior motives. Selfish motives. He wasn't fucking Superman.

Even if he was, how did he even know she needed saving? Her mother didn't know. Lexi was good at making sure nobody knew. Except Billy. He was the only one who knew how deep the rabbit hole went. How tight Vicodin's hold on her was.

* * * *

The churning tumbler of the door lock alerted Lexi of Mark's return a few seconds before the door swung wide.

"Breakfast is served." He swept into the room holding a tray encumbered with steaming plate of succulent smelling food, and a white ceramic mug Lexi prayed contained coffee.

He moved to the dresser to unload his burden. A small black bag draped from his shoulder.

More therapy?

Her cheeks heated. "What's in the bag?"

"Pressure cuff and a stethoscope. I need to check your vitals."

She joined him by the dresser, refusing to let him see how their interlude had affected her. She plucked a strip of bacon from the plate and quirked a brow. "You weren't *that* good. I'm sure I've recovered from the ordeal." She popped the strip of bacon into her mouth and held it between her teeth while she added cream and sugar to the coffee.

"Funny. No. I want to make sure your body is handling the methadone properly before you get another dose this afternoon."

After giving the coffee a quick stir, she set the spoon aside, grabbed the bacon perched in her mouth, and tore a healthy bite free. She brought her drink back to the bed with her, sitting as she chewed. A sip from the mug rinsed her mouth before she answered. "You said you'd be back with breakfast and medication. If the Methadone is in the afternoon, what am I taking now?"

He came about with a paper cup of water. He extended a hand in her direction, a pair of round white pills resting on his palm.

A tingle of warning danced down her spine. Lexi knew pills, was more of an expert on them than she preferred to admit, and she had no idea what these were. "What is it?" She made no move to take them.

He chuckled. "Such a cynic. They're just Vitamin D pills. Not really a suitable replacement for UV light, but it should help make up for the lack of windows."

Lexi frowned. "How long do you plan to keep me locked up down here?"

"That really depends on you." He moved his hand closer and held out the paper cup. "And how willing you are to participate in your own sobriety."

She popped the pills into her mouth and swallow them down with a drink from her mug. "Speaking of my sobriety, what difference does it make to you?"

Mark set the paper cup back on the breakfast tray. "Don't deflect, Alexis. This isn't about me."

"Isn't it? Doesn't it have to be? At least in part? Why else would you go through all this trouble? Why me? I'm not the only addict at the university. Hell, I can give you a list, and it's a long one. So why is it me who's imprisoned in what I assume is your basement? At first, I thought you were attracted to me. That you wanted me. But this morning's therapy, as you call it, burst that fantasy bubble pretty effectively. So, now I'm obsessed with knowing why."

His brow furrowed. "And why have you determined I'm not attracted to you?" He folded his arms over his chest. "You have me quite curious."

"Now who's deflecting?" She met his gaze over the rim of her mug. "I'll tell if you will."

"I told you. This isn't about me." He slid the bag from his shoulder and removed the stethoscope, settling the earpieces around his neck. He fished out the blood pressure apparatus. "This is about seeing you well and back to your old self."

"What do you know about my old self?" She scoffed. "All you know about me is I took your class sophomore year."

The mattress sagged as he sat, the shift in weight distribution bringing her shoulder into contact with his. Tingles raced along her arms. She straightened quickly, as if scalded by the incidental touch.

Mark's warm fingers caressed the sensitive flesh of her upper arm as he wrapped the cuff around it. "When you took my class, you were impossible to ignore. So vibrant. Sexy in an understated way." He put the ends of the stethoscope in his ears and rested the cool metal disc at the end to the pulse of her arm. His concentration fell to the dial affixed to the air tube. "There was just something about you, a spark of fire, a light in your eyes that drew me to you." He pumped on the ball at the end of the tube, filling the pressure cuff with air as he spoke. "I couldn't get you out of my thoughts. I wanted you like I have wanted no other woman I've known."

The pressure on her arm increased, but his words had their own effect. Her chest tightened, and a ball of heat unfurled in her stomach, spiraling outward until her whole body bathed in its warmth. Her cheeks flushed when she realized he'd notice the uptick in her pulse.

He released the tiny metal valve and the compression on her arm slowly decreased. He watched the gauge. "You were the only one who ever tested my resolve to avoid relationships with students. The only one I imagined bending over the arm of the sofa in my office." He nodded at the dial before removing the stethoscope from his ears. "Anyway. I saw you on campus last month and the light in those beautiful blue eyes was gone. Instead, dark circles sat beneath them. You were"—his expression clouded—"are a specter, just a skeleton of who you were. You reminded me so much of my sister. And I admit, it terrified me." He removed the cuff from her arm and returned it to the bag along with the stethoscope. "One sixteen over sixty. About perfect." His smile didn't reach his eyes. They still churned like a brewing storm.

Terrified?

Lexi swallowed the lump in her throat. "Your sister?"

"Yes. The light in her eyes died, too. About two months before she did. She was twenty when she overdosed. I was only twelve. Too young to understand what really happened to her. Why she changed so much when she went away to school. Why she withdrew from us. From me." He took Lexi's hand in his. "The moment I saw you in the campus center, I knew I had to do something. I wasn't prepared to watch drugs destroy someone I care for again. Not when I actually had the power to help this time."

Holy fuck. He really was Superman.

And he thinks of me like a sister.

But he'd said he was attracted to her earlier. Confusion muddled her thoughts.

Past tense. Before the pills destroyed her.

"So you kidnapped me just to save me from ending up like your sister?" It explained why he hadn't screwed her earlier, but didn't explain the teasing...the exquisite torture. "Then what was this morning about?"

Mark released her hand and got up from the bed. He pointed at the tray. "You need to eat your breakfast before it gets any colder." He faced her. "This morning was about therapy, just like I said. About you and only you, and showing you new ways to find the highs your body has grown accustomed to. It had nothing at all to do with my needs, or how badly I wanted to bury my cock in that delectable pussy of yours. And trust me, sweet Alexis, that is exactly what I wanted to do."

Lexi gaped at him, mesmerized, his words setting loose a swarm of butterflies in her stomach. She marveled at how they managed to survive the inferno blazing in her core, swallowed her fear, and met his gaze. "I'm not sure I believe you." She got to her feet and stepped closer, lifting her chin to keep eye contact. Her next words were barely more than a whisper. "Prove it."

He startled her with the force he used to pull her to him, but his low growl urged her on. She slipped her arms around his neck and her mouth sought his, her lips challenging him to deny her.

It seemed he had no intention of doing so. Vicelike hands wrapped around her wrists and jerked, drawing Lexi's arms down and pinning them behind her back. His sharp white teeth bit down on her lower lip, eliciting a squeal.

He trailed hot kisses down the side of her neck.

Lexi let her head fall back, giving him full access to her throat. Her fingers curled to fists and her nails dug into her palms, useless, frustrated in their need to touch.

With a groan and a suddenness that startled her, Mark released his hold, spun, and stalked from the room without uttering a single word, slamming the door so hard the walls shook. The click of a lock followed.

Lexi slumped onto the bed, breaths coming in gasps. Her lips tingled where'd he'd ravaged them. She let out a deep sigh. "That went well."

* * * *

The day ticked by in agonizingly slow minutes. Mark didn't return to remove the breakfast tray Lexi had long since occupied with emptying. Anything to keep her from obsessing over the cause of his hasty departure. If he wanted her as badly as he professed, why didn't he take what she had so obviously offered?

She forced her idle fingers to stop picking at the mattress and cast a quick glance at the ever-watchful camera in the corner. Was he watching? Did he enjoy toying with her?

Over the course of the past hour, the dull ache in her head had returned, and the room's temperature seemed to have increased at least ten degrees. A beaded line of sweat insisted on returning to her upper lip each time she swiped it away.

She glanced at the door. He would have to come with her methadone soon. Wouldn't he? Maybe he would punish her by withholding the medication she needed. Let her feel the full effects of withdrawal to keep her beholden to him. Was that his end game? To make her dependent on him for relief?

No. She reminded him of his sister. He'd said as much. From what she knew of Professor Foster, he'd not make her suffer needlessly.

The longer the door separating them remained intact, the less confident Lexi became with that assessment of her situation. She glared at the camera, annoyed with his game. Her skull pounded in time with her pulse.

Before Lexi could unload her opinions on the unsuspecting mechanical voyeur in the corner, the door to her prison unlocked and swung wide.

Mark swept inside, all smiles, another tray in his hands. "Time for your next dose." He looked her over from toe to tip. "How are you feeling? Any symptoms?"

The concern in his tone took the edge from Lexi's anger. "Headache for sure. And either I'm having a hot flash, or this room is about eighty degrees right now."

His chuckle sparked a fire in her belly. "Not bad as withdrawal goes." He set the tray down and withdrew the methadone from his pocket. "We'll stick with the same dosage as yesterday. Do you want some ibuprofen for the headache?"

She shook her head and grabbed the water from the tray. "I'm okay. Thanks." She scooped the pill from his palm and tossed it back, washing it down with a long gulp of water. She returned the glass to its place on the tray. "About earlier…" She pivoted toward Mark.

"I owe you an apology," he said, his expression blank. "I shouldn't have lost control the way I did. Lost focus. I'm sorry."

Lost focus? She frowned.

He's sorry he kissed you. The knife of reality slashed at her insides. "Oh, uhm, apology accepted, I guess." She glanced at the floor. "But I don't really understand what you are apologizing for. I was glad you lost control, or whatever you want to call what happened." She forced herself to look at him.

"I liked kissing you. And…" Her voice trailed off and heat flamed her cheeks.

"And?" he asked, his voice soft, like a gentle caress.

"And…" She wasn't sure what had transpired between them earlier. "My therapy." Her heart thudded against her rib cage, threatening to expose her need for him. "Even though I'm not entirely sure what it was supposed to teach me."

Mark grinned, awarding her with the briefest glimpse of his delicious dimples. "Ever the blunt one. I've always liked that about you. I'm glad to know you enjoyed yourself, although your orgasm sort of gave you away there."

The fire returned to her cheeks. "Funny."

"In all seriousness, I explained the point of the session this morning, and what it was meant to show you." He tilted his head and a smile tugged at the corner of his mouth. "What still has you confused, sweet Alexis?"

"That's all it was then, really? Just therapy? Clinical, emotionless, and detached therapy." She sighed. "It didn't feel like any therapy I've ever had before."

"I can understand that. It's not like you'll find any studies on using the Dom-Sub lifestyle in addiction recovery." He pushed his hands into his pockets, appeared pensive. "For this to work, I have to remain detached. Clinical, as you call it. It's important our time together is focused on your recovery, and teaching you new ways to cope with stressors."

She swallowed hard. "You stress me." She waved an arm and gave her leg a wiggle, bringing the chain to life. "This stresses me. What happened this morning was anything but stressful. Quite the opposite in fact."

His smile warmed her. "That's good. Your body will learn to crave those sensations as much as it does your Vicodin." He stepped closer, his overwhelming presence stealing the air from her lungs. She had nowhere to go, her back pressed against the dresser. He reached up and brushed a lock of hair from her face.

She sighed. "I crave you." Her gaze dropped from his. "I…really thought you wanted me, too."

He grabbed hold of her arms as a growl rumbled from him. "You just don't get it. Do you?"

She hesitated, fear and excitement churning her insides. "No, I guess not. Make me understand." Lexi wasn't sure she was truly ready for what she asked for, but she didn't care. She wanted him.

He released her abruptly and stepped back. "Obviously, we are not going to be able to move forward until we put this point to rest." He inclined his head toward the bed. "Get over there. Hands on the bed and spread your feet."

Breathless, Lexi did as told. Her palms pressed into the mattress. She moved her feet wider apart.

The sound of his zipper echoed in her skull, followed quickly by a condom wrapper being torn. His warm hands caressed her hips, and she moaned in anxious anticipation.

"It's time we put the whole desire debate to rest once and for all." He stepped closer, his hard cock pressing against her wet opening. Without further fanfare, he drove himself deep inside her. His fingers sunk into the soft flesh of her hips, holding her in place. He didn't withdraw, but remained buried inside as he bent over her back. His heated breath caressed her nape. "Don't for one second doubt my desire for you." His hips rolled against hers, fanning the flames of her need. He pulled his hips away, stopping just short of a full withdrawal. "Ever." He slammed back against her ass, earning a whimper of sheer pleasure from her. "You're mine."

She arched her back, giving him better access to her already throbbing center. "Oh, yes, Mark, yes. All yours."

His hips pumped against hers while his hands found her breasts. He kneaded the tender flesh, and pinched the tight nipples, driving into her again and again, setting Lexi's entire body aflame. He drew her up against his hard chest, palms molding and teasing her tender flesh while he plunged into her at a faster pace. His heated exhales kissed her shoulder, driving her wild with lust.

Her pussy throbbed and pulsed in time with his thrusts. "Oh, yes, please." Her thigh muscles quivered. "Please, can I come?"

His grip on her breasts tightened and his pace quickened. "With me, sweet Alexis, with me." His voice arrived thick with desire, sending Lexi into a swirling chasm of bliss. Her nails dug into the flesh of his hips as he held her in place and drove into her again and again. "Now, baby girl," he cried out, pumping his throbbing shaft into her. He growled his climax into her hair.

The blinding white light of orgasm overtook her, sending Lexi over the chasm behind him. Her pussy contracted around his throbbing cock as she spun out of control, blind to everything but the soaring pleasure electrifying every beat of her racing heart.

With one last thrust, Mark bent her over the mattress once more and released his tight grip on her breasts. His fingertips slowly traced along the sides of her waist to her hips as he withdrew from her. "So beautiful…so hard to resist." He sighed and stepped back. "Now stop fucking around and eat your lunch, Alexis."

Without another word, he pulled up his pants, fastened his belt, and left the room. His departure was followed, as usual, by the sound of the door lock clicking into place.

She ate her lunch, not tasting any of it. She was too preoccupied with what had just occurred to care. When she'd finished everything on the tray, she settled on the bed and stared a hole into the ceiling.

Her body ached from the vigor of Mark's not-so-gentle fucking, a constant reminder of his proven desire for her. But why had he left so abruptly? Was he angry with her? Or with himself for wanting her?

The more she tried to untangle her thoughts, the more jumbled they became. Finally, she gave up, and turned her concentration to the tranquility swimming through her limbs. Contentment washed over her at the memory of his soft words as he'd driven inside her, making it impossible for her to deny their truth, even if she'd wanted to.

You're mine.

* * * *

Lexi woke and stretched languidly, not quite willing to emerge from the bliss bubble the dreams of Mark's strong arms had offered. She sat up and tried to determine how long she'd dozed. Without windows, her small prison made it impossible to mark the passage of time. She could have slept fifteen minutes or fifteen hours. Improbable, since Mark hadn't yet returned to collect the meal trays. Had he?

She glanced at the dresser. The empty trays were gone, and a pile of folded clothing sat in their place.

She checked the camera perched in the corner. He must have taken them away while she slept. She pushed up from the bed and crossed to the dresser.

Sitting atop the clothing—her clothing, was a folded piece of paper.

She snatched it up and unfolded it.

Get dressed. Meet me upstairs.
~M

The clouds of confusion returned. Lexi put on her clothes and headed for the door. Hesitantly, she tried the knob. The door popped open.

She eyed the opening, her teeth worrying her lower lip. Was this some kind of test? More odd therapy?

Determined to find out, Lexi dressed in a hurry and ran nervous fingers through her sleep tangled hair. She cast a quick glance at the camera perched in the corner and took a deep breath. "Ready or not, here I come." She squared her shoulders and went in search of Mark.

Finding the stairs leading up from the basement was easy, but when she pushed through the door at the top, she glanced around, unsure. Which way to go?

She'd emerged through a door at the back of a massive, well-appointed country kitchen, but a long hallway stretched to the right, a closed door waited to the left, and across from her, an archway led to what appeared to be a formal dining room.

Mark's brief note didn't tell her where to find him, and the idea of wandering aimlessly about his home held no appeal.

"Hello?" she called out, taking a few tentative steps into the kitchen.

"In the library." Mark's reply floated to her from the corridor on her right.

The coolness of his tone sent a shiver of apprehension down her spine. Why did he seem angry? What had she done wrong?

She scoffed at the thought. Because she allowed herself to be captured? Let him tease and torment her. Fuck her.

Oh, the horror.

If anyone should be angry about anything, it was her.

With defiance blooming in her chest, Lexi headed in the direction of his voice. She found him behind the third open doorway on the left, sitting at a large mahogany desk, surrounded by shelves upon shelves of books, his hands folded on the desk's smooth surface.

"Come in." Mark indicated the empty chair across from him. "Make yourself comfortable."

Her apprehension spiked as she stepped into the library and planted herself in the seat. She glanced at his intertwined fingers, and thoughts of how his hands felt on her flesh swarmed her mind. Her gaze shot to the shelves and the watercolor painting on the wall behind him. Safe places to look. Unlike the stormy, intense eyes that seemed to be able to see her very soul. She gnawed at the inside of her cheek.

"I guess you're probably wondering why I've allowed you out of your room," Mark began.

The corner of her mouth quirked. "The thought crossed my mind."

He leaned back in his seat, his expression unreadable. "I made a mistake bringing you here the way I did, Alexis, and I've decided it is best if I allow you to leave."

She frowned. She should be thrilled to hear of her impending freedom, but she wasn't. Not at all. Despite the odd circumstances that brought her here, she genuinely enjoyed Mark's company and wasn't ready for their time to end. She liked that he seemed to give a shit about what she'd been doing, and wanted to help cure her of an addiction she had no chance of beating on her own. Then, there was the sex. Her body warmed, driving home the sense of loss growing within her chest. "Why the sudden change of heart? I don't understand. Did I do something wrong?"

He awarded her with a paternal smile, one reserved for a pouting child. "No, not at all. In fact, it's me. I did something wrong. Something I promised myself I wouldn't do even before I brought you here."

She still didn't understand and opened her mouth to say so, but as he lifted a delaying hand, the words stalled in her throat.

"Let me explain. I will answer any questions you have once I've done so, I swear."

She clamped her jaw shut and nodded.

His slight smirk revealed the elusive, heart-stopping dimple. "Thank you." He took a deep breath, expanding his already broad chest to distracting proportions. "You know by now that I brought you here to help, and, that is and always will be, the complete truth. My intentions were infinitely more honorable than my methods, granted, but I have always had your best interests at heart."

"Yes." She kept her response to one word, her curiosity almost overwhelming.

"Before I made the decision to take you, I promised myself I would remain clinical in my approach to you. That despite my unorthodox therapies, and my admitted desire, I would keep myself distant, and not allow my needs to factor into our interactions. In that effort, I have failed miserably."

"Bu—"

"Let me finish," he admonished.

"Sorry."

"What happened this morning was a big wake up for me. And a humbling one. No matter how much you asked for it and how much you wanted it." His gaze took on a devilish glint. "Wanted me. I never should have lost control like that. I gave in to my own desires and forgot what we're both here for. I forgot all of this is about, and for you. Or maybe I just didn't care. Either way, I've lost my objectivity when it comes to you, Alexis, and I've come to the realization that not only do I have no desire to remain detached and clinical with you, I am fairly certain it would be impossible to do so after..." He hesitated, and for the first time since she met Professor Foster in her Western Civilization class freshman year, he appeared unsure of himself. "After I experienced the mindless bliss associated with your pussy contracting around my cock."

Fire singed her cheeks, and the warmth coiled in her stomach drifted lower.

"I want more of that, my dear. So much more, and acknowledging this truth has brought me to a stark realization. I need you to be here because you choose to, not because I've forced you to remain."

He wanted more. Of her. Her skin tingled.

"I am sure I have made clear I enjoy the BDSM lifestyle, but I misled you when we first spoke. I have never had a slave. Submissive girls eager to please?" He winked. "Absolutely. My fair share. Not all of them were girlfriends in the typical sense, but most were. A dominant submissive relationship requires an intimacy beyond the norm, one that fosters a strong bond, even when it comes to no-strings playmates."

Her thoughts tumbled to their first session. Blindfolded. Tied and at his mercy. His.

Mercy.

Lexi gave herself a mental shake and fixated her attention on his lips, praying it would help her focus on the words.

"I won't allow you to be a slave to me any more than I will allow you to be a slave to your addiction, Alexis, so I'm letting you go. You are no longer a prisoner here. If you choose to go to the police, I won't lie about what I've done. Nor will I lie about why. I'm not sure your life choices could withstand the scrutiny, but everyone has choices to make. I'll leave that one to you. But, should you choose to stay, which I sincerely hope you do, you will do so as my girlfriend and fledgling submissive. I won't be able to treat your addiction anymore, but I will find a suitable therapist who can. One who works more in the confines of acceptable methods." He grinned, flashing a row of perfect white teeth, and, of course, the disarming dimple.

"And you will need to go to rehab. The whole point of all this was for you to get well. To have the light return to you, so, on that subject, I will not bend. If that doesn't work for you, then I have to walk away from the potential I see, and ask that you leave with my hope you find a path to sobriety. No one can force you to get better. I know you know that. So I need you to be strong enough to choose to."

Lexi sat dumbfounded. Girlfriend? Rehab? Was he for real?

Superman, remember?

After a few moments of silence, Mark spoke again. "You can speak now. I've had my say."

She thought she nodded, but wasn't sure. Her brain moved a mile a minute and she had trouble nailing down a rational thought. "Uhm...wow." She glanced at the polished desk top. She wanted nothing more than to stay, to spend more time with Mark, and the idea of doing so without the walls of therapy held its appeal, but rehab?

"You must have questions."

She shifted her attention upward. "About a million." He chuckled and prickles of pleasure danced along her spine.

"I've got time."

"How long do I have to decide." Maybe she could kick the Vicodin without rehab.

"I'm afraid I'll need to know your answer now. You can have a few hours to make arrangements if you decide you need to go, but I'm local, and happy to pay for a cab if you need one."

"Can I agree to get clean without rehab?"

"No. I'm afraid my sister has taught me better than to believe you can do that from where you are right now. I'm sorry."

Lexi tried to shake off the terror surging through her veins at the thought of rehab. What if it didn't work? What if she hated it? Besides, it was a lot like trading one prison for another, wasn't it? But a stint in rehab held a reward beyond sobriety. A dangling carrot she wasn't sure she could deny. She'd have Mark. He'd be her boyfriend. Her lover. Her dominant? "What exactly does being a fledgling submissive entail?"

"It means you're willing to learn. To explore more of what we've shared. You'd need to be willing to concede that I am capable of deciding what's best for you, of protecting you. You'd have to be able to trust me. Do you trust me?"

"Yes." Without hesitation. She'd been at his absolute mercy for two days. If he'd planned to hurt her, he'd have done it long before now.

"Would I call you sir?"

"Eventually. Sometimes. When appropriate. You'd learn when that is."

"I can't afford rehab."

"I can. And if that poses a problem for you, we'll find you a suitable job once you're out and you can repay me the cost." Mark got up from his chair and came around the desk, resting his bottom on its surface. He took Lexi's hands in his. "I want you to stay, in case that hasn't been clear enough."

She got lost in twin pools of unmasked desire. As the heat of his palms warmed her, fear evaporated, and she knew what she wanted. If she were brutally honest, exactly what she needed.

Lexi stood and maneuvered into his embrace. He wrapped his strong arms around her waist. She was sure of where she belonged. Her arms drifted up to encircle his neck. She pressed her lips against his in the softest whisper of a kiss. "I think I'd like to stay."

Mark's grip tightened. He took her mouth in a soul-searing kiss, his tongue branding her as his.

Her fingers tangled in his hair and her heartbeat quickened.

By the time he drew his lips away, Lexi was lightheaded and breathless.

The dimple appeared at the corner of his brilliant smile. "I was really hoping you'd say that. I wasn't sure I would be able to let you go. I fear I may have developed an addiction to you."

Lexi returned his grin with one of her own. "Well then, we can work on our recovery together."

The End.

ABOUT THE AUTHORS

D.C. "Desi" Stone is a best-selling romance author and full-time fraud investigator. She lives in California with her incredibly supporting husband, two kids, and the ever-growing family of cats. After serving eight years of service with the United States Air Force, she went on to transition into the world of financial crimes and became a lead investigator for many years. Reading has always been a passion of hers, getting lost in a good, steamy romance is one of her favorite past times. She soon after discovered her own love for writing and recreating stories and characters in her head. Her writing concentrates on romantic with specifics in paranormal, suspense, and erotica. Now, when she isn't trying to solve a new puzzle in the world of fraud, she is engulfed with coffee, her laptop, and all those crazy characters in her head.

Find her on http://www.authordcstone.com/

Kastil Eavenshade is a multi-published author pandering her romantic shenanigans. When not catering to the whims of three rescued kitties, she's dreaming up her next heart-beating tale. No period in history—past, present, or future—is safe from the clutches of her muse. Her passions beyond writing are drawing, cooking, and watching Pittsburgh Penguins hockey. She credits her parents for her free spirit as they've always supported her in every aspect of her life. Without them, she wouldn't be here. She finds pleasure in writing anything from fantasy to romance-which sometimes parallel each other.

Find her on https://kastil.wordpress.com/

Award-winning author **Lea Bronsen** likes her reads hot, fast, and edgy, and strives to give her own stories the same intensity. After venturing into dirty inner-city crime drama with her debut novel Wild Hearted, she divides her writing time between psychological thriller, romantic suspense, and erotic dark/contemporary romance.

Find her on https://leabronsen.com/

R. Brennan is a subbie brat with a bitch streak, an IT geek for the state of New York, and reformed gaming addict living in the rolling hills of Upstate NY. (You know, where it takes a ten minute drive to buy a gallon of milk, and the smell of cows lingers on the breeze.)

Find her on https://bexbooknook.wordpress.com/